BURNING UP

BURNING UP

A FLIRTING WITH FIRE NOVEL

JENNIFER BLACKWOOD

Montlake
Romance

Published by Montlake Romance, Seattle

www.apub.com

Amazon, the Amazon logo, and Montlake Romance are trademarks of Amazon.com, Inc., or its affiliates.

ISBN-13: 9781503901414
ISBN-10: 1503901416

Cover design by Letitia Hasser

Printed in the United States of America

To the heroes who run into burning buildings
when everyone else is running out

Chapter One

It was a well-known fact that when in search of incontinence products at the grocery store, Erin Jenkins would pick the squeakiest cart known to mankind. First mistake: picking the stray cart pushed off to the side like a dreaded yellow Starburst. But twelve aisles from the front of the store, she'd gone too far. Okay, fine, pure laziness stood between her and going back to the entrance.

The Bluetooth headpiece nestled in her ear beeped, and she clicked the "Call" button.

"What's the status on the contraband?"

Erin rolled her eyes as her sister's voice carried through the speaker.

"This isn't a drug deal, Andie." Although she'd likely be getting fewer side-eye glances with *those* types of items in her cart rather than Preparation H. This was Portland, after all. "Do you need something? Or just want a direct play-by-play of my shopping trip?"

"I need something to keep me entertained while I make tea for Mom. She called my steeping skills subpar. Can you believe that?"

Erin side-eyed her headpiece. "How can you screw up Lipton?"

Plates and silverware clanged in the background, and she could picture Andie clattering around in the small galley kitchen, her curls curtaining over her inked shoulders as she searched for more tea products in the lower cabinets. "I'm just that talented."

"You're something, all right." Erin chuckled but then focused back on the job at hand. With her mother out of commission because of her hernia surgery, Erin was tasked with shopping for her grandmother. So that left her rolling her squeaky cart down the incontinence aisle.

Mission: Acquire Depends, bunion pads, hemorrhoid medication, and age-defying wrinkle cream.

Casualties: Self-pride.

She loved her family. To the point where she slapped a carefully practiced grin on her face to do yearly photos with matching plaid shirts. Yes, they were *that* family. The type that re-created throwback photos of embarrassing pics that were really better off collecting dust in an album. But there had to be a line drawn somewhere, and a cart full of incontinence products at her old stomping grounds came awfully close.

"Any chance of you picking up some tea on your way home?" Andie asked.

"The odds are about as good as you learning how to brew a good cup before I get back." She'd drop the groceries off at her grandma's house, lay low at her mom's house, and then pray that her purchases lasted until she skipped out of town in six weeks.

"I thought I was your favorite sister."

"You're my only sister," Erin said.

Erin crumpled the grocery list in her palm and shoved it into the side compartment of her purse. Hemorrhoid and age-defying cream, check. Bunion pads, acquired. All with the stealth and precision of a seasoned FBI operative. She'd managed to strategically drape a cluster of bananas over the items, but that wouldn't cut it for the jumbo 120-pack of adult diapers she'd soon be rocking in her cart. Maybe she should buy a few new beach towels. That would cover the box.

As she turned down the aisle, her cart decided to act up again, the wheels emitting a high whine. A group of guys in their early twenties breezed past her to the beer section, each giving her an amused smile as she squeaked along. This day could end anytime now.

Squeak, squeak, squeak.

"What the hell is that noise?" her sister said.

On the other end of the line, fine china clinked together, and Erin could picture her sister roughly handling her mother's tea set. "The slow death of my emotional stability." Her fingers dug into the cart handle as she took a calm, steadying breath.

"I thought you'd lost that years ago."

Six weeks. Six excruciating, long weeks and then you'll be back in San Francisco. That was what she'd written in her teacher planner, and by golly, if it was in there, it was going to happen. She'd used ink and surrounded the words with star stickers: *August 1, setting up my classroom.* Positive thinking put plans into motion, right?

Then again, no amount of positive thinking would reverse the million-dollar budget cut to the city's education fund that had left six teachers, including Erin, without jobs this fall. No amount of planner decorating could save her old position. Hopefully one of her interviews would pan out and get her back on track to return to her old apartment in the city.

"Very funny, smart-ass," Erin said. "Remind me why you called again?"

"Someone has to keep tabs on you to make sure you're not skipping town again."

"Ha ha." Although it was a valid statement, because Erin did, in fact, want to bail.

Positive thoughts. She'd had a job interview yesterday, four hours before she'd driven home. The optimist in her had hoped they'd offer her a job on the spot so she could take her packed suitcase back to her San Francisco apartment. The realist in her knew that there had to be phone calls conducted and references checked before they could offer anything. So, here she was. Back in Portland, the town she hadn't called home for more than a decade.

As long as her latest job interview panned out, she'd be set to decorate her new classroom at the end of the summer. This one felt right, the principal telling her how much she loved the lesson plan Erin had shared during the meeting.

Erin narrowly avoided bumping into an older lady as she passed on the right. The lady shot her a look. The *I got you figured out, your stupid bananas hide nothing* look. Or maybe she was becoming paranoid. Luckily, she hadn't run into anyone she recognized. She'd made sure to go to the supermarket on the outskirts of town just so she wouldn't encounter any neighbors.

Squeak, squeak, squeak.

Erin cringed and muttered a few choice words under her breath. Her sister continued chatting about the tea, banging more cabinets in the process.

She glanced sideways at the endcap, spotting the Depend logo out of the corner of her eye, and scooped it into her cart faster than her favorite mascara at a Sephora sale. Add a couple of boxes of Rolaids, and she'd be bringing all the blue-pill-popping boys to the yard.

"Mission accomplished. And a bonus—I don't think the cartel will be hunting me down anytime soon," she told her sister.

"Good to hear. Which means you still have time to get that tea . . . you know, if you want to be a good sister and all."

Erin managed to make it down the fourteen aisles to the checkout stand without bumping into anyone she knew. Luck must've been on her side today. "Not happening. Read the instructions on the back of the package."

Another beep came through on her headset.

"Hold on. I have another call coming in," she said, and then clicked to the other line.

Erin didn't bother checking her phone to see who it was. Chances were pretty high it was her mother. Probably complaining that Andie was taking too long with the tea. Or making sure she hadn't fled town yet. Both viable options.

"Hello?"

"Ms. Jenkins?"

Erin stopped unloading her grandmother's groceries onto the conveyer belt, frozen in place. "Yes?"

"This is Linda Murphy from Dennison Middle School."

Holy crap. So soon? Either they really liked her, or this was a pity rejection call.

Her lungs couldn't decide whether they wanted to zip off to warp speed or stop working altogether. It had been the fourth and final interview she'd managed to snag before her trip back home. The last three had called to tell her the positions had been filled by someone else. This was her last shot. Fourth time was a charm, right? "Uh, hi. Hello."

She cringed as soon as the words left her mouth. *Lame.* Seriously, she worked with people for a living. At the very least, she could strike up polite chitchat.

The cashier waved a hand in front of Erin. "'Scuse me, miss? There's a two-for-one special on all Depends products. Do you want me to send a checker to get another box?"

"Sorry, I didn't catch that. What did you say?" Linda asked, her voice crystal clear in Erin's Bluetooth.

No. A potential employer did not just hear she was buying adult diapers.

Erin shook her head at the cashier, praying he didn't say anything more about her grocery items, and focused back on her call. "Nothing. I'm so sorry. You were saying?"

The cashier glared at her but grabbed the package and ran it over the scanner. It emitted an angry *beep, beep, beep.* First, the squeaky cart from hell; now the loudest checkout stand in existence. Seriously, what was with her and these sounds at this supermarket? The checker tried again, and it made the same noise. He picked up the microphone and announced, "Price check for Depends, Fit Me Snuggly."

For the love of all that was holy.

Erin's lower back broke out in a cold sweat. She dug her toes into her sandals, and it took everything in her power not to shrivel up and die of mortification. Gaze trained on the cashier's name tag—Clint— she fought for a calm, happy place. A box of newly sharpened number-two pencils. Planner stickers. A completely untouched whiteboard.

"Are you sure this isn't a bad time, Ms. Jenkins?"

"No, no. Perfect time." As in perfect time to bang her head into unconsciousness and forget this ever happened. She swallowed hard.

The cashier picked up the ringing phone a moment later and then said, "Ha! I knew there was a sale going on. Sure you don't want me to have someone grab you an extra box?"

"No," she growled. She shot him a look that promised mental death daggers to fly his way if he asked again. If it scared a class of thirteen-year-olds into not torching the science lab with Bunsen burners, it'd work on pretty much anyone.

Cashier Clint with the Mohawk wasn't getting the memo. "I mean, if it were me and I had a leaking problem, I'd want to stock up. Just sayin'."

She muted the speaker to her Bluetooth. "What is this? A used-car lot? What did I ever do to you?" She sighed and counted to five in her head. She looked at Clint and his ridiculous Mohawk and decided to give in. "Fine. Give me the extra box."

"Sheesh. Just trying to help you out, lady." He shrugged, then picked up the courtesy phone and said, "Bring that package of Depends up to the register, Larry." He hung up, and a loud thud reverberated over the speaker system.

Erin cringed and focused back on the conversation, unmuting the call. "I'm so sorry. What were you saying? Someone ahead of me is having trouble at the register."

Um, yeah. Nobody with a brain would buy that garbage she was selling.

"Admin at Stephens Middle School sang your praises when we called for your references. We know you'd be a fantastic addition to any school . . ." She trailed off.

Erin swallowed back the sudden thickness in her throat. There was a *but* coming. The looming *but* was as obvious as a cart full of incontinence products being wheeled around at the grocery store. No. *No.* She needed this job. Teaching was all she knew, and if she didn't get a position by the end of the summer, where would she be? Unemployed? Extending her stay at her mom's house? She shuddered.

Linda sighed. "But we needed to hire from within. I'm so sorry, Ms. Jenkins."

"I understand." And she did, but that didn't ease the sting in her eyes.

"I really wish you the best of luck in your job search."

She swallowed past the thick lump in her throat and managed a thank-you before clicking to her sister on the other line.

"Andie?"

"About time. I'm so bored I almost started doing the dishes."

That cracked a smile on Erin's wobbly lips. "I'm going to head to Barry's Bakery and go eat my feelings now. Be home later." She turned off the Bluetooth and dragged her groceries to the car. Six weeks might seem like forever at the moment, but it wasn't very much time to find a job for the upcoming school year.

Chapter Two

"Ready to head back to the station, Bennett? C shift's here to take over," Reece called from across the street.

Jake Bennett nodded to his buddy and fellow firefighter and made his way to the apparatus. "I was ready two hours ago." His muscles were tight and heavy with every movement. Finally, this forty-eight-hour shift of torture was over.

In order to get time off for his sister's wedding this weekend, he'd covered for another guy on A shift. It wouldn't have been so bad if the charity event hadn't happened right after the brutal night where Jake had spent the majority of it in his turnouts rather than the cot at the station.

He swiped a hand across his forehead as the unforgiving midday sun beat down on his face. He was decked out in his turnout gear—everything except his mask—and sweat trickled down his neck as he walked the riverfront with a black-and-yellow rubber boot in hand. Wads of money crested the rim, the rest of it packed tightly into every crevice of the shoe. All he had to do was drop off the money in the cash box in the engine parked a few blocks away, and then his shift would almost be over. And after working a double twenty-four-hour shift, he was ready to pass the hell out once the clock hit eleven.

Jake locked up the cash and began to unhook the hoses and wind them back onto the engine his team had dubbed the Intimidator. During any charity event, kids loved to explore and take turns pretending to use the equipment. Jake enjoyed this, but it meant an extra twenty minutes back at the station checking twice to make sure everything was ready for the next shift.

Making his way back around to the cab, he straightened the headsets and closed all the compartments. His eyelids continued their descent, and he fought the urge to fall asleep right where he stood. The engine door would make a fantastic pillow.

After a normal shift, he'd pass out for a good eight hours, but he was needed for a final tux fitting at two. Compared to provoking the beast better known as his Bridezilla sister, sleep deprivation and potentially getting stuck with pins while he tried on the monkey suit seemed like the safer option. His future brother-in-law, Tom, had achieved saint status this past week when Josie pulled *Exorcist*-level scary shit when the florist had to back out at the last minute. Tom was most likely the only reason Josie's head hadn't made a full revolution.

He hoisted himself into the passenger seat as Reece climbed into the driver side of the apparatus. They both threw on their headsets, flipping them to transmit.

His eyelids fought to snap shut again. Just seven hours earlier, he'd been called to an apartment fire. Carried a woman and her child over his shoulders as his crew raced to get the family dog stuck in a back bedroom, blocked by flames. With the lifting he'd done yesterday, paired with carrying two people sixteen flights of stairs, he was long overdue for a massage.

He stretched his neck from side to side again and glanced around to the back of the cab. "Where's Hollywood?"

Reece shrugged. "Knowing him, he's convincing the women roaming the riverfront to throw the deeds to their houses in his boot. He'd better hurry up, because I need to jet once we get back to the station."

Their rookie, Cole Gibson, always managed to raise the most money during these events. It wasn't an accident they'd nicknamed him Hollywood when he transferred to Station 11.

"What's your hurry?" Jake said.

"Mom's in meltdown mode because Erin is home," Reece said. "She wants everything to be perfect, which means I am needed to, and I quote, 'woo my sister into staying.'"

Jake noted the grimace on Reece's face. Reece and Erin had always had a rocky relationship—at least they had ever since Jake had moved in two blocks away in the fourth grade. Most would chalk it up to good old sibling rivalry, but it'd become more strained since Erin had moved to California. That'd been over a decade ago, when she'd started college.

"Isn't wooing saved for relationships?"

"Who knows? Mom's loaded up on pain meds from her hernia surgery." Reece scratched his chin. "Which might explain a lot."

"How long is Erin in town?"

"Just for the summer. Don't think she could handle our mom for any longer than that."

Jake nodded. Erin had always been the beach-going type, complaining that there was never enough sun in Portland. With the sun only making an appearance in July, August, and part of September, he'd have to agree. But he liked that about Oregon. The change in the seasons. The hustle and bustle of the small metropolis he'd called home for the majority of his life.

"You're more than welcome to stop by. Just might save one of us from killing the other," Reece said.

"Can't. Have to run some errands for Josie."

Reece shook his head and smiled. "Still can't believe she's getting married."

"Figured it was about time one of us Bennetts tied the knot." *Thank hell it isn't me.* He had one girl in his life already, and she maxed out every bit of patience and commitment he could muster.

The back door to the cab flew open, and Hollywood's voice carried past Jake's headset.

"Were you assholes going to leave me stranded here?" Hollywood wagged the money-filled boot in Jake's and Reece's faces as he slid into the back of the apparatus. He plunked the boot on the floor and pulled on his headset. "I was doing my civic duty by encouraging people to make healthy contributions to raise awareness for muscular dystrophy."

"You made it, didn't you?" Reece said, twisting the key in the ignition. "And don't give me that altruistic crap. How many numbers did you get along with donations?"

Jake turned around in time to see Hollywood put his hand to his chest in mock horror. "I take this job very seriously. And I'm offended you'd even ask."

Jake cocked his brow. "Do you smell that, Reece?"

Reece made a show of sticking his nose in the air and taking a grandiose sniff. "As a matter of fact, I do. Smells like a pile of shit."

Cole sighed and knocked his head into the back of the seat. "Only four numbers this time. I'm losing my touch."

Both men up front chuckled. It'd be a cold day in hell before Hollywood ever lost his touch.

The three of them had worked B shift together for the past two years. Reece was their engineer while Jake was the lieutenant. Add Cole as their firefighter on duty, and they'd been a tight trio since day one.

A few minutes later, Reece pulled the apparatus into the station, and they all began their end-of-shift routine of checking supplies and prepping for the next shift. They slid past each other without a second glance, the movements so natural and rehearsed they were as simple as breathing. At a quarter till twelve, later than Jake had anticipated, they'd finished their duties.

"See you guys on Monday. Don't have too much fun without me," Jake said.

"Try to survive Bridezilla," Reece said, clapping Jake on the back.

Jake flipped Reece the bird. "I guess you'll know if you need a new lieutenant by Sunday."

He walked out into the parking lot, the sun blazing against his tired eyes. As Jake slid into his truck, he pulled out his phone.

His daughter, Bailey, had stayed with her grandmother for the past two days since Jake had offered to fill in for someone else, taking a double, not realizing that his shift for Fill the Boot was right after that.

She picked up on the second ring. "Hey, Dad."

"How are you, princess?"

"Dad." He could practically hear her eyes rolling. Something that was happening with alarming frequency lately. "I'm not seven anymore."

Yep. He knew this. And even on the off chance he'd suddenly forgotten, his twelve-year-old made it abundantly clear that she was 282 days closer to becoming a teenager. Lord help him. But she'd always be his princess, even when she turned forty. And was still single and angelic.

"I was talking to Aunt Julie last night at dinner . . ." She trailed off.

Every muscle in his body tensed. He stretched his neck from side to side, waiting for whatever crazy scheme was about to be thrown at him. *Talking to Aunt Julie*, a.k.a. Jake's free-spirited sister, was always code for *bringing up something that 100 percent will not be okay with Dad*. He loved his sister, but she liked to play the fun aunt card more than Jake appreciated. Last time they'd called from a tattoo parlor, Bailey begging for a nose piercing. Solo parenting was hard enough without three sisters, Julie in particular, trying to undermine his authority every time he turned around.

"Yes? What about Aunt Julie?" he managed to get out through gritted teeth. The coffee he'd picked up on his way out of the station wasn't nearly potent enough.

"Can I bring a date to the wedding?"

Jake nearly aspirated on the coffee he'd just taken a sip of and placed it back in the cup holder before he did something stupid like crush a cup with scalding hot liquid all over the interior of his new truck.

Just a phase. Just a phase.

Shit. Boys weren't a phase, not even close. He knew just what reckless ones were capable of. He had been one. Which was how Bailey had come into existence. Best thing to ever happen to him, but he'd rather that she not follow his same path.

He swiped a hand over his face. Boys. There was no way they were to that stage already. It felt like just last week Bailey was fake-gagging over people kissing on TV. Installing a tracker on her iPhone would qualify as overkill, right? Just when he felt like he had this parenting gig on lockdown, Bailey had to go ahead and throw him through yet another loop.

"Dad," Bailey said. "You still there?"

No, Dad's not here right now. He's busy having a brain aneurism.

Hell, he'd just had the period talk, even YouTubed videos to make sure he was giving Bailey the correct information—he'd spent thirty minutes in the feminine-products aisle of the grocery store helping her figure out the difference between ultra and super. And what was up with wings versus none? He still didn't understand the difference, but they'd decided on the pink box, which he had then bought enough of to skyrocket the brand's share on the stock exchange. There had to be a parenting rule out there that a single dad was allowed at least a six-month reprieve before the next catastrophic event.

He turned onto Twenty-First Street, making his way toward the bakery to pick up a treat for Bailey and his mother as a thank-you for watching her the past two days. "I thought you wanted to take Rochelle." They were best friends as of today. Tomorrow it could be another debacle about who stole whose contouring brush. The Internet had saved his ass so many times when he'd had to Google all this makeup lingo he barely understood.

"Aunt Julie said Rochelle was already invited. I figured if you get a plus-one, I do, too." If Jake was in the same room as his daughter right now, he'd put money on her batting those big blue doe eyes at him. "There's this guy . . . Zack."

Nope. Not happening. Not in a million years. Or at least until she was twenty-seven. That seemed like an appropriate age. "Let's just stop right there. I'm not even using my plus-one, which means you aren't either."

She huffed, and her words were laced with venom as she said, "Just because you have a loser love life doesn't mean I have to."

Jake rested his head on the steering wheel and closed his eyes as he sat at a red light. His heavy lids fought to stay shut. Sleep. He needed sleep. Hell, maybe he *was* sleeping, and this was all just a shitty dream. Bailey's exasperated huff cutting through the stereo system proved otherwise.

Middle schoolers. They'd been the worst when he was in school, and if this was any indication, they still were. Before Jake could say anything, Bailey cut in.

"Hold on. Grandma wants to talk to you."

Two women ganging up on him while he was sleep deprived? Now that was just fighting dirty. Luckily, his other sisters were out of state because they'd never miss out on a chance to dog-pile him.

"Well, if it isn't my hero son. How were your shifts?"

"Just fine." They were brutal. He'd had an especially bad call involving an infant that made him want to hug his daughter tight and encase her in Bubble Wrap. "Is everything okay with Bailey? She was good for you?"

"She's always a peach. We're not here to talk about her."

"Then who are we talking about?"

"You."

She never did beat around the bush. "Can't this wait until I pick up Bailey?" At least then he could pound back a sufficient amount of caffeine and be somewhat awake for whatever she wanted to discuss.

"No, this can't wait." Nothing could wait with Sadie Bennett. He loved his mom, but she was the type who had to speak her piece the instant she felt the need to. And apparently now was the time he'd be getting an earful.

"I was talking to Julie last night."

"Seems like everyone was," he murmured.

"You might be thirty-two, but I am not above taking out the wooden spoon."

He smiled and shook his head. His mom loved to joke about whacking them with a wooden spoon, but he could count on his one hand the amount of times his mother had ever followed through with that sentiment. "Fine, Mom. What's up?"

"We're worried about you. With Josie getting married, this is a good opportunity to think about getting back in the game."

He knew where this was going. He'd tried the whole dating thing after Bailey's mom had left them high and dry when their daughter was three months old. Bailey had been six when he'd started dating someone seriously. Jake was cursed with shitty luck in picking women, apparently, because that one had left as soon as it had gotten too serious. The look on Bailey's face when Jake had told her Brittany wasn't going to be around anymore had been enough to reinforce that he wasn't going to seriously pursue anyone until Bailey was out of the house. Protecting her was his number one job.

"Mom, you know how I feel about that," he gritted out.

"You deserve to have some happiness, too. I talked to Melissa. You know, the pretty blonde who lives down the block from me."

"The one with twenty-nine cats?" No, really. Twenty-nine fucking cats in a tiny one-bedroom bungalow. The stench of cat piss wafted clear down to the other side of the street. Even the neighbor kids gave wide berth to Melissa's property line. He might have been in a dry spell, but he was nowhere near desperate enough for his mother to play matchmaker.

"What does that matter? Anyway, I was talking to her and said you might be interested in taking her as a date to Josie's wedding."

Christ.

Jake was thankful his drink was shoved into the center console as he wrung his hands around the steering wheel. "You didn't." His mother and daughter were going to be his demise.

"I did." She even managed to sound offended at Jake's comment. "She is perfectly suitable. I even did some . . . What do you call it? Stalking on the Facebook. She posts an awful lot of quiz results about Harry Potter, but literacy is a noble hobby."

Idiot move setting up a Facebook profile for his mother.

"Mom," he warned. There wasn't enough coffee in the world to make this morning better. Somehow he kept his car from veering off the road as he navigated downtown Portland. "As much as I appreciate your"—*meddling, absolute lack of consideration of my privacy*—"kindhearted gesture, I'm going to be busy enough helping Josie out. No need for a date."

"I'm just concerned." Her voice wavered, which was as effective as a sucker punch to Jake's gut. "I'm not getting any younger, you know. I just want to see my boy as happy as he deserves to be."

Straight for the jugular. His mom was the ultimate tour guide down Guilt Trip Lane. If he hadn't been up for almost three days straight, he could probably have thought of a better defense. Instead, he let out a sigh. "You want me to find a date for the wedding? That would make you feel better?"

"Yes, it would." The wobble had completely disappeared from her voice, and Jake gritted his molars together. Jake: 0. Mom: 1.

Fine.

What could one date really hurt? A date for his sister's wedding meant absolutely nothing. He could ask around the station. It wouldn't be too hard to find someone with a sister or a friend of a spouse.

"Fine. You tell Melissa you're sorry, but I already have a date. I will find someone else." Even if a wedding date meant nothing, he still didn't want to go with the crazy cat lady.

"Promise?"

"Yes."

Great. Now he needed to find someone to travel to the other side of the state for Josie's wedding . . . in two days.

Bailey came back on the line. Damn. He'd been played. His mother always was good at that. "Does this mean I get to bring Zack?"

Zero chance in hell, kid.

"We'll talk later when we get home."

Another petulant sigh. "Fine. Can you pick me up a bagel from Barry's? Cinnamon raisin, please."

"Already on it. See you soon."

He pulled his truck into Barry's Bakery and cut the engine. Where the hell was he going to find a date to his sister's wedding?

Chapter Three

"Everything bagel with a small coffee," Erin said to the lady at the counter. The woman poked the register keys with a fluorescent-pink nail, the chipper color offset by her black shirt that read MY CITY'S WEIRDER THAN YOURS. Rows of beautifully glazed doughnuts and bagels outlined the back of the register area, all nestled in rustic wicker baskets lined with white linen. Erin swiped at the drool pooling at the corner of her mouth as the barista plucked a bagel with a set of tongs and placed it in the toaster.

Nothing like garlic, poppy seeds, sesame seeds, and onion slathered with cream cheese to momentarily forget she was back home for the summer after a ten-year hiatus. And to alleviate the sting of still being jobless. The only thing that would make her feel better at this point was the smell of Chinese food and the sight of thick fog blanketing the Bay Area. Yes, she was homesick enough to miss the daily weather system.

She tossed down the proper amount of cash, grabbed her coffee cup, and went to the counter across the room to fill it with the strongest drip she could find. Barry's Bakery was a gem on Mississippi Avenue in downtown Portland. Bold, rich coffees. Fluffy, decadent pastries. The line to get into this building, which was nothing more than a hole in the wall, wound around the block well before six in the morning most days. That was the way most of the downtown food establishments worked.

Because if Portland was known for one thing, it was great food, beer, and coffee. At least that was a plus.

Erin pumped the coffee into her cup, replaying every single interview she'd had in the past week through her head. All positive. All seeming to go well. And yet she wasn't the perfect fit for their school. *Your luck's run out. You'll be stuck here forever now.* Seemed like her worst fears were about to come true.

Coffee drizzled onto her fingers as her cup moved out of the trajectory of the pump. *Damn it.* She really needed to stop zoning out. She grabbed a few napkins from the basket next to the half-and-half and whole-milk containers and dabbed at the liquid on the lacquered wooden counter.

A text buzzed through her phone as she filled her to-go cup with her favorite tortoiseshell blend and a dash of cream. She grabbed a lid, popped it onto the cup, and pulled out her phone.

ANDIE: SOS. I'm going to jump out the window if Mom makes me fluff her pillow one more time.

Erin imagined her sister's lip curling before sticking out her tongue the second she was out of view of their mother. She would have done the same at nineteen. Possibly still would at twenty-eight if she was around her mom for long enough. Because even though she'd been back less than twenty-four hours, she could feel herself slipping back into that role of the daughter still viewed as six in her mother's mind.

I love my family. Love them.

She'd chanted that through her five-hour shift at their family gourmet PB&J food cart downtown because when you were a grown-ass woman, you hiked up your big-girl panties and didn't complain when family needed you most.

ERIN: Dude. Five hours in an Airstream scooping peanut butter.

Which she'd done before she'd endured the grocery shopping trip from hell.

ANDIE: Mom asked me to file her toenails. I REPEAT. FILING TOENAILS. Must. Save. Me . . . Withering away.

Dear Lord. If her sister decided to finally get her butt to college, she should major in theater.

ERIN: This is me playing the world's tiniest violin.

Her sister sent back a middle-finger emoji.

You're just back for the summer. Take care of Mom post-op and then pack your bags, she reminded herself.

Enough time for Erin to do her daughterly servitude and find a new job down in San Francisco, since her teaching license was restricted to California.

She'd think of these next six weeks as a holiday. An extended one. One that made Quantico seem appealing. As she said, she loved her family, but there was a reason she lived six hundred miles away. And it included appreciating her family to the max in small doses. The kind that could be measured in those infant liquid-medicine cups.

Please. Someone—anyone, take her out with a hammer. Make it quick.

"Bagel for . . ." The barista muttered the last word, but she could have sworn she heard her name. She strode up to the counter, still staring at her phone, at her sister's message.

Barry's was the best in downtown Portland because not only did they have the best pastries, but they were also very liberal with their cream cheese. She didn't even want to think about how this little indulgence capsized her healthy-breakfast streak. Okay, fine, she'd done the whole yogurt-and-granola thing for a whopping two days . . . and it was absolute torture. In fact, if she didn't get a bagel in her mouth in the next two minutes, she might spiral into a state of despair. Because, if anything, being under the same roof as her mom again really put her in the mood for overdosing on calories.

She grabbed the to-go bag on the counter and, without another look, peeled back the paper and took a bite . . . and fought the instant urge to dry heave.

Cinnamon raisin. Her nose wrinkled. Worst flavor ever.

She knew the barista had been distracted when she'd taken her order, but that didn't sound anything close to *everything bagel*.

She shrugged it off and took another bite. Right now, carbs were carbs. She'd take this one over waiting in line another half hour. She was about to leave the shop when she heard a gruff voice ask, "Where's the bagel I ordered?"

"Which one was it, sir?"

"Cinnamon raisin," someone said, the gravelly voice sending a curl of pleasure licking down her spine.

Erin swallowed hard, the two bites of bagel sinking like concrete in her stomach.

"No worries. We'll get another one started for you . . ." The barista frowned, her hand clicking the metal tongs together. "Sorry, sir, we just toasted our last one."

She looked down at the bag, examining the name scribbled in black Sharpie. Maybe there was a *J*, but the rest of it looked like a two-year-old had decided to scribble across it. Yeah, nothing resembling her name in there.

Affirmative. Not her bagel.

Heat prickled her cheeks, and she looked around to see if anyone had noticed her, anyone to call her out on her bagel thievery. Maybe if she just slipped out without anyone noticing . . .

She started toward the door, trying to play it cool. The worst she'd ever done was walk out of the grocery store with a ChapStick once. Didn't even realize it until she made it to her car, then felt so guilty she went back in and bought it.

"Bagel for Erin!" the barista shouted, and tossed a white bag onto the counter.

She stopped, steps from the door. *Crap.* Now they were calling her for her actual bagel. While she had one in her hand. How was she going to play this off? The cinnamon scent of the stolen goods wafted under her nose, taunting her.

"Is there anything else I can get for you?" the other barista asked the man. The poor man she'd stolen from. Oh, why did she have to have a conscience?

"No. I only needed that kind," he said. She could tell he was trying to be polite, but annoyance laced in his voice nonetheless.

And here she thought her mother was the only one who could make her feel guilty as hell.

Erin got a better look at the man. He was in firefighter blues, the uniform molding against his broad shoulders, the name Bennett stitched across the pocket on his chest.

Her heart skipped three beats.

No. It couldn't be.

She hadn't seen Jake in years, not since late-night sleepovers with his younger sister, Hazel, at the Bennetts' house. Wistful glances were as far as she'd ever gotten. Jake and Erin's brother, Reece, had been inseparable. Jake had been the wild child. Reckless. Hot in that bad-boy type of way that Erin only liked from afar.

He was a boy then. Now, well . . . now there was little resemblance to that carefree heartbreaker. Her heart had never been in the cross fire, both because she was four years younger and also the fact that braces and acne didn't exactly scream *sex goddess*. Luckily she'd gotten over that phase. The sex-goddess situation was still to be determined because Lady O had been hibernating for the past year.

He shoved a hand through his jet-black hair, irritation written across his features. Very nice features at that. A strong stubbled jaw, cheekbones that were supremely unfair, and piercing blue eyes that glinted in the morning sun trickling in the storefront window.

She was going to hell. The man risked his life in the line of duty every day, probably saving children and puppies. And she'd just stolen his bagel.

"I'll just go somewhere else. No problem."

Standing forty minutes in line for a breakfast item constituted a big deal in her book. That pang of guilt twisted tighter in her gut.

Just let him walk out the door. He has no idea what you did.

"Bagel for Erin," the barista called again.

Erin shrank into herself as the woman said her name even louder this time. The hairs on the back of her neck stood on end, and she looked around the bakery. C'mon, didn't someone want to hop on the opportunity to claim the best damn bagel in the whole city that she should be eating instead of cinnamon raisin?

No takers.

Damn.

She strode up to the counter and grabbed the bag just so they'd stop calling her name. And now she was in possession of two bagels. What the hell was she going to do with this?

Before Erin could stop herself, she ran after Jake's retreating figure, coffee in one hand, two bagels in the other. "Jake," she called.

He turned around, and a shuttered breath escaped from her mouth. Frontal view was way better than the profile.

What was that old saying? Aged like fine wine? Erin was more of a beer girl, so she didn't get all the hype of vintage years. But cheese? Now that was speaking her language. And Jake had aged to perfection, like a great parmigiana reggiano.

Jake did a double take as recognition washed over him. "Erin? Wow, I haven't seen you in—"

"A while." A little over ten years. Not since she was seventeen, and he'd gone off to fight forest fires in central Oregon during a particularly dry summer.

"I heard you were back up from San Francisco."

What was that? Oh, just her pulse ratcheting up ten notches. He'd kept tabs on her? Not that she didn't do her own social media stalking every once in a while.

He cleared his throat, and his fingers combed through his thick black hair. She clenched her fingers tighter around the bagel bags before she did something stupid like scale him like she was a friggen mountaineer. "Reece mentioned you were teaching down there," he amended.

"Yeah, I'm just up for the summer to help out with my mom's surgery and fill in at the food truck."

His lips tugged into a smile, and creases formed in the corners of those ice-blue eyes.

Um, yeah, the whole lady-bit region was totally on board with that grin. Hot men were a staple of California life, but Jake didn't fit the mold of what she'd become accustomed to over the past decade. He didn't emit the expensive salon-haircut pampering vibe. No, his mussed hair and the way-past-five-o'clock shadow elicited thoughts of rugged, filthy desire. A man who didn't mind getting his hands dirty. Someone capable of taking care of a woman's needs.

Hello, ten years of pent-up imagination. Nice to meet you, old friend. Yup. Somehow, standing in the middle of a coffee shop, holding his stolen bagel, didn't seem like an appropriate time to fantasize about her brother's best friend. Try telling that to the sudden need pulsing between her legs.

"I always loved their peanut butter."

"Thanks." Erin hid a smirk by taking a sip of coffee. Truth circle? She'd kept a jar of Jif stashed under a floorboard in her room throughout high school. Homemade peanut butter was okay, but nothing compared to Jif, in her mind. She was a traitor to her own family.

What the hell was she supposed to say again? Her brain had fuzzed over after he'd first looked at her. She gripped the bags in her hand, and the plastic crinkled, cutting through the Jake Bennett haze that was as thick as Bay Area smog. Oh, right. Bagels.

She cleared her throat. "I didn't just stop you to catch up, though. There was a mix-up, and I grabbed your bagel instead of mine." She held up the bagel, a bite mark marring the fluffy bread.

His lips spread into a wide grin. "You know, if you wanted to talk to me, there are easier ways than bagel thievery."

Jake stared down at the bagel that Erin held in front of her. Or at least he was trying to focus his attention there. Instead, his gaze kept drifting to the black tank top that conformed to every luscious curve. She'd just been a kid when he'd last seen her. Since then, everything had been replaced with a feminine softness that he wanted to bury himself in.

"I'm sorry." A flush filled her cheeks and ran along the delicate column of her throat. *Damn.* Reece's younger sister was no longer little. And he was a shithead for even having thoughts like that about her. In fact, Reece would probably throat-punch him if he'd been in the vicinity.

"No problem." His daughter would just give him more of the evil eye he'd become accustomed to lately. "I'll head over to Patsy's on Albina."

They didn't have nearly as good of a selection, but it'd have to do. Because if he spent any more time with Erin, he might do something stupid, like reach out and tuck that stray strand of hair behind her ear. He clutched his hands into fists.

Jake could be counted on for a lot of things: a ride home from the bar, a perfectly grilled steak, keeping his men safe on the job. But most of all, he kept his word. Even a promise made to his best friend years ago, swearing that not a damn hair on Erin's head would be touched by Jake.

That day still rang clearly in his mind. They'd just gotten home from a varsity baseball game senior year, and Reece had fled to the kitchen to grab a couple of sodas from the fridge. Erin had come downstairs, her hair dripping wet, fresh from the shower. At the time, his first thought had been, *She's cute.* But more in a little-sister way because she had just been a freshman at that point. Reece had walked back in the room, tossed him a Coke, and said, "Don't mess with my sister." And that'd been the end of that. Bro code was in full force, and he didn't intend to break that, no matter if it was more than a decade later.

"Did you want this everything bagel?" She held up the white bag, her red painted nails biting into the paper.

"I appreciate the offer, but I needed a cinnamon raisin."

Erin nervously tucked the strand of glossy hair Jake had eyed earlier behind her ear, teeth raking over her bottom lip, which proved to be very distracting. "At least let me give you some money to pay for it. I feel terrible. It looks like you just got off work."

Normally he'd be wearing his civilian clothes when he finished a shift, but he'd been too tired to change out of his blues after the charity event this morning. "A double, actually."

Her frown deepened. "I think I've just been moved up a circle in hell."

A smile twitched at his lips. "If we're really getting into semantics, I think that means you moved up two circles, since it was a double." Teasing her was one of his and Reece's favorite pastimes. She was easy to rile up, but the true definition of a firecracker. She had no problem handling herself.

She put the bagel-wielding hand on her hip and pursed her lips. "I'm at least attempting some bagel diplomacy over here."

"Anyone not related to Reece and I might almost believe it." He was shitting her, of course. Reece was one of the good guys. He'd managed to keep Jake from doing anything too stupid in high school. He most likely owed the guy for keeping him out of jail with half the harebrained ideas he'd come up with. Bumming a police scanner off his older cousin and following around police cars when he was in high school? Probably not the smartest of choices. Though, nothing catapulted you into adulthood like a positive pregnancy test and a disappearing baby mama.

"You know, you're probably right." She gave him a mischievous smile. "Why even bother? I know who I'm dealing with." She brought the bag up to her face. Those pretty pink lips wrapped around the bagel as she took a bite. Jake's throat went dry.

She wiped a crumb from her lip, and it took every bit of self-control to tear his gaze away. Seemed that feisty streak in her hadn't been extinguished over the years. He liked that in a woman.

Reece's sister. Off-limits. Stop, idiot.

"This is how you treat a friend you haven't seen in ten years? California turned you into a cold woman," he teased.

"I'm sorry. What were you saying? I can't hear you over the crunching of this delicious bagel." She licked a dab of cream cheese off her finger. "So good."

He chuckled. She'd be eating her words if she knew this was for his daughter. He was gentleman enough not to make her feel bad. But as much as he was enjoying this chance meeting with Erin, he really needed to get back to Bailey and give his mother a reprieve. Even if Bailey was a good kid, a twelve-year-old was a lot to handle by anyone's standards.

"I'm glad you take satisfaction from my personal pain."

"Payback for all those times you called me Heron Erin." She gave him a playful shove, and Jake kept his hands firmly in his pockets because the alternative was pinning those hands to the nearest storefront wall and devouring that mouth of hers.

"I guess the nickname doesn't apply anymore," he said. Jake and Reece had been inseparable when they'd met in elementary school. During the summers, Erin had liked to follow them around when they'd played out in the neighborhood. She'd tagged along in that annoying little-sister kind of way. At the time, they had come up with Heron Erin because her neck was a little long, and it had stuck over the years. But the kiddish nickname didn't fit now.

"Assholes." Her smile faltered a fraction. "I really am sorry, though. My offer still stands to buy you another bagel."

They'd made it to the edge of the storefront, brushing past customers waiting in the line snaking down the side of the building. For late June, the weather was uncharacteristically warm, and Jake cursed himself for not changing into his basketball shorts before he'd left the station.

Erin didn't look like the heat bothered her at all, which wasn't surprising since she'd always loved the sun. Sunlight streaked through her blonde waves, creating a halo around her face, and her red skirt rustled in the light breeze, kicking the material up to the middle of her toned thighs. The coffee from earlier must have taken effect because his pulse pounded in his ears.

He thumbed the coin in his pocket, giving his hands something to do. *Leave before you do something stupid.*

"It's fine," he said. He just needed to get down to Patsy's, grab something for his daughter, and pick her up from his mother's house. Even if she didn't show that she missed him, he sure as hell wanted to spend some time with his daughter before she completely shut him out once she got to high school. Time seemed to speed up the older she got. "I'll catch you around."

He made it a few paces, and she was still at his side, taking a deep pull from her coffee cup, looking up at him with rich hazel eyes. She arched her brow.

"What are you doing?" he asked.

"What a coincidence. I happen to be walking in the direction of Patsy's, too."

"Oh, really. Where is your car parked?"

"Right in front of Patsy's, of course." She smiled sweetly.

"You never were a good liar."

"And you were never good at shaking me when I tailed you and Reece. Trust me. I've had years of experience keeping up with you guys. Just watch me."

He picked up the pace, just to see her little legs move double time. Okay, so he still got a lot of satisfaction out of giving her a hard time. Sue him.

To his surprise, she kept pace with him, even though she only came up to his shoulder.

"You're going to have to try better than that. I've got ten years of long-distance running under my belt. I can do this all day," she said.

The whole damn family had a persistent streak as wide as the Columbia River. He couldn't say he didn't mind the company, even though his head was aching to make contact with his pillow.

"You're not going to let this go, are you?"

Her toned thighs flexed with every step, and it took every ounce of concentration not to fall flat on his face or run into a parking meter. He shoved his hands in his pockets and focused his gaze to the sidewalk.

"Not a chance. I also can't help it if one of my twenties hops onto the register when you're ordering."

They were still speed-walking down the street, Erin clutching her cup of coffee in one hand, the two bagels in the other, her cheeks turning a deep shade of pink. She looked up at him with a look that screamed *Try me. I won't take your shit.*

And there came that word again popping into his head. *Cute.* But this time there were a few more adjectives tacked on. "Did anyone ever tell you that you're stubborn?" He slowed his pace, and they settled into a lazy walk. They were two blocks away from Patsy's, and Jake wasn't ready for their time together to end just yet.

She took another sip of coffee, and Jake caught himself staring at her lips again. He'd been out of the dating game for a while, but he could appreciate a beautiful woman when he saw one, and on a one-to-ten scale, Erin ranked a solid fifteen. Five bonus points for humor.

"You say it like it's a bad thing," she said.

"I say it as an objective bystander."

She chuckled, and they fell into stride next to each other, walking down the bustling city block. "People here just have a hard time appreciating a thing called tenacity."

"Is that so?" They made it to the front of the shop, and Jake made a show of looking around. "Hmm. Where's your car, Erin? You said you parked in front of the shop, right?"

She swatted him in the biceps. "Let me buy you your damn bagel, and then I'll walk you back to your car."

The next fifteen minutes passed by in a blur, and before he knew it, they were steps away from Jake's truck.

He leaned against the tailgate, not in as much of a hurry as he'd been when he'd first parked on Mississippi Avenue. Why the hell was he stalling for time?

The best answer he came up with was that he found himself doing the gentlemanly thing of keeping up polite conversation. He'd keep telling himself that was the reason he hadn't hit the "Unlock" button to the truck yet.

Erin's gaze took one long sweep across the length of the truck. "A step up from the beat-up Camaro you used to drive back in high school."

He'd forgotten that he'd given Erin rides to school when she'd missed the bus, and she'd tagged along to movies at the drive-in. The Erin standing in front of him was practically a stranger. A ten-year absence would do that, he guessed.

He sighed. "That was a great car." Women tended to prefer the back seat in his more rebellious days. But when Bailey had come along, he'd needed something more practical, so he'd grown a pair and sold it for a truck. He didn't often let himself think back to those days. What was the point when he had so much to focus on now?

Erin shuffled from side to side, gripping her coffee cup between her hands. "I should get going. You sure there isn't anything else I can do to make up for the earlier mishap? I'd take a few more bites of this, but I won't give you the pleasure of seeing me choke on my own guilt." Her eyes glittered with amusement.

The tongue on this woman. Yeah, he pushed any further thoughts about that portion of her body out of his mind before he needed to punch himself in the face. He'd grown up with her. Played laser tag in their backyard on long summer nights. This was obviously his body reacting to sleep deprivation. "Always a pleasure, Erin."

Before he thought better of it, he scooped her into a hug. Yup, that was a key mistake. He inhaled the tantalizing scent of coconut as her hair brushed the bottom of his chin. He definitely wasn't paying attention to the way her breasts brushed against his chest. Five seconds into the hug and he was contemplating making up a reason to stop by the Jenkins house sometime next week.

And then it clicked.

He did need her to do something. She'd be the perfect candidate to take to Josie's wedding. It was a lot to ask. But his family already knew her—she was friends with Hazel, another bonus. Her family wouldn't even think twice about Jake bringing her as a date because the Jenkins family had been a big part of his and Hazel's life years ago.

A safe choice. And it beat the hell out of Melissa from down the street with the cat-hoarding problem.

"Actually, there is something that you can do."

Chapter Four

"Slow down there, Speed Racer."

Erin shot her sister a look and continued wearing a path into the dingy beige carpet of the attic she'd converted into her personal woman cave in high school.

Her breath came out in shallow huffs as she continued to the closet. She shoved hanger after hanger to the side, not happy with any of the selections. Seriously, when did she have such poor taste in clothes? Her hammering pulse beat wildly in her temples. In fact, her heart hadn't stopped the damn palpitations since the moment she'd laid eyes on Jake. Pathetic? Yes. Bad for her health? Possibly. Those two crappy yogurts that were part of her stay-somewhat-healthy-while-in-carb-mecca plan weren't even worth choking down if she went into cardiac arrest. In fact, she could totally use another bagel.

No. No time for food. She was a woman on a mission. One that involved her not looking like a complete slob at Josie's wedding.

She may have had no chance in hell with her high school crush, but at the very least, she should have a killer outfit for the wedding.

Andie sidled up next to her as she continued to stare into the closet.

Cute dresses appropriate for a wedding: zero.

She may as well call Jake right now and tell him that she was sick. Came down with a bad case of I-officially-have-a-lame-wardrobe-itus.

Andie tapped a finger to Erin's forehead, jostling her out of her thoughts like she'd pulled a rip cord. "Earth to Erin. Anyone home?"

"What am I going to do? I don't have time to go shopping before tomorrow."

Andie cocked her head, the disbelief written clearly on her face. "You don't have anything? Not even a hoochie club dress?"

"Do I look like I'd own a hoochie-mama dress?"

Her sister gave her a once-over. "Good point. Haven't you been to any other weddings?"

She shrugged. All of her teaching friends had either already gotten married before she'd met them or were still unmarried, like she was.

Yep. She was as surprised as her sister. How had she made it through her late twenties without owning a proper cocktail dress? Now, shoes on the other hand, she had that on lockdown. It was her personal vice.

Erin motioned toward the closet. "Take a look for yourself."

Her sister dug through the closet, grunting and giving a few *Oh my Gods* when she ventured deeper. She came out seconds later holding up seven sweaters, all the same style, just different colors. "Dude. How many cardigans does a teacher need?"

She shrugged. "They were on sale."

"You could have worn this today, and then you wouldn't have to worry about the wedding."

Erin stuck out her tongue and grabbed the hangers from her sister, cradling the clothes to her chest. "Hey, don't diss my cardigans. They have feelings, you know." *Wow.* She'd really hit a new low if she was defending the merit of a sweater.

Clothes. She needed formalwear that she didn't own. For a wedding she hadn't even known about until yesterday. This was crazy talk.

"Plus, we're going as friends."

Andie let out a dry laugh, which was muffled because she was back in the depths of Erin's closet. "Sure you are."

"What is that supposed to mean?"

"You were all heart-eye emojis when you walked in the door. I don't blame you. He's hot."

"And way too old for you."

Her nineteen-year-old sister didn't need to be noticing men more than a decade her senior.

"Not like you know what my type is, anyway. Maybe I'm into older men." She reemerged from the closet, no miraculously awesome outfit in hand.

Erin let that comment slide. Her relationship with her sister had more twists and turns than Space Mountain. One day they'd be laughing their butts off over Skype, and the next, Andie was screening her calls. Erin would like to say it was teenage hormone crap, but she had a feeling that there might be more to it.

"If that's the case, good luck bringing one home living under Mom's roof," Erin said. Their mom was suffocating on the best of days. The boa constrictor of love. "Have you thought any more about college?"

"I don't think you checked in the back here. Maybe there's a dress tucked away." Andie disappeared into the back of the walk-in closet, completely ignoring Erin's question.

Okay. Guess she didn't want to have the college talk. Fair enough. It had devastated her mom when Andie had turned down a full ride to Portland State University on a track scholarship. Erin knew all about avoidance, though. She'd been doing it for the past decade. And had been successful so far.

"You could always go in a paper bag. It might be an improvement on some of these outfits."

Erin sighed. "You're a lot of help."

"Like you said. You're going as friends, so does it really matter what you wear?"

"Yes." The answer came out so suddenly that Erin wasn't sure if she was the one who'd said it.

An entire weekend spent with the Bennett family. For a wedding. Sure, she'd known the family well when she was a teenager, but this was Josie's special weekend, and she didn't want to impose. Then again, the palpable relief on Jake's face when she'd agreed . . . Well, she wasn't thinking about the bride's opinion at all. Hell, with those eyes on her, she'd be hard-pressed to say no to any request.

Down, girl.

He'd asked her as a friend—nothing more. Plus, she didn't even want to entertain thoughts of Jake in any capacity, not when she'd be back in California in a few short weeks. There was nothing to worry about here. Except for looking like she was living in a van under a bridge when they traveled to one of the fanciest resorts in central Oregon. In front of a guy who'd played front and center in High School Erin's fantasies.

Erin peeked into the closet and eyed her sister. She wasn't the same size as Andie, or else she'd bum clothes off her. And with her shift at her family's food truck starting in forty minutes, that left her zero time to head to the mall . . . unless . . .

She stared at her sister, who was still riffling through the closet. "I need a favor." She'd already managed to get her to cover tomorrow's shift, so this was asking a lot.

Andie gave up on digging through Erin's closet and plopped down onto the bed, squishing a few of her cardigans in the process. "The answer is no."

Erin tossed a shirt into the open suitcase. "You don't even know what I was going to ask you."

"I don't have to. You only ask for things that completely suck."

Damn it, she was right. But there wasn't anyone else to run the food truck if she bailed tonight. One of the college students who worked part-time for her mom had called yesterday and said he'd be back in town Saturday morning, which meant he could take over. Their mother was almost back to normal, just not able to lift anything for the next few weeks. And as much as she wanted to go to a wedding, she'd call Jake and tell him she couldn't make it if it meant saving herself the embarrassment of showing up in her chalk-marred wardrobe. Even her best peep-toe stilettos couldn't hide the glitter crusted into her dress slacks. Ah, the glamorous life of a teacher.

"Are you free tonight?" Erin asked.

Andie managed to look bored. A lioness toying with its prey. "Depends." Erin hated these games because her sister was a much better negotiator. She'd suggest Andie enroll and major in law, but she didn't want to piss her off, especially when she needed a favor.

Familial bond only went so far. Then came bribery. "On?"

Her sister pushed at her cuticle. "Can I borrow your Jimmy Choos on my date next weekend?"

Erin would not whimper. Nope. Wouldn't happen. Not like she'd poured half of her first paycheck from teaching into buying those babies—they had sentimental value at this point. Just one of many milestones she'd achieved in her career. Her lips wobbled at the thought of not seeing her students next year, how she felt like she had so much more to give to that school.

"If you promise not to scuff them."

The shoes in question sat tucked away in their original box in the back of her closet. She wore them on days her supervisor assessed her classes. During state testing week. Hell, she wore them whenever she needed that extra lift to feel strong. Badass. Invincible. Like Saturday night when she'd surely need the ego boost because first dates were not her forte. Not that this was a date. Just two people going to a wedding.

Hopefully the bar would be well stocked.

Jake smoothed a hand across the back of his neck. *Shit.* It'd been a while since he'd taken someone out. Years. Now he'd be spending an entire weekend with Erin. Hell, he didn't even know her anymore—it was practically like taking a stranger to the wedding. The idea seemed a lot better in the heat of the moment, when they were joking around like the good old days. But now, with an overnight bag stowed in the back of his truck and time to think about all the ways this situation could go sour, he wasn't so sure.

Chances were slim that he'd really screw it up too much since Josie had packed the itinerary so full that there were designated bathroom breaks listed. Even with the overscheduled weekend as a buffer, that didn't stop the sweat from slicking his palms.

He cut the engine as soon as he pulled onto the street in front of Erin's house. There were two cars parked in the narrow driveway. One was the same minivan Mrs. Jenkins had used to pick Reece and Jake up from soccer practice.

The air-conditioning unit in the first-story window hummed loudly as he shut the door to his truck and walked toward the porch. Ivy twisted around two pillars bracketing a cheery yellow-painted door.

From the street, this home resembled many of the downtown bungalows—well loved, preserved through decades of city expansion, a house similar to what he'd grown up in. A few years ago, he'd decided to move to the suburbs on the outskirts of town, because after a long day, the last thing he wanted was to be caught in the middle of the hustle and bustle of downtown.

Jake crossed the front porch and stood on the doormat. He peered down and chuckled as he scanned the cursive print that read Hi, I'm Mat.

Corny as hell, but it was similar to his mother's humor, and heck, the woman who'd raised him drove him up the wall, but he still held a soft spot in his heart for her.

Before he could lift a hand to the doorbell, the door swung open, and Erin's mother stood with her arms spread, a smile on her face.

"Jake Bennett. Come here and give me a hug."

He wrapped his arms around the woman who'd treated him like he was family growing up. She still smelled the same—lavender, with a touch of vanilla. It was a nice fragrance, one that was both motherly and comforting.

She held him at arm's length and blew out a whistle as she gave his arm a firm squeeze. "Christ, boy, what are they feeding you at that fire station? I could bounce a quarter off those biceps."

"Mom!" Erin groaned.

"What?" She shot her daughter a look. "I'm menopausal, not blind."

Jake had the good sense to hide his amusement and instead politely smiled. He wasn't going to get in the middle of this, especially when he was about to get a similar dose of his own mother's comments when they arrived at Three Sisters Resort.

A tinge of pink spreading across Erin's cheeks was the only response to her mother's question. Damn, she was adorable.

Did Erin notice? Jake wondered. He worked out daily in order to keep fit for his job. But he'd long since stopped the peacocking he'd done in his early twenties. Something about Erin's flustered expression sent a jolt straight to his cock.

"To answer your questions, I'm the one that cooks during my shifts at the station. It saves me having to bust out the fire extinguisher." Cole and Reece were great at a lot of things, but cooking wasn't one of them.

"A man who can cook"—she turned to her daughter—"Erin, this is the kind of man you need in your life."

Erin smoothed her thumb and her index finger along her brows and muttered, "Please ignore my mother. She's still on pain meds from the surgery. I'll be back on Sunday. Love you. Bye." She gave her mother a hug and murmured something in her ear, soft enough so that Jake couldn't hear from across the room.

And with that, Erin rolled her suitcase out the door and gave a quick wave before wheeling down the walkway.

"It was a pleasure seeing you, Mrs. Jenkins."

"You tell your mom that we need to get together to play bridge one of these nights."

"Will do."

She shut the door behind him, but not before giving him a little wink.

Jake grabbed Erin's suitcase, carried it down the driveway, and hoisted it into the bed of the pickup. For a two-night trip, her bag weighed enough that it might accrue overage fees on an airline.

He rolled his shoulders back before opening the door. This was no big deal. Just one weekend out of his life. The festivities would blanket most of the awkwardness.

As he slid into the truck, he was immediately hit with the fragrance of Erin's coconut shampoo. His goddamn eyes nearly rolled back in their sockets as the intoxicating scent hit his nose.

Friendly wedding date. Emphasis on *friendly*. It was a safe assumption that weddings ranked somewhere along the lines of running stair exercises in full gear, but this time he just might look forward to putting on his rental tux. Or maybe he was experiencing a contact high from all the coconut in the car.

He glanced over to Erin's side of the truck. Her face was still bright pink as she leaned into the headrest. "So sorry about that," she muttered.

"I spent my entire childhood at your house. Nothing your mom says will faze me." In fact, he clearly remembered her giving the sex talk one night after she'd had one too many glasses of wine. She'd told them that in order to stay safe, they had to double-wrap it. With that logic she had bestowed on them, it was a wonder there weren't more Jenkins siblings.

"Really? Because the older I get, the more I wonder if that is my future."

"Unless you start pinching guys on the ass, I think you're good."

Her hands shot up to cover her mouth. "Oh my God, did she do that to you?"

"Not today."

She groaned. "Glad I got you out of there before she had the chance, then."

He turned the key in the ignition and glanced over at her. Jean shorts, a tiny black tank top, and dark red lips. His personalized version of temptation. He gripped the steering wheel tighter. "Ready to hit the road?"

The gravity of that statement hit him harder than a battering ram. He'd be spending the weekend with Reece's sister. He'd run it by him the other day after he'd asked Erin, and Reece had texted back: That's fine. Just as friends, right?

"As soon as we find a good station." She went to reach for the presets for the radio.

He intercepted her hand before she could hit the buttons. "Whoa, whoa, whoa. Hold on there, Heron."

"Oh, so we're back to name-calling?"

Yes. Because it was a reminder of who she was. Who she'd *always* be in his eyes.

Jake would first and foremost never cross his friend, but there was also the fact that he had his daughter, Bailey, to think about. And that he didn't even know Erin anymore. She was doing him a solid by filling in to appease his mom this weekend, but that was it. End of story.

"If you're going to mess with a man's stations, then yes, Heron. The name is making a comeback."

"That is the most ridiculous load of crap I've ever heard. Everyone knows it's the copilot who picks the tunes."

He cut his gaze to her. "*Tunes?* Okay, Grandma."

"Holy crap. I *am* turning into my mother."

"If you start pinching my ass, I'm going to have to pull the car over."

She gave him a playful shove.

"Okay, fine. Pick the music. Let's hear what you're going to subject me to for three hours." He gestured to the radio with his chin.

He put the truck into gear and turned off her street, toward the highway. Three hours. What the hell was he going to do with three hours? As long as he kept his eyes on the road, he should be fine.

To his surprise, she picked a local country station that was already on Jake's presets. He wouldn't have pegged her for a country fan, but then again, the woman sitting next to him was not the same person he had grown up with.

After a few minutes of listening to George Strait and Reba, Erin splayed a hand over her tanned thigh. "So nice to get out of there for the weekend."

"Haven't you only been in town two days?"

"You have met my mother, right?" She smiled and shook her head. "I think she's just getting a little antsy because she doesn't have any grandchildren yet."

He laughed. "Word of advice: once you start, they just keep asking for more." Even though he'd never married, his mother still asked when he'd give her another granddaughter. He loved the close-knit community his family had built. When he had been growing up, he'd never felt lonely because there had always been someone to throw a ball with. Someone to run around downtown with. Someone to get in trouble with. He wanted that for Bailey but had never found the right woman—or had stopped trying a long time ago.

A long stretch of silence passed that tripped Jake up on his momentum. It was easy talking to her once they found a rhythm, but right now it was as erratic as an EKG during a heart attack.

Erin's muscles in her toned legs flexed as she bobbed her knees. Nervous. She was just as nervous as he was, he decided. Asking her along had seemed like a sensible choice at the time, but what was he supposed to do with her all weekend when he wasn't busy running errands for his sister? He'd hung out with her brother all these years, not Erin. And then there'd be a million questions from Bailey. Maybe he really would have been better off going with his mother's neighbor.

This was a bad idea. A code 10-50 bad.

More awkward silence.

Jake made the swooping loop, entering the interstate. *Talk. You've done it before. One word after another.* Before he could say anything, a semitruck moved into his lane without a signal, and Jake had to cut a hard right in order to avoid colliding with ten thousand pounds of metal. Erin squeaked, fumbling her phone. It bounced off the center console and landed somewhere near his feet.

He righted the car, his heart pounding. "Sorry about that," he said. Worrying about the damn weekend wouldn't do him any good if he and Erin were pancaked into US-26.

"Who needs coffee when adrenaline amps up your heart rate?" She let out a nervous laugh. She shifted in her seat, peering around the truck. "Huh. Where did my phone go?"

"By my feet."

"Here. Let me get it before it slides under your pedals." She reached over, gripping the armrest between them, fishing for her phone. Her hair splayed across his jeans as she pawed around. Jake kept his eyes on the road instead of the view that would surely be seared into his brain for the next year. Lush fir trees, the sun peeking over Mount Hood. Yes, if he focused on the top of the ski run, he could effectively shut her out.

"Of course it's all the way in the corner." She unhooked her seat belt, bent over even farther, this time gripping Jake's leg for support. Her red nails bit into the fabric of his pants, and she let out a tiny grunt as she managed to grab her phone. An image of her nails digging into his back as he took her against a wall flashed in his mind, and he gripped the steering wheel until his knuckles ached.

Holy hell.

He was going to need to keep his distance this weekend before he did something *really* stupid.

Her fingers left his thigh as Erin popped back into her seat and buckled herself back in. "Good thing they make protective cases, right? I drop this thing like ten times a day," she said, smiling over at him.

"Right. Good thing." Phone cases were the farthest thing from his mind right now, but he was trying his damnedest to be a gentleman. And failing.

After another moment of silence, Erin cleared her throat and asked, "How old is Bailey now?"

The subject of his daughter doused all his previous thoughts. "Twelve." *Twelve and 192 days, Dad. Get it right* is what Bailey would say if she were in the truck with them right now. Was it bad that he would kill for his daughter to act as a buffer right now?

"Same age as my students." Jake caught the frown out of the corner of his eye. Something had happened with her job, but he didn't feel comfortable enough to press the issue.

"Then you know what you're getting into." He loved his daughter, but preteen girls were a scary breed, especially for anyone who wasn't related.

She turned to him, those red lips twisted into a wicked smile. "Trust me. I'd take them over high schoolers any day of the week."

That was not comforting.

One phase at a time. It was the only thought that prevented him from waving the white flag in regard to parenting.

"Where is she?"

"She wanted to ride up with Julie. They're getting pedicures with Hazel and Josie."

"Sounds like she's in good hands."

"She is. They love spoiling her." As much as he gave his sisters shit, he knew they were taking good care of her. He'd painted Bailey's nails when she was younger and played princess tea party, but nowadays, he had no clue how to even pique her interest besides sending her into Sephora with his credit card.

When he'd gone out with his buddies after a shift and he'd met the occasional woman, he'd kept his daughter out of the equation. He wanted to keep her safe and protected, especially after the whole Brittany debacle and the disappearance of her mother, Maisey. It had been a long time since he'd opened up to anyone besides his family and his unit. But he found himself swapping preteen horror stories with Erin as they drove over the mountain pass and the lush greenery turned to high desert, and he felt lighter than he had in years.

Erin stared at Jake's hand as it gripped the gearshift in his truck. His thumb made slow, lazy circles around the notch of black plastic. Jake had dressed casually today, in a navy-blue T-shirt and well-worn jeans. The material of his shirt stretched to capacity around the arms, giving way to tanned skin corded with muscle. Jake had the type of biceps that Erin wouldn't even be able to fully encompass with both hands. That, paired with the veins snaking up his forearms, and she was going to need to find something else to focus on the rest of the weekend. Perhaps the lovely high-desert scenery. Ruddy rocks and ridges were just as appealing. *Yep.*

She'd already made the cardinal mistake of touching the guy. The way his solid quad muscles had jumped under her touch had nearly sent her spiraling. That was it. A million and one fantasies unleashed, ones she couldn't unsee even if an industrial-size container of bleach was involved. One minute she was trying to get her phone, and the next, *Pow, hello there, Mr. Firefighter, I think my house is burning down. Please, carry me to the safety of your bed.*

She focused back on their conversation. She'd managed to bring up a safe topic—his daughter. That effectively stopped the whole arsonist scenario she'd toyed with for a hot second.

Just as Jake finished telling a story about how Bailey's recent foray into contouring was an absolute bust, he turned down the drive of Three Sisters Resort. Both were silent as they wound up the inky black road. Her gaze settled on the landscape, the dusty clay, the abundance of firs. The type of beauty that would be perfect for a panoramic postcard.

The elegant Three Sisters Lodge spanned the length of at least two football fields. A sprawling lawn of lush grass and flowers rolled down the hill, ending at a gazebo area filled with twinkling lights and white folding chairs. Erin presumed this was where Josie would be saying her vows the following evening. Canopied sitting areas were located in several spots on the grassy expanse, so inviting—the perfect spot to read a book. Or down a few margaritas. It was a charming place to have a wedding and undoubtedly cost more than her teaching salary. When she'd gotten her first paycheck, she had been stoked. Until she had realized 90 percent of it went to rent and food in the city. Nothing quite took the wind out of a newly graduated person's sails like being thrown into adulthood.

She turned back to Jake, whose white knuckles had a death grip on the steering wheel. Tendrils of tension wound around her neck. It wouldn't just be them in the truck anymore. Which was a shame, because even if she was fighting the whole awkward "I'd dry-hump the crap out of you" urges, it was surprisingly easy to slide back into the comfort of talking to an old friend. Now it was showtime.

"Looks like everyone is here already," he said.

Jake pulled the truck into the large gravel lot next to the main resort entrance, parking next to a silver Mercedes. He hopped out of the truck and wound around to her side and opened the door before she had the chance to unbuckle her seat belt.

"Oh, thanks." *Oh boy.* She was not expecting that sweet gesture. Neither were her ovaries. They might have been giving him a standing ovation.

To make things worse—or maybe better?—he held out his hand to help her down from the truck.

Seriously, where were these guys back home? The last guy she'd dated honked the horn instead of coming to her door when picking her up. He'd also taken her to In-N-Out for her birthday and forgotten his wallet. With everything that had just transpired in the last thirty seconds, she was 80 percent of the way to an orgasm.

Friends, she reminded herself. She was here on friend duty. She'd mingle with people, drink enough beer to alleviate the awkwardness, and then go back to bingeing on early-2000s shows, caring for her mother, and job hunting once she returned to her mom's house.

They extracted their luggage from the truck bed. As they meandered down the walkway, Erin glanced at Jake's overnight bag that wouldn't even fit her hair products, let alone a weekend's worth of clothes. *Men.*

She wheeled her suitcase up the cobblestone path, the wheels rolling loudly over each groove. Jake gave her a lazy smile, the skin around his eyes crinkling. *One foot in front of the other. Left. Right. Left.* Multitasking had always been her strong suit, but with one look at his lips, she was reduced to single-digit functions. Jake turned her into a certifiable mouth breather.

She chanced another glance at him halfway down the sidewalk. Such a deep red. They stood out against the closely trimmed beard. Erin had never been with a man with a beard. She wondered if it would tickle the inside of her thighs.

Wow.

That thought process derailed off course faster than traffic during a rainstorm in the city. *Smile does not equal face time between the legs, girl.* She brought her iced coffee to her lips and took a deep pull. *So hot out here.*

He held the door open for her as she walked through the massive entryway, rich red carpet hushing her tread as it squished beneath her sandals. If the outside looked like a small rustic palace, the inside reminded her of an elegant tree-house heaven. Wooden beams criss-crossed along the ceiling. A massive stone fireplace took up almost the entire left side of the room. Lacquered wood-and-leather chairs curved in a semicircle, facing the unlit hearth. For the middle of the day, it was surprisingly empty, only a couple of people filling up water cups out of a crystal decanter in the sitting area.

They made their way to the front desk in the center of the room. The concierge greeted them with a beaming, if somewhat forced, smile. "Welcome to Three Sisters Resort. Can I have the name of your room reservation?"

"Two rooms. Both under Jake Bennett." Jake had insisted that there be two rooms in order to make her feel comfortable with the whole voyaging-halfway-across-the-state-to-stay-at-a-luxury-resort thing. Twist her arm a little harder, please.

The concierge entered the information and nodded. "Lucky you got here when you did. Seems we've had an issue with overbooking for this weekend. These are the last two rooms available. One has an excellent entrance to the butterfly garden."

Erin and Jake quickly glanced at each other, and by the visible sag of relief in his shoulders, she could tell Jake was thinking the same thing she was: that the concierge might say something ludicrous like they'd have to share a room. Not that she'd really put up that much of a pro-test. But for the sake of making this weekend as painless as possible, it'd be safe not to be in a room alone with him for more than ten minutes. A girl had only so much willpower before things like *Please, show me what those biceps would look like as you press me up against a wall* or *Can I smack your ass as you fireman-carry me to my bed?* word-vomited out of her mouth. Yeah . . . this was going to be a long weekend if corny one-liners were already winning out over coherent thoughts.

"Let's put the bags in our rooms and meet back here in twenty. Sound good?" Jake said.

She cleared her throat, hoping her thoughts weren't etched on her heated cheeks. "Works for me."

They v-ed off at the entrance to the suite area, and Erin took a deep, calming breath as she walked down the hallway alone. Yes, she could do this. She wouldn't make an ass out of herself. She definitely wouldn't end up in Jake Bennett's bed, no matter how active her imagination was. And, oh, she was thinking up ten different ways to incorporate those sexy turnouts in the bedroom.

A quick glance at the door at the end of the hall told her she'd arrived at her destination. Shaky hands excavated the key from the pocket inside the complimentary pamphlet, and she slid it into the lock.

The mechanism beeped, and she jiggled the handle and swung open the door.

She stared.

And stared some more.

No.

She swiped at her eyes, just to make sure she wasn't somehow hallucinating.

Nope. They were still there.

Two raccoons scampered across the bed—her bed—over the night-stands, along the headboard. They both chittered at each other, and oh my, were they pooping as they ran? The fatter raccoon shredded the fluffy white duvet, ribbons of fabric flying into the air. The other one clung to the telephone and knocked it off the nightstand. Both landed on the floor with a *thud*.

The door to the garden was wide open, and insects had decided the cool air-conditioned room was preferable to the midday heat.

Erin didn't even bother stepping foot inside the room. Instead, she turned back toward the front desk and let the door slide shut behind her.

Chapter Five

Jake paced the spacious suite wondering what the hell he was doing. It'd been a mistake to invite Erin. He realized that the second he couldn't tear his gaze away from her smile.

Not like he could do much about it now, especially since they were three hours from home and out in the middle of nowhere. He'd make the best of it, he decided. All he needed to do was keep his distance. That was the smart thing to do. Just as he made another lap around the room, a knock came at the door.

He shook his head. His sister couldn't know that he'd already arrived. He'd be on wedding duty the rest of the weekend—at least give him a few minutes to get acclimated. Instead, when he opened the door, he was greeted with the one person he should be staying away from.

"What's up, Erin?"

She clutched at her overnight bag, her fingers straining against the strap.

His gaze landed on the two other bags beside her. Including her roller.

"There's an issue." From the way she worried her bottom lip, and the fact that she had everything in front of him, this couldn't be good.

"What kind?"

"My room is currently occupied by raccoons."

"Raccoons." He'd heard of a lot of things left in hotel rooms. Most of them falling under the do-not-use-a-black-light-on-this category. Raccoons were a first.

"Yeah, you know. The creatures that like to dig in trash cans and carry rabies. Although, I doubt these ones were rabid. I didn't see either foaming from the mouth."

She was rambling. Damn it, she was cute when she got nervous.

She cleared her throat and looked expectantly up at him with those big hazel eyes.

The concierge's words echoed in his head. "And there are no other rooms in the hotel . . ."

She mashed her lips together, and her knuckles turned white around the grip she had on her suitcase. "Yep."

A long, awkward pause ensued.

Shit.

If anything, Jake was a fixer. Busted pipe? All he needed was a wrench and caulking. Missing parts in an Ikea product? He'd make do. Making a hotel room appear out of thin air? He'd rise to the challenge.

"No problem. I can see if I can put you with Bailey and Julie," he said. Those were safe choices. He at least trusted his daughter not to traumatize Erin.

"Would you? Oh, thank you." She breathed out a sigh of what looked to be relief.

Jake grabbed his cell from the nightstand and dialed his sister's number. She picked up on the second ring.

"Shh . . . turn down the music or your dad will know that we're getting matching tattoos. Oh, hi, brother. Bailey and I are having zero fun over here." His daughter giggled in the background.

Jake shook his head and smiled. "No tattoos till she's eighteen." That had been his mom's rule in high school. He'd abided by it until the second his birthday hit. Then he had gone to the parlor and started on his half-sleeve tattoos—ones that were still a work in progress to this day. His mother had cried.

"What can I do for you?"

"Have any extra room in your suite? Erin is roomless at the moment."

"We don't. We already have four people in the room. Why don't you try Aunt Vikki?"

And so it went. He called Aunt Vikki, who had brought two of her great-nieces. Aunt Susan said her room came with only one bed. And that was it. He'd exhausted his list of people to call. He glanced at Erin, who sat at the edge of the couch, wringing her hands. He'd sorely overestimated his fixing abilities.

He took a seat next to her and blew out a breath. "So we got a problem."

"No room?"

"No. But I do have room here. I can sleep on the couch, and you can take the bed."

Bad idea. Horrible. He briefly entertained sleeping out in his truck.

Her brows gathered together. "You're sure? That won't bother you?"

It scared Jake how *not* bothered he was at the thought of Erin sleeping ten feet away.

"I insist." Hell, her brother might bust his kneecaps if he even looked at her the wrong way, but what was he supposed to do? Make her sleep in the hall? He'd rather drive her back home now and risk the wrath of his sister than contemplate that option.

"Make yourself comfortable. I have to go check and make sure that my sister isn't murdering the groom."

"If you need a hand burying a body, just give me a text. I've been doing CrossFit."

He cocked his brow, smothering his grin.

"Don't let the short stature fool you. Tire-flipping, butt-kicking machine at your service." She shoved up an imaginary sleeve and flexed her biceps.

There was that word again. *Cute.* Every muscle in his body tightened as he resisted the pull to reach out and caress the exposed sliver of skin between her shorts and tank top. "Put those away before you hurt someone," he said.

Manicured fingers hooked around the loops of her shorts as she smiled up at him. She moved across the room, dropping to the edge of the bed. It was amazing how much Erin had changed over the past decade. At seventeen, she'd been pretty in that sweet-girl-next-door kind of way. Now her blonde beach waves, cutoff shorts, and toned legs screamed anything but sweet. He pushed back thoughts of those legs draped over his shoulders.

As if her body was in tune with his thoughts, she uncrossed her legs and recrossed them in the other direction. The material rode up even higher, exposing more tanned skin. He bet her skin was as silky as it looked. Desire prickled down his spine, quickly going to other areas that did not need any excess blood flow at the moment.

Yeah, he needed to get the hell out of here. And fast.

He cleared his throat. "I'll have my phone on me in case you need anything," he said, patting the pocket of his jeans and coming up empty. And then he remembered that he'd plugged in his phone to charge since it was almost dead when they'd arrived. He pointed to the nightstand. "Just need to grab that and I'll be on my way."

Taking the safe route, he walked the perimeter of the room, trying to stay as far away from Erin as possible. Too bad he had to reach over her to get to the phone.

"Here. I got it." She grabbed for the phone and stood abruptly. In the span of a breath, her body pressed against his, her breasts brushing against his chest. He retreated a step, and his back hit the wall. *Christ.* Her body felt good against his. Too good. It took every ounce of restraint not to grab her arms, spin her around, and pin her against the wall.

She handed him the phone. "Sorry. I'll get out of your way now."

She mashed her lips together, and pink rose in her cheeks. What he wouldn't give to see where that flush ended, below the deep swoop of her top.

He gripped the door frame to the bathroom and clenched his jaw tight. *Get it together, asshole.* He hated that he had to keep reminding himself of who she was and just why it was such a bad idea to be sharing a room with her. And to think, given any other circumstances, he'd be getting ready for his shift tomorrow. With her brother.

"Right." He cleared his throat. He was doing that often enough now that it could be considered a chronic condition. "Well, I better get going."

Twenty minutes later, not even setting the table decorations on fifteen tables was enough to dull the memory of her curves. He shook his head and re-formed another ribbon on the centerpiece. He just needed to make it through the next forty-eight hours, and he could get back to his normal routine, one that did not include any thoughts about Erin Jenkins.

He never was good at lying to himself.

Erin sat at the edge of the bed and stared at the door. It'd been an hour since Jake had disappeared in such a hurry, one might think his pants were on fire. At least the guy knew how to properly stop, drop, and roll.

Her phone buzzed on the nightstand.

JAKE: Meet me at the barn in twenty? Got caught up in decorating.

Erin stared at the text. It'd be easy for him to come back to the room and pick her up for the rehearsal dinner. So what was up with him? He'd been acting weird ever since the ride up.

She stood and walked over to the window. She was done being the little sister, the third wheel. She'd make the best of this weekend, with or without Jake Bennett.

ERIN: No problem. C U there.

Chapter Six

Erin slipped into the corridor of the artfully distressed red barn that had been turned into an event hall. Cool night air whispered across her skin as the door swished shut. Goose bumps flecked her forearms and legs, and she held the tiny excuse of a shawl wrapped around her arms tighter as she took a moment to breathe. It wasn't that she had an issue with crowds—she worked with six classes of forty students every day. Or even the fact that it'd be the entirety of Jake's very large, equally loud family at the rehearsal dinner. It was the fact that he'd looked at her with such . . . she didn't even know how to explain it, besides the fact that he looked like he was going to eat her alive. Not that she'd object. It'd be a hell of a way to go. The fact that a single touch sent him running for the hills didn't bode well for her, though. There was a good chance that if the resort wasn't tending to her raccoon-infested room, she might have preferred to keep the wildlife company. It seemed like a safer option.

Jake had been helping his sister set up for the past hour, and Erin had taken the opportunity to take in the grounds of the sprawling resort. Crazy to think a mere three-hour ride over a mountain pass put them in high-desert conditions, and the fragrant Japanese maples and oak trees were now replaced with red rock, dirt, a smattering of ponderosa pines, and the occasional tumbleweed. White-tipped mountains towered in the distance behind the lake Josie and Tom would be married in front of tomorrow. If Erin had to pick a destination for her future wedding and had access to unlimited funding, this place would rank high on the list.

Booming laughter swelled in the hallway, and Erin's fingers bit into her palms as she convinced herself to walk into the room of people she knew so well yet who were also complete strangers, since she hadn't talked to them in the past decade.

As soon as she rounded the corner to the expanse of the main room, her gaze immediately connected with Jake's. Even from across the room, his baby blues blazed brightly against his shirt, the color a carbon copy of his eyes. His tongue ran across his lower lip, and there her lady bits went again, sounding the alarm. *Danger. Danger. Panties may disintegrate if you get within five yards of Jake Bennett.*

He scooted out from the table and quickly made his way over to her.

"You look"—he swallowed hard, his eyes a little wild—"gorgeous."

Erin smoothed her hands down the skirt of her dress. She'd been working hard lately to take compliments. Years of nitpicking every detail of her appearance was a tough habit to break. "Thank you."

More of that weirdness from before filled the air between them. Was it just her? Or did he also feel as if plucking out her eyebrows one by one would be more pleasant than this?

"You're not having seconds thoughts, are you? Because if you leave, my mother threatened to set me up with the neighborhood cat lady."

"What's it worth to you to keep that suit cat hair–free?"

"I can promise a slice of pizza and a beer," he said.

A smile tugged at her lips. What type of monster could pass up two of God's greatest gifts, right next to DQ Blizzards and dry shampoo? "Make it two slices and a Hefeweizen, and I promise I won't duck out."

"Deal."

Whatever it was that hovered over them dissipated as soon as Hazel sprinted up to the two of them.

She had the same raven-black hair as the rest of the siblings, but unlike Jake's baby blues, Hazel's eyes were a dark green. "Erin! I was so happy to hear Jake brought you as his plus-one."

She and Hazel had kept in contact over social media—the occasional comment or like on a picture or wishing each other happy birthday. But, besides her best friends, Sloane and Madison, she had let other friendships fade away over time. Her ten-year reunion was set for this winter, and other than Hazel, there wasn't really anyone else she wanted to catch up with. Bonus points—now she wouldn't have to spend extra money on a flight for the reunion because she was about to catch up with her now.

"This resort is absolutely gorgeous," Erin said.

"It might be a crime scene by morning with the murderous looks Josie was giving Tom earlier. Who knows," Hazel said.

Their oldest sister, Josie, had always been a little high-strung. One time when Erin had stayed the night, she'd grabbed a hairbrush out of Hazel and Josie's bathroom to brush out a few knots. Josie had lost her mind when she found one of Erin's blonde hairs in there the next morning. So it didn't surprise her that the planning and executing of a wedding was cause for some stress.

"I'll make sure to watch out for the chalk markings and evidence tags," Erin said.

"Crap." Hazel looked around toward the entrance of the barn. "I have to go help get the pizza. Catch up in a bit?"

Erin nodded.

As Hazel disappeared through the barn doors, Erin turned back to Jake, who looked more uncomfortable by the second.

"Ready to head to the table?" he asked.

As long as they kept talking, they seemed to be going back to their normal selves. Totally fine. She had this handled. She was a teacher, after all. Talking was her forte, and if she needed to spend the rest of the night talking about layers of the earth and the solar system, well, Jake would be a very informed individual.

"Lead the way." She motioned toward the table, where guests now boomed with laughter.

His palm pressed into the small of her back as he led her to the table that seated more than thirty of Jake's relatives and the wedding party.

The laughter died down as soon as Jake and Erin made their way to the foot of the table. Things like *This is so awkward* and *I really hope I remembered to blend my makeup into my jawline* played in a loop while the party looked her over.

"Everyone, you remember Erin," Jake said. "She's back from California for the next few weeks."

Shouts of "Hello" and "Welcome" echoed through the barn. A little too loud, but she could attribute that to the half-empty pitchers of craft beer and bottles of wine on the table. *Right.* Who needed to be nervous when the whole wedding party was tipsy?

Jake guided her to the empty chair next to his, and to his right sat a girl around the same age as most of Erin's students. With her bright blue eyes and dimpled chin, the girl was the spitting image of Jake.

"Erin, I'd like you to meet my daughter, Bailey."

"Bailey, this is Reece's sister, Erin."

Bailey gave a small smile. "You don't have a menagerie of cats, do you?"

Erin held up her hands. "I can't even manage a houseplant. Cat-free zone in my apartment."

His daughter punched his biceps and smiled. "You found a normal one on your own, Dad. I'm so proud of you."

Jake shot a pointed look to his daughter. "What Bailey means to say is that she's pleased to meet you."

Bailey shrugged and pulled out her phone, her smile fading. "That, too."

"She's a little upset because her best friend bailed on her last minute," Jake murmured into Erin's ear.

Erin couldn't help but notice the protective growl in his statement. What a complete 180 from High School Jake. Even though he was plenty nice back then, just the way he looked so tenderly over at his daughter ratcheted his hot points up several more notches.

The double doors on the opposite end of the barn sprang open, silhouetting Jake's older sister, Julie. "Pizza's ready!" she shouted as she cradled several boxes in her arms.

She, Hazel, and a few other people who also held several pizzas set the boxes down on a buffet table and popped them open. The smell wafted over to Erin, and it called to her like free Jamberry samples in her favorite Facebook groups. Her stomach gurgled in response.

"Your pizza bribery awaits." Jake jutted his chin toward the table.

Being hooked up with a cat lady seemed like unfortunate happenstance. But she wouldn't leave Jake up shit creek without a paddle in terms of wedding-date status this weekend. Plus, who couldn't be won over by deep-dish pepperoni? A monster.

She scooted back from the table and made her way to the food, standing in line behind the rest of the family members eager to snag a few slices as well. Jake stood directly behind her, and their bodies were close enough that the heat from his body warmed her skin. Just one step back and she'd be pressed against his chest. It didn't help matters that every time he moved, she'd get another quick whiff of his cologne. The subtlety of it made her want to bury her face into his shirt. Which . . . would 120 percent be a bad idea.

Wedding date. That was it. Just as a favor for a stolen bagel.

Stop being stupid. She quickly brushed the thought away because all it would do would put her in a spiral of angst that rivaled how she'd felt in high school. She'd had ample opportunity to date these past ten years. None of her boyfriends had even come close to making her feel the way Jake did when he was in the same room. *Desperate.* The kind that made smart women turn stupid. And, boy, was her dating IQ dropping at an alarming rate.

Yup. Closing in on the single digits.

She focused on the six boxes of pizza sitting atop the white linen-covered table. So many choices. They all looked delicious in a definitely-nose-diving-the-healthy-eating way.

Jake's breath whispered along the shell of her ear. "You can have anything you want."

She jumped in response. *Earth to Erin. Don't just stand here like an idiot.* She grabbed the pizza server and reached for a slice of pepperoni.

They were discussing pizza, right? Because "anything" might really stand for "shoving all these pizzas to the ground and being ravished on the table" instead. That'd work for her.

He chuckled. "Yes, I was talking about the pizzas."

Oh no. The pizza server clattered to the table, the slice of pizza going with it. She quickly grabbed the slice and shoved it onto her plate and inwardly groaned at the stain she'd just left on the pristine white linen.

"Did I really just say that out loud?" she asked.

"I don't know what you're talking about. I'm just here for the pizza." He grabbed the server off the table and plopped a couple of slices of some type of meat overload option onto his plate.

Please, let the floor just swallow her up right now. She managed to make it from the buffet to the table without talking, spilling anything, or telling her deepest, darkest secret. No one needed to know about her obsession with watching those oyster-shucking videos on the Internet with all the gorgeous pearls.

Erin shifted on the folding chair, placing a napkin over her lap. Most of the party had already made it back to their seats and were gorging on their slices of pizza. Smiles and laughter floated around the room, sending warmth radiating through her. She bit the inside of her cheek. Jake's family had always been nice, welcoming. Their motto was *The more, the merrier.* Which was a good thing, because there were enough grandchildren, cousins, aunts, and uncles to cover every event at the Olympics. This was in stark contrast to her family. Sure, she had her mom and Andie and Reece. But besides their grandma, they saw extended family only every few years.

Josie and Tom sat at the head of the table. Her pale-blue sundress matched his button-up, and she wondered if they'd planned this or if it was just coincidence. "They look so cute together."

Jake followed her gaze and bit back a laugh. "Bridezilla over there color-coordinated their outfits."

"I think it's sweet. It'll make for some great pictures." Erin should be taking notes because Josie had this wedding on lockdown.

"That's what she said. Although not as nicely as you." He pointed to the groom. "See the way Tom's clenching his fork? That's a cry for help."

She giggled. "You're awful."

Erin reached for the silverware set to her left just as Jake reached for his water. Warm fingertips brushed against the back of her hand, and Jake pulled back immediately, like she'd shocked him. Or she had bubonic plague. *Awesome*. Add this to how he'd practically run out of his—*their*—room earlier, and this was ego-boost central tonight.

He cleared his throat. "Sorry," he murmured.

"Jake, honey, can you get more ice?" Jake's mom called from down the table. Sadie had the voice of someone who smoked a couple of packs of cigarettes a day. She was a delightfully round woman who came up to Erin's shoulders, which wasn't saying much since she was five foot six on the best of days.

Without as much as a glance, his chair scratched against the hardwood floor as he backed away from the table. "Sure."

Erin caught his hand before he could make it past. "Mind if I come, too?" The thought of sitting at the table and making small talk was enough to give her hives. Plus, she'd get this weirdness all out in the open because she wasn't going to spend all weekend with him if he was going to act like a spooked horse.

Jake looked from the hallway back to the table, clearly debating his strategy. After a few moments, he nodded.

"I think it's in the storage room over here," he said. It was to the point where he wasn't even looking at her now. What the hell had she done?

Before he could disappear into the room, she grabbed his arm again. "Jake."

He swiveled to face her, his eyes nearly melting her into a puddle of goo. *Girl. Get ahold of yourself. It's just a freaking man.* Her body and mind were obviously on different terms. "Yeah?"

"Listen, this is just getting weird. Right? It's not just me?"

He quirked a brow. "Weird how?"

"Don't you play it off like it's all me." Erin did have a knack for making situations awkward, but there was no way she was the only one experiencing this level of discomfort. She put her hands on her hips. He had to feel this, too. One minute they were laughing like old times, the next, she was subject zero of an infectious disease. "It's like I have the plague or something."

"Do you have the plague?" he asked, clearly amused.

"No." Copious amounts of hand sanitizer ensured that. "But you're treating me like I do."

"I'm not treating you like you have the plague."

"Poisonous warts? Dengue fever? Halitosis? Take your pick," she said.

He moved closer to her, his scent a mix of cologne, beer, and mint encasing her. She'd like to say she didn't inhale it creepily, but she was still Erin Jenkins.

"None of the above." He swallowed hard, his Adam's apple climbing his throat.

"Then what is it?" She was at the point where she almost wished she hadn't come. At least then, she could live in her delusional bubble of reminiscing about the way things used to be, when he actually hung out with her.

Perfectly straight teeth raked across his bottom lip. "Being around you just brings back a lot of memories."

"Hopefully not embarrassing ones."

"Those are the best kind, Heron."

"I see." That was not an answer she'd been expecting. *Play it cool.* Yeah, she was never good at listening to her inner chi.

"Erin, as gorgeous as you are in that unfairly tight dress, you are my best friend's sister. I work with Reece. I don't want to lose my kneecaps because of something stupid I'd do."

"You want to do something stupid?"

He grinned, his eyes lighting up into the dangerous glint he used to have when he was younger and about to do something that he'd absolutely regret. The one that always made Erin's knees wobble like jelly. "Yes. Insanely stupid."

His fingers brushed against her cheek, scorching a trail down her jawline.

"Tell me, Erin. Do people still use the word *ravish*?"

Damn it. So he *had* heard her earlier. When she thought she'd kept her thoughts in her head—where they belonged. She fought back a cringe and squared her shoulders. She was a grown-ass woman and would own up to it.

"Those who read material other than *Firefighters Monthly*, yes."

"A lesser man might be offended." He took a step forward, and she parroted the move, taking a step back, her back hitting the wall. His arms bracketed her head, caging her in. "Feel free to peruse my science-fiction selection anytime you want."

She rolled her eyes. "If I didn't know you better, I'd call that for what it is—the worst pickup line in existence."

"Trust me, Erin, even if I dropped my best pickup line on you, it wouldn't work." He closed his eyes and took a steadying breath.

"Is that so?" Little did he know that he could use single-word commands and she'd be playing her own version of "What Would You Do for a Klondike Bar?" Except instead of ice cream, her prize would be in the form of licking other things.

He tucked a stray strand of hair behind Erin's ear, and she nearly bit back a groan as the calloused pad of his thumb brushed mere inches from her lips.

"You must hear dozens when you go out in California. All those pretty boys with their manicures." He looked at her, eyes searching, and if she went up on her tippy toes, her lips would be at the perfect position to meet his. As if he could read her thoughts, his teeth raked across his bottom lip.

Oh, girl. Shit was getting real up in here.

She swallowed, trying her best to play this off the coolest she could. Inner Erin was hyperventilating into a paper bag. "Can't forget the hair wax. And Armani."

"Is that what you like?"

She looked at Jake, in his button-up and dress slacks. If they were out in Portland, he might cause traffic accidents by the number of women who'd be rubbernecking to check him out. She preferred the Jake who wore faded jeans and a baseball cap.

"No," she admitted.

"What does a woman like you want?"

You.

"Why? You aiming to deliver?" she asked.

He moved in closer, his scruff brushing against her cheek, his leg pressing between her thighs. Her eyes fluttered shut, and she swallowed hard, leaning into his touch. *Oh boy.* This was not what she had been expecting.

"I—"

"Dad?" Bailey's voice came from around the corner, and the hairs on the back of Erin's neck stood on end.

Quicker than lightning, he separated from her, making his way into the storage room. He came back out moments later with a pack of ice over his shoulder, like he hadn't been about to kiss her.

As soon as Bailey rounded the corner, she continued, "Can I go out with Aunt Julie to the Little Roadhouse tonight?"

"Isn't that a bar?"

Bailey did that eye-roll sigh combo that most of her students had mastered. "No, it's a family restaurant and has karaoke. I want to hear Julie sing 'Baby Got Back.'"

Jake huffed out a laugh in response. "I'm surprised you even know that song."

Bailey shrugged. "I can rap the whole thing."

His brows pinched in response. "You memorized that song but refuse to listen to AC/DC? I've failed you as a parent."

She rolled her eyes. "So can we go?" She looked up at him with those same blue eyes. "Please?"

Jake dragged a hand through his hair. "Fine. But Julie needs to have you back at a decent time. I don't want you dragging for the ceremony tomorrow."

She bounced on her toes and flung herself at Jake. "Thank you, thank you, thank you."

He wrapped her in a hug and kissed the top of her head. "Yeah, yeah. Get going before I change my mind."

Seconds later, Bailey was bounding back down the hallway and skidded to a halt in front of Julie and the rest of Jake's sisters.

Jake loosed a heavy sigh. "She's going to be the end of me."

"She seems like a pretty decent kid in my book."

"Growing up too fast. She asked to bring a *date*."

Erin grinned back at him. "And what were you doing at thirteen?"

He groaned. "You really are trying to kill me, huh?"

"Let's get this ice to the party."

And just like that, the moment, whatever it was between them, was broken. It was probably for the best. Because what if he actually had done something like kiss her? Well, if that were the case, she probably would have welcomed it and locked them both in the utility closet. But that was a moot point now that they were back to the rehearsal dinner, and she was three slices past feeling sexy. She might have done that on purpose, but she was regretting it because a full stomach while sharing a small room with Jake now seemed like a bad idea.

Two hours later, Erin was helping pack up the leftover pizza with Jake and his mother.

"We're so happy you could join us," Sadie said, patting Erin's hand as she slid the last piece of meat lovers' extreme into a plastic bag. Her fingers were warm as she squeezed Erin gently. Tom was a lucky man marrying into this family. She'd always heard horror stories about mothers-in-law from hell, ones who made it their mission to fray the newly minted member's resolve. But Sadie defied societal stereotypes. She'd even sent care packages back when Erin had moved to California when her mom had been too upset to even speak to her for the first six months. Those jars of peanut butter and *Cosmo* magazines had been a godsend, especially when she had been stressing out about classes.

She tossed the bag of pizza onto the table. "Thanks. I'm glad I can see Josie walk down the aisle."

"It's going to be beautiful." Sadie beamed. "Still waiting for this guy to get his happily ever after." She wrapped her arm around Jake, who looked like he wanted to be anywhere but there at the moment.

"Bailey keeps me more than busy."

"Just saying, there's more to life than parenting."

Jake shot his mother a look, which seemed to go unnoticed as Sadie zipped up the plastic bags.

"And on that note, I think I'll take these back to the fridge." He grabbed the bags and made his way to the small hallway in the back of the barn.

Sadie's gaze lasered to the hallway, and she sighed. "He's a good man. Just wish he'd put himself out there."

Erin didn't know what to say to this. She wasn't one to put herself out there either, much preferring the simple routine of eat, sleep, and teach. "Somehow I don't think Jake will have any problem finding someone once he's ready."

The thought of Jake ending up with someone and having the 2.5 kids and a minivan made Erin's stomach churn.

"I'm just going to make sure all the lights are shut off and head to my room. Thank you again for your help," Sadie said.

"Of course." Erin gave her a hug and went to find Jake, who was still placing plastic bags of pizza into the fridge.

"Coast is clear. You can come out now."

"Who said I was avoiding coming out?" He closed the fridge and faced her, his broad shoulders straightening.

She swallowed hard, momentarily forgetting her train of thought. "It takes an expert to know one. Did you already forget who my mother is?"

He shook his head and smiled. "C'mon. Let's get back to the lodge."

They walked back in silence toward the main portion of the lodge. Most of the party had already returned to their rooms, and only a few hotel guests roamed around the front lobby.

"I appreciate you helping out tonight. You didn't need to do that." His voice was a soft rumble in the quiet courtyard, making every single hair on her arms stand on end.

"I know. But I was more than happy to."

For a moment, she saw the same flicker of desire cross his gaze. But as fleeting as a Southern California rainstorm, it was gone again. Obviously she kept misreading his cues. She didn't know why she expected any less. It had been the same thing that had happened years ago. Door shut. No interest. Get over it, girl.

Except this time it would be ten times more humiliating if she put herself out there and he turned her down again. How about a "Hell no" to that.

Jake bit the inside of his cheek as he regarded Erin. Her dress hugged every curve, the tight fabric landing midthigh, just begging to be pushed higher. Even if she'd claimed she was completely fine, her swaying while just standing upright spoke otherwise. *Definite hands off.*

"I had a really good time tonight," she said. Her head rested in the crook of his arm, and he guided them back to the room. Crisp mountain air ruffled her hair against his chin, and goose bumps flecked her skin as they made their way across the grounds. He pulled her tighter as she started to shiver. He hated to admit it to himself, but she felt damn good, her soft curves pressing against him. He slowed down his pace, taking his time to get to the room. Because once they got there, he wouldn't have an excuse to hold her anymore.

When they made it to the room, he led her to the bed. He guided her down on top of the comforter, propping her head on the pillow. She looked up at him, giving a sleepy smile that made his heartbeat quicken. He'd take the couch tonight—he'd already decided that much when she'd shown up earlier with her ridiculous amount of luggage in tow.

"I don't think Cat Lady would have been able to put up with my family for an entire evening."

She turned around, fluffed the pillow behind her, and leaned against it so she was sitting on the bed, her legs crossed. "Don't sell them short. Your family is awesome. Unless Cat Lady has hearing sensitivities." Erin was way too generous. His family was nice, but they were a lot to handle. Even as a blood relative, Jake needed a break sometimes.

"Not to my knowledge. But I doubt she'd be half as good a date as you are." He looked down, unable to hold her gaze. Yeah, that hadn't meant to come out. He was trying to keep things light, but after their interaction in the hallway, Jake didn't know what the hell to feel at the moment.

Her eyes widened in response. She sat up higher on the bed, her wavy hair swishing along her shoulders. One of the thin straps from her dress fell to the side, exposing the delicate dip of her collarbone. The red lace molded to her breasts, the fabric moving up and down with every breath. It'd take ten steps to get to the bed, maybe fewer.

"I have to make a confession."

"You do know I'm not a priest, right?" he said.

"I kinda had a thing for you all through high school. I know. Silly, right?" She bit her lip, and her cheeks bloomed a deep shade of red that matched her dress.

He should end this conversation right here. Tell her that he needed to get some sleep for the big day tomorrow. That would be the sensible thing to do. Instead, he said, "Why is that silly?"

"You were so far out of my league in high school."

"I was a stupid shit who didn't deserve someone nice like you." While Jake had participated in activities that had turned his mother's hair gray, Erin had volunteered her time at soup kitchens and knitted hats for homeless shelters. Even at fourteen she had been kind.

"Do you remember your senior winter formal?"

"Yeah." He'd been named winter-formal king, and his date, Janet Thompson, had been making out with his best friend in the guys' bathroom during the award. Shortest date of his life. Really, Janet was just the beginning of the string of women who would leave in his life. "What about it?"

"You gave me a ride home because I got sick."

Honestly, the night was a blur. Anger had taken hold after he'd found Janet, and he'd effectively blocked everything else out after he'd been crowned. He vaguely recalled driving her home. "Okay, yeah, I remember that."

"Do you remember what you told me in the car?"

"No. What?" Probably nothing useful if he'd been that upset. Plus, he'd been eighteen. Nothing remotely insightful had come out of his mouth at that point.

"Well, first, you told me liquor before beer, in the clear."

He laughed. That would be something that would have come out of his stupid teenage mouth. "I was a wise man back at eighteen. What was the other bit of wisdom I imparted on you?"

"Never trust a woman in a red dress." She smiled. "I'm pretty sure that was because your date was wearing red, but, regardless, I never had an issue with the last bit of advice."

"Wiser Jake would like to amend that statement to include all women. No matter what they're wearing." He had learned the hard way, but it was better to have no relationship than one that would let you down.

"Am I included in this lump generalization?"

"Especially you, Heron," he teased. But there was some truth to his statement. The only women who didn't apply were his sisters.

"You know, that nickname can die a fiery death anytime now."

"Where's the fun in that?" He shoved off the couch to get a glass of water from the bathroom.

"You're impossible." She threw a pillow at him, and he caught it inches from his face. "Why did I say yes to your wedding-date proposition again?"

"Because of my charming disposition and witty intellect."

"Those were not the reasons," she mumbled. She eyed him, steps from the bed, her gaze taking a long perusal of his body.

Damn.

"I'm not really tired. Are you?" She mashed her lips together. Her legs parted a fraction, a sliver of her black panties now in plain sight.

Blood rushed directly to Jake's cock. More than anything, he wanted to make his way to the foot of the bed, strip Erin of that dress, and show her just how *not* tired he was.

Do it. Go over there. Tear her clothes off. Make her scream your name. Every damn cell in his body told him that was exactly what he should do.

"No." He was not tired. At all.

Jake shoved his hands in his pockets, attempting to subtly readjust himself. His pulse pounded in his temples as he took the handful of steps needed to get to the bed. *Do it. Get into bed with her. It's been so damn long. Too long.*

His shins hit the edge of the bed, and his gaze met hers. Her eyes traveled down the length of Jake's body, her cheeks blooming a deep crimson. The way she looked at him made his temperature kick up a few degrees. His knees sank onto the down comforter, and she moved higher up the bed, her dress hiking to her hips. *Shit.*

Jake swallowed hard and continued his ascent up the bed. Erin's hands fisted the sheets, and her breathing seemed to become more rapid the closer Jake got. He stopped at her feet, sitting back on his knees. "I—"

His phone buzzed in his pocket. If his daughter weren't out tonight, he would let whoever texted go unanswered. But he couldn't do that—not when someone might need him, and he needed to make sure his daughter was okay. He pulled his phone out of his pocket.

BAILEY: Back at the resort.

The momentary relief that his daughter was in for the night vanished as the weight of the situation came crashing down on him. What was he doing? What did he expect to happen? Fuck Reece's little sister and have everything go back to normal like nothing ever happened?

He shoved his phone in his pocket and glanced back at Erin. Her brows pinched together as she watched him. "Hey, what's going on?"

Even though he wanted Erin so damn bad, he had other people to think about.

He cussed under his breath. "I can't do this." He couldn't believe he was saying this. Such a gorgeous woman in front of him. Wanting him. "I'm going to grab some water. You need any?" What a fucking cop-out. By the drop in her smile, she knew it, too.

"I'm good," she said.

And there came the uneasy silence again, filling the room like a box alarm fire. They'd keep it at bay the entire evening, and Jake had a feeling he'd need to work double time to get back to an easy groove with her.

Jake managed to pull himself off the bed and disappear into the bathroom. He splashed his face and came back with a glass of water. Erin had already straightened her dress and was tucked underneath the covers. He decided it'd be safer to take a seat on the couch, which sat perpendicular to the bed, about five feet away.

"Maybe we should chill out and watch some TV?" Anything to ease the tension in the room. Or avoid doing anything he'd regret.

"Sounds good to me."

Good. At least they were in agreement about something. Maybe an hour or so of *CSI* and a cold shower would douse these feelings.

Jake found the remote and sank down into the couch. Nothing like something mindless to lose himself in for a few minutes.

With the click of a button, the jumbo flat-screen TV lit up with more tits, ass, and dicks than he could count. Loud moaning blasted from the speakers, and he quickly went to change the channel. He hit the "Up" button and the "Down," and nothing worked.

"Jesus. What the hell is this?" Erin balked at the screen, to where the woman wearing cat ears was now crawling around on the floor, meowing while one of the men barked. He even had a studded collar around his neck.

"I—I don't know." Crap, why wasn't the "Channel" button working? He pushed down on the volume, and nothing happened again. None of the buttons seemed to work besides the "Power" button. Another loud groan came from the woman, loud enough that Jake was worried whoever was staying in the next room would call the front desk and complain.

"Can't you change the channel?"

"I'm trying." Shit, he hadn't felt this embarrassed since his mom had found his dirty magazines underneath his mattress as a kid.

"Meow, baby. Your stroke is purrrfect," said the woman on the screen.

"That's right, kitty cat. Now it's time to get your milk." The man spanked her.

For fuck's sake.

Finally, he was able to get the "Up" button to work, and it turned to *another* adult program. And another. What was this? Porn hour?

"Forget this shit." He clicked the TV off.

Erin looked over at him, and a smile twitched at her lips. Then she burst out into laughter, buckling over, her shoulders shaking. Jake couldn't help himself, and he found himself cracking up at the situation as well.

As their laughter died down, Erin wiped tears from her eyes. "Well, that was . . . enlightening. I didn't know animal erotica was coming back into fashion."

"Was it ever in fashion?" If so, he didn't want to know.

"Touché."

He stretched out on the couch while Erin rustled in between the sheets on the bed. She still had a grin plastered to her face. He hadn't been wrong earlier. Erin was sin and heartbreak. Two things he'd steer clear of this weekend.

Chapter Seven

Jake had managed to keep himself busy with wedding decorations the majority of the day. Now, he had to go back into the room to grab his suit for the wedding. Which was a blessing, because he'd woken up with a throbbing erection and the remnants of a dream about Erin's legs wrapped around him. Hell, he couldn't even escape her in sleep now. His sisters might say that this was his subconscious trying to tell him something. Luckily, he didn't believe in that crap. He was no stranger to compartmentalizing, and he'd do that in regard to Erin. Sure, she was tempting, but he could push those thoughts away.

He slipped the key card into the slot and opened the door.

A faint *tap-tap-tapping* caught his attention, and he turned to find Erin on the bed, her laptop on her lap.

"Don't teachers get the summer off?"

She looked up from her computer and gave him a bright smile that made all his earlier irritation melt away. "Not this one. Looking to see if there were any job openings since yesterday." She frowned, her eyes scanning her screen.

"Any luck?" He grabbed the suit from the bathroom and pulled his shirt over his head.

She shook her head, her shoulders drooping. Just like that, it was like a cloud had passed in front of the sun, darkening the mood. He didn't like to see her this way. Would do anything to erase that hurt in her eyes.

"We'll get extra drinks tonight at the wedding. Maybe we can go hiking tomorrow." He knew that look. She needed to get out of her head. Usually Jake's way of blowing off steam would be hitting the weights at the station, but he supposed any type of physical activity would do.

"I did bring a pair of hiking shoes."

He jutted his chin to the overnight bag and the carry-on. "You probably packed your whole wardrobe in that monstrosity of a suitcase."

She wagged a finger at him. "There's nothing wrong with having options."

He just nodded. Give him one or two choices and he was set. It seemed that Erin's life was one of those destination signs pointing in all different directions, with every city imaginable listed.

"Can you help me with something?" Erin called from the bathroom. Jake already had his suit on and had helped with the last-minute preparations. Now he was free for the next hour until the ceremony.

He walked into the bathroom and swallowed hard. Erin's dress was open down to the small of her back, tan smooth skin on full display. No bra. The thought made his dick twitch.

"Will you help zip me?"

It was one of those dresses that had the big opening in the middle, the zipper starting at her shoulder blades. "Sure thing." He grasped the delicate zipper between his fingers, and his thumb grazed her bare skin. A soft whimper escaped Erin's lips, and he bit down hard on his tongue. *Nope. Do not picture what sounds she'd make if your hands were other places.* But hell, he was only human. His mind went there. It went a lot of places, including what type of sounds she'd make if he took a nip at her neck.

She cleared her throat, snapping him back to the present. He'd been standing there for who knows how long, closer than he should have been standing. Just an inch closer and his chest would be flush with her back. It'd take less than two seconds to have her dress pooled on the floor—he'd put money on that.

Back. Off.

Reluctantly, he released her zipper and backed away. "I need to make sure my sister doesn't need anything else before the ceremony. I'll see you at the wedding?"

He shoved his hands in his pockets and thumbed the coin that was practically searing a hole through his pants. He had no right to be thinking those things. Not when this was Erin. Hell, he owed it to her to show her respect. She was here as his friend, and he'd like to keep it that way. It didn't matter that she'd admitted to liking him in high school. He planned on ignoring that for the remainder of the weekend.

She looked at him through the reflection of the mirror, her expression unreadable. Ever since last night, everything had felt different. Tighter. Like whatever was between them was seconds away from snapping. "Yeah, I'll sit by Bailey," she said.

"Great." He hadn't seen his daughter since last night. She'd sent him that text at midnight that she was back safe from her escapades with his sisters, but that was it. A pang of guilt hit him that this had been the last thing on his mind all day. "I'll see you soon."

He took one last look at her, blonde hair swept over her shoulders, her black dress hugging every mouth-watering curve.

He made it out of the room and loosed a breath, banging his head against the wall. This woman was his damn Achilles' heel. Twenty-four hours and then he'd be in the clear. Until then, he just needed to repeat to himself that he had enough willpower to stay away from her. He hoped it was true.

Erin chewed on her bottom lip as she sat on the bed, staring at the door.

"You're an idiot, Jenkins." Of course she had to go and make things awkward by blurting out that she'd had a thing for Jake since prehistoric time. There was a lot of last night that was fuzzy, but she remembered that part. For a second there, she thought she'd hit the jackpot, especially when he'd joined her on the bed. And then his phone had gone off and, boom, reality check.

Beer? No longer her BFF.

She pushed off the bed, strode over to the mirror, and gave one more look-over, deeming herself made up enough not to be given major side-eye by any of the wedding party.

Now all she needed to do was make it through this evening and never show her face around town again, and she'd be good. It was a solid plan. Mostly. Besides the fact that she was here in Oregon for another month.

She stood in front of the mirror, putting her hair into a half pony. Then down. Then all the way up into a bun. Then half down.

She let out a frustrated groan. "Come on."

Nothing looked right. Or maybe she was just freaking out and her hair was the only bit of control she had left.

A knock came from the door, along with a muffled "Housekeeping."

She shuffled around the bed and opened the door to find someone from the hotel staff standing behind a cleaning cart.

"Come on in. I'll be out of your way in just a second." She always felt awkward being present while someone came to clean the room because she always had the urge to help them pick up. "Just need to grab my bag, check my lipstick one more time, and should be good to go." Why did she feel the need to give this poor woman the play-by-play commentary? Maybe she really was starting to lose it.

Bag. Now. Go.

Making her way across the room, she searched for her little wristlet that contained her ID, cash, and aspirin in case the headache from this morning decided to make a reappearance. Her clutch sat on the coffee table by the couch, along with Jake's glass of water from last night.

He'd been in her bed. For less than two seconds, but still. If that text message hadn't come through, they might still be in there. Maybe.

She glanced at the clock on her cell phone. *Crap.* Fifteen minutes until the ceremony. She quickly backpedaled out from the tiny space when her legs hit the couch and she went down, ass first. She landed on something hard, and then the moaning came. Not from her, but from the TV.

"For the love."

She clicked the remote, and this time the "Power" button didn't work.

A woman dressed as a wizard stepped into the frame, wielding a wand. "You've been a very bad boy, Harry."

Oh dear God.

"This isn't what it looks like. This was the only thing that was on." She winced. Nope. Not the right thing to say. That would imply she *wanted* to watch the freaky-deaky debauchery of her favorite childhood series. "Not that I'm into this kinda thing. I mean, if you are, more power to you."

"Is that a wand in your pants, or are you excited to see me?" came from the TV, full blast. Erin cut her gaze to the plug in the wall and debated tearing it out.

"I mean, this is the only channel we were able to look at because the remote is broken."

Erin smacked the remote against her palm and tried the "Power" button again. Nothing.

The housekeeper stared at her, arching a brow. Yeah, she wasn't buying it. Wasn't it in their job description to not pass judgment on hotel guests? Because Erin would put money on this woman witnessing weirder stuff than role-play porno.

"I've been a bad little wizard and cheated on my exam. Punish my chamber of secrets, baby."

Come. On. Stupid. Button. Her zero chill factor made a brief drive-by, and now Erin was in full-on meltdown mode.

She tried the remote one more time, and the button remained stuck inside. She raced to the wall and ripped the plug out, closing her eyes, and then turned slowly toward the housekeeper. "Can we just keep this between us?"

The housekeeper held up her hands, a scrubber in one hand, a bottle of cleaner in the other. "I didn't see anything."

Well, at least she wouldn't have to worry about that anymore. One more night and she'd be out of here. It was bad enough she had to skirt around Jake in the room while they pretended not to be in each other's space.

Enjoy the wedding, be a good date, then it was back to the grind with job hunting.

As soon as she walked out to the main area, her breath evaporated from her chest. Across the grassy expanse, chairs had been set up to face the deep-blue lake that glistened in the afternoon sun. A wooden pergola, intricately carved with vines and leaves, was set up in the center, twined with exotic flowers of various shades of purples and blues. Five rows of white chairs were laid out on either side of the makeshift aisle, and rose petals lay on the runner covering the lush green grass. A dream wedding, Erin decided. On a teacher's salary, she'd either need to not buy food for the next five years to save for this or marry into a really, really rich family. So basically it wasn't in the cards. Which was fine. Erin wasn't one for glitz and glam—because, let's face it, dry-clean-only clothing did not mix with Crayola products or science experiments.

Josie and Tom's wedding was set for six o'clock on the dot, leaving them in the last hours of the summer heat. Today was a minor miracle, the temperature touching only past the seventy-degree mark, which promised for a chilly night. She'd spent time in Bend during a Fourth of July celebration once, and it'd been ninety during the day, and then a light dusting of snow had come in the evening. High desert was nothing if not unpredictable. With the flimsy excuse of a shawl she'd packed, she prayed there'd be no snow in the forecast tonight.

Ten minutes before the wedding, she checked her hair one last time in her compact mirror and walked down the main lawn.

The sun had dipped below the tree line. Laughter bubbled through the outdoor area as kids chased each other through the grass. Twinkle lights hung like falling stars from tree branches. Erin's hand flew to her chest. Everything about this was so . . . perfect. Like she'd been transported into a fairy tale, and any minute a prince and princess would be holding hands at the altar.

"There you are."

Jake walked up behind her and placed his hand on the small of her back. Warm calloused fingers swept across her bare skin in a delicious caress.

Oh, hello there, lady bits.

She glanced up at him, his hair artfully tousled, his blue eyes standing out against the navy button-up and blazer.

"Ready to take a seat?" he asked.

"Sure thing." He led her down the aisle, this part of the grass covered in a pristine white runner. Four rows from the front, they took a left and grabbed the two available seats next to Bailey.

Bailey sat low in her seat, her phone wedged between her crossed arms. Erin's heart lurched a bit as she regarded her. The same age as all her students. The same I'm-too-cool-for-this/why-does-everything-have-to-be-so-boring facade. And at the same time, that awkward quirkiness that only a preteen could manage. God, she missed her students. Erin smiled and gave her a tiny wave before taking her seat.

As soon as her back hit the white folding chair, the threat of waterworks pressed against her sinuses, just from one glance at the altar. Erin didn't know what it was about wedding ceremonies, but no matter whether she knew the bride or not, tears would be flowing before the bride made her way down the aisle. Call her a sap or whatever, but she loved the idea of love. The thought of two people coming before their closest friends and family to pledge their love for one another remained one of the top romantic gestures in her book. That and flash-mob proposals.

From the swans in the lake to the ornate flower arrangements at the ends of each aisle, this place screamed love, and, by golly, the tears might start even before the bride made an appearance.

"Everything looks perfect," she said.

Jake's gaze dipped to her dress, and her skin burned from her ears down to her toes. "Yes, it does."

Erin fanned herself with the program that was propped on the seat next to her.

Music from the nearby DJ station started up, playing a soft melody, and Julie began her descent down the aisle with one of the groomsmen from the party the previous night. Next came Hazel, arm in arm with another groomsman.

Erin was doing good. Not a tear in sight. She even managed to keep her laugh contained when the flower girl chucked her basket of flowers at someone's head in the audience. And then Josie appeared from behind the barn and linked arms with her father. Her sweetheart-cut dress swished across the grass in dramatic arcs. The gauzy fabric floated in the breeze, and with the sun setting behind her in the distance, she looked like she'd floated straight down from the heavens. Her father's bottom lip quivered as they reached the top of the white runner on the ground, pulling his daughter closer.

And, yep, her throat constricted, and the tissues came out. From what she saw, it was a beautiful, albeit blurry, ceremony.

Thirty minutes later, Jake took a seat next to Erin at one of the tables in the barn. Bailey was at another table with Hazel and Julie, taking selfies on her phone, completely in their own little world. Which suited him just fine at the moment. He wasn't one for weddings. The idea of finding someone to spend the rest of your life with just seemed like a load of crap to him. But Josie looked so damn happy standing up there with Tom that he had to believe they'd be part of the small percentage who were actually able to keep their marriage afloat.

"Looks like Tom is stuck now," he said.

Both their gazes moved to the groom, who was beaming ear to ear. "I think he's happy with his decision," she said.

"A little liquid courage also helped." Tom had taken a few swigs of scotch before the photos this morning. The poor guy didn't know what he was getting himself into. It also didn't help that the photographer was up in his face the entire day. He felt for the guy.

"You are terrible." A smile twitched at her lips.

"Just callin' it like I see it," he said. He was a realist. Why spend so much on one day that they probably wouldn't even remember twenty years from now? He'd rather use that money to pay for an exotic trip.

"Such the romantic," she mused.

"Hey, I can be romantic."

Erin arched a brow.

"Did I tell you that you look beautiful tonight?"

A flush crept up her neck and filled her cheeks. "Thank you."

She stared down at the hors d'oeuvres on her plate. In fact, she hadn't really said much the past few minutes since they'd taken their spot at the table. It might have been the weird TV mishap last night, but he wasn't delusional. He saw the look in her eyes when he'd caught her gaze in the mirror earlier. There was so much want and desire. And every single neuron in his body shouted to give her exactly what she needed.

She picked up a small tart off her plate and took a tentative bite. And then she moaned, and her eyes fluttered shut.

Jake's fingers clutched the fork until the metal dug into his skin. Did she realize what that was doing to him? She had to.

"Oh my Lord. Have you tried these?" She pointed to the pastry.

"No." His mouth was so damn dry. He took a sip of water, but it did nothing to help.

"You need to. Here." She brought it up to his lips. He thought about saying no. But what was the harm in taking a bite from her dessert?

He bit into the flaky crust, a mix of cherries and something he couldn't place rushing past his lips. "Shit. That's really good."

Her eyes crinkled in the corner as she smiled at him. His jaw tensed as he fought back thoughts of last night. His composure came so close to crumbling. In fact, the more time he was around Erin, he realized this might be a losing battle.

She fumbled with the pastry, and it dropped in his lap and then made its descent to the floor. Cherry and powdered sugar streaked his dress slacks like a red-and-white starburst, and Erin grabbed for the napkin next to her place setting. "Oh, I'm so sorry."

She rubbed the white napkin vigorously across the top of his thigh, dangerously close to other areas. Back and forth, her fingers continued to work along his leg, her red nails digging into his pants. *Shit.* He was trying his best, he really was, but it was absolute torture to resist her. His fingers wrapped around her hand and stilled her motions.

"You need to stop that."

"Why?" She looked up at him, confusion crossing her features.

"Because if you keep that up, I'm going to take you back to the room and finish what you started."

Confusion etched across her brows, and Jake knew the second she'd finally processed his statement. She looked from him to his lap, and her eyes widened a fraction. Then that sexy little half smile graced her lips as she realized just what was happening. "Is that so?" Her fingers brushed against the evidence that she was, in fact, affecting him.

His eyes fluttered shut. When he finally opened them, he turned to find Erin staring at him, heat and wicked desire laced in her gaze.

"You're playing with fire, Erin." The little voice in the back of his head warned him. *Wrong. Don't take this any further.*

"Good thing I have someone professionally trained in my presence."

He chuckled. "You know, I've heard a lot of firefighter jokes, but that one ranks possibly the worst." A feather-light touch of his finger traced up the inside of her thigh, and her knees parted infinitesimally as her body begged for more.

Fuck. What was it about this woman that he couldn't resist? He couldn't even keep his damn hands off her.

Everyone around them made their way to the dance floor at the start of a song that Jake had heard at every wedding. Even most of the men knew the moves to this. He'd memorized Bailey's dance routines when she was younger, so his fatherly dance duties had been paid in full. No more dancing for him.

A warm hand slid up his thigh, bringing his attention back to Erin, who was looking at him through hooded eyes.

"Want to go someplace quieter?" she asked.

He couldn't ignore the heat in her gaze any longer.

"Yes," he said. *No* wasn't an option anymore.

She pushed back from the table and stretched out her hand. They were going somewhere quieter to talk. Yes . . . just talk. He glanced down at Erin's dress, the material hugging her ass. There was nothing friendly about the way he was feeling for Erin at the moment. Nor did he feel like talking.

They managed to make it to the hallway they'd been in last night, before his daughter had interrupted and brought him to his senses. But everyone else was out on the dance floor right now. There was no one coming to interrupt this time.

The bass of the music pulsed down the hallway. Darkness swelled around them as they entered the little room where Jake had gotten ice the night prior. Erin's hair fell loose around her shoulders, her blonde waves teasing at the straps of her dress, ones he desperately wanted to rip off.

"Not in the mood for dancing?"

"Not in the least bit." Dancing was the furthest thing from his mind at the moment. Especially when Erin moved in that damn dress. It made him want to rip it down the middle until the two pieces of fabric floated to the floor. Then it'd just be Erin in a pair of sky-high heels. The thought of every inch of her skin on display forced him to surge closer, caging Erin in.

"That's too bad. It's a good song." Her hips swayed to the music. So confident. He liked that about her. He bit back a groan as he watched her, wondering just how good that would feel if he pushed her against the wall and took her right here.

"What is that look for?" she asked.

"Nothing."

She arched a brow. "And you called me a bad liar."

Screw it. She wanted honesty? He'd give it to her.

"I'm thinking how you in that dress is driving me absolutely insane." He moved his head down to the shell of her ear. Her hair brushed against his nose, that delicious coconut scent shutting his brain down even more. She reminded him of a goddamn tropical drink. And with the sweltering heat, he could go for a cold one right about now.

She shivered under his touch, but she continued to dance to the music. Her body arched as she turned around, now giving him a perfect view of the backside of the dress. The fabric dipped to just above her ass, two dimples on full display. Judging by how the fabric stretched across her, there was a matching set of nothing on underneath. *Christ.* He was in so much trouble.

She turned to look at him, a sly smile spreading across her lips. "What's the matter, Jake? Something got you scared?"

He laughed but was a little unnerved that she could tell what he was feeling without even looking at him.

Her ass brushed against his pants as she reached her hands up and around the back of his neck, pulling him closer. She moved against him, and there was no hiding his reaction to her as she brushed against it.

Fuck it. He was already going to hell. His hands slid down the side of her silky dress, his fingers bunching the material until the hem moved up her thighs. Might as well do something worth going to hell for.

Erin was going to burn alive. Heat traveled from her head to *other parts* as Jake's hands coasted over her hips. Her pulse galloped wildly as calloused fingertips dipped under the hem of her dress, tracing circles up her thighs. She continued to move against him, letting the beat of the song guide her movements.

"You're making it very hard to be good, Erin."

"I'd hate to see what bad behavior looks like." Ha ha. Just kidding. Load her up with a bunch of Benjamins because she'd make this place rain in order to see what *bad* looked like on Jake Bennett. She brushed against him again, and there was no ignoring his hard length that bulged against his dress slacks. Heat slicked the spot between her thighs, and she thought she just might break out in a sweat if the temperature ratcheted up any higher between them. Heat poured through his dress shirt, and his scent wrapped around her. A hint of cologne, a bit of body wash. She wanted to turn around, fist his shirt, and press her nose against it, memorizing this scent. Heck, if she could get away with it, she'd rip it right off his body and roll around in it until it was permanently etched into her skin.

"You'll find out soon enough if you keep doing that," he said.

"I don't know what you're talking about." She smiled. Did it make her a bad person that she was totally turned on by the fact that he was reacting to her like this? It'd been forever since fire hummed in her veins. Need pulsed deep in her belly, and if his hands coasted any higher, he'd find out she was just as affected by him.

His fingers edged up her dress, high enough that if anyone came into the tiny room, she'd be flashing a good amount of skin to them. "Tell me, did you really think about me in high school?"

Her eyes fluttered shut. "Yes."

"What types of things?"

"Your hands between my thighs." She unhooked her laced fingers, and one hand traveled between them, brushing against his hard length. "Other things between my thighs."

His breath hissed through clenched teeth. "Christ, Erin. You're going to kill me."

Her fingers wrapped around his hardened length and moved up and down his shaft through the coarse fabric. "I think you said something similar in my daydream. Except there was a little more profanity."

"Did I do anything else with my mouth?" he growled in her ear, still pressed up against her. His chest brushed against her back, the lean muscles of his stomach rubbing against her.

A second wave of heat bloomed between her thighs. Just the sound of his voice short-circuited her brain. Made her desperate with need. Was it possible to orgasm from a sexy voice? She'd bet that Jake reading the phone book could get the job done. "Your mouth was relentless."

Too tight. Everything in her was coiled so tight, she felt like she might explode at his next touch. Her dress pressed painfully against her aching breasts.

Her breath hitched as his fingers brushed against the aching spot between her thighs, slicking against her arousal.

"Shit." He groaned. He ground into her harder and flattened her into the wall.

Her legs parted as Jake's thigh slipped between, shoving her dress even higher. The song outside in the reception switched to something faster. She ground against him, and pleasure sparked in her core as her center rubbed against his dress slacks.

"You keep doing this to me and I'm going to take you right here against this wall. I don't care who sees."

A thick finger teased at her entrance. Every muscle in her body tensed as her aching breasts brushed against the wall. Her nipples puckered against the silk as Jake palmed one of them, rubbing his thumb in maddeningly slow circles.

She chanced a look back at him and was met with intense eyes. Ones that promised he wouldn't stop until he'd wrung out every possible bit of pleasure Erin was capable of experiencing. Every muscle, every bit of flesh and bone inside her body, turned to smoke, floating, hovering.

She turned around, the motion doing nothing to stop his two hands from working over her body. "And here I thought you were doing everything in your power to make sure we don't get together."

"We shouldn't be together," he said, but even she could tell that his resolve had strained too far, like a rubber band that'd been pulled too far and lost its elasticity.

"You're absolutely right." Bad idea. So bad. But the train had left the station, and it was heading right toward I-don't-give-a-shit station.

He leveled her with a look. One that spoke of want. Need. Desperation. "I want to make one thing clear. This is a onetime thing. I can't give you anything more than tonight."

"Who said anything about attachments? I'm not looking for anything either," she said. This was a chance to be with her high school wet dream in living color, who currently looked like he might devour her. One fantastic night, then she could get on with her life and stop wondering just how good he'd feel between her thighs.

She pressed the flat of her palm along the tented fabric of Jake's pants and gave a long stroke. His head knocked back, his brows pinching together. This man's resolve buckled under her touch, and she couldn't wait to bring him to his knees.

The song out in the reception changed again, another fast one with a deep bass beat. And it was just her and Jake, tucked away, out of sight, bodies sliding against each other. She continued rubbing her palm along his erection, her fingers wrapping around his impressive length.

"Shit, Erin." Jake's legs shook and tensed, seeming to fight for control. "You can't keep doing that."

Can't wasn't part of Erin's vocabulary.

Challenge accepted. Up. Down. Up. Down. She continued her pace as Jake knocked his head back against the wall.

His hands moved from her hips to cup her ass. He pulled her up, and her legs wrapped around his waist.

She bucked against him in response, her center riding along the expanse of the bulge. A flicker of ecstasy sparked in her core. His fingers dug into her hips, and she bucked into him again. His hand slipped between them, his thumb finding her clit.

A cry escaped her lips as he circled the sensitive spot.

"Is that what you want? You want me to take you right here?"

She rocked against him, the pressure between her legs building. So close. She was so damn close.

One finger, then two, dipped into her, and theme-park-worthy pyrotechnics exploded behind her eyes.

Yes. Please. Take her up against the wall. Make it quick and dirty, with clothes pushed hastily to the side.

His lips met her neck, teasing, nipping, and she didn't know how much more of this she could handle. Her nails raked into his back, fighting for control. But she was falling, falling, falling, letting the build between her thighs take over. Every muscle in her body quivered, every synapse hyperfocused on the two fingers, curving to hit the exact spot that sent her spiraling.

"Oh, Jake," she cried. Her back arched, and she rode his hand, wringing out every last bit of ecstasy.

He lowered her until her wobbly legs hit the ground. Her pulse drummed in her ears as Jake looked down at her with wild eyes. She needed more of him.

"Room. Now," he growled.

Those two words promised exactly what she needed, and her stilettos couldn't move fast enough as they beelined it down the hallway. They brushed past the double doors, back through the main barn area where the reception was still going strong. Erin's pulse hummed in her ears, and she didn't dare look anyone in the eye, because if they were stopped for a conversation, she might self-combust.

Twenty paces from the door.

Fifteen.

Ten.

They both looked at each other and grinned. The chattiest family in the world was none the wiser that they were skipping out on the reception.

They slipped out of the barn and into the cool night. The music thumped quietly in the background, the only other sound their breaths as they did Olympic-worthy speed-walking to the main lodge.

Jake fumbled for his key when they rounded the corner to his room. "Shit, I didn't bring any condoms."

"I'm on the pill. I get tested regularly. Yadda, yadda. Now would you please hurry up with the key?"

He smirked. "Just want you to know, the only crabs I've gotten were at Joe's Crab Shack."

She smacked his chest.

He grabbed his wallet from his back pocket and came up empty in terms of key cards.

Damn it.

"I gave my key to Bailey so she could grab something from my room. Do you have yours?" he said.

Erin nodded and pulled one out of her purse. She had just slipped the card into the mechanism when he heard it. Moans. And not just subdued ones, but loud shrieks that sent the hairs on the back of his neck on edge. And it was coming from his room.

They looked at each other with wide eyes.

"Did someone turn on our TV?" he asked.

They barreled into the room just as someone on the screen was deep-throating an eggplant. What the hell was wrong with this channel?

"Take that purplelicious D for me, baby," a guy as short as he was round said, rubbing the woman's back.

Jake's grandma was frantically clicking the remote to no avail, muttering something under her breath. "Where's the damn *Wheel of Fortune*? I want my Pat Sajak."

"Here, Grandma, let me get that for you." He sprinted for the remote, gave it a hard smack, and then successfully hit the "Power" button. The screen went black, and Jake drew a long breath. Traumatizing his grandmother wasn't on his to-do list for this weekend.

"Just wanted to see my Vanna." His grandma fanned her face with the hotel pamphlet. "Bailey gave me your key. She said it was okay if I took a rest in your room." His grandma lived a few towns over, only staying for the day. Jake chucked the remote on the couch and rubbed her back.

"We've had issues with our TV. Sorry about that."

"I've never seen vegetables used that way."

What was he supposed to say to that? The woman had a picture of the Pope above her bed. She sent him crosses made out of palm fronds for Ash Wednesday and sent little prayer cards with his birthday presents. Man, was he going to hell for everything tonight.

"This is no way to court a young lady, Jake." Her gaze slid from Jake to Erin, and he couldn't tell if that was a smile or a grimace. With the way his mom and grandma talked on the phone, it was only a matter of hours before he got the third degree from his mother.

"It's not like that, Grandma. The TV has been stuck on the same channels, and the front desk was looking into it."

She gave him a look that obviously meant *Sure, sonny. If that's the story you're sticking to, then we'll just go with that.*

"I'm going to find your grandfather. Already ate cake, so guess it's time for me to go home."

"Would you like me to walk you back to the party?" Anything to try to smooth this over.

"I'm fine. Maybe you should call the front desk again."

He nodded, and out of the corner of his eye, he caught Erin smothering a smile with her hand. "Will do."

"Wasn't even using the right technique, that idiot. I could show her a thing or two," Grandma muttered under her breath as she grabbed her walker and made her way out of the room. "See you tomorrow."

Jake exchanged a glance with Erin, and the horror he felt was written all over her face.

"Did she just say . . . ?"

"Those words never need to be repeated. Ever." His lips pressed into a hard line. He did not need to hear that from the woman who should be associated only with snickerdoodle cookies and fishing at the lake.

"This resort is obviously out to get us."

It'd been so damn long since he'd been intimate with anyone, but it looked like it was going to be a bit longer. His need for Erin had evaporated. "I don't think I can do this."

Chapter Eight

Light slashed through the curtains as Erin woke the next morning. Jake was wrapped in a blanket on the sofa, his arm hanging off the edge. His lips were plumped into a pout, and Erin had to grip her sheets in order to hold back from going over there and taking them between her teeth.

In a few hours, she'd be back to normal life. Well, if moving back home and living in her childhood bedroom fell into the normal category.

It was for the best. She needed to get back and fill out some more job applications. Hopefully there'd actually *be* jobs to apply to, unlike when she had last checked yesterday. Plus, she wanted to see Sloane and Madison, who would no doubt hound her for every damn detail of this weekend.

Jake rustled, and his blanket fell to the floor. He was wearing only black boxer briefs and apparently having one heck of a dream. A massive bulge tented the material, and all of Erin's thoughts cut to static. His man-bulge game was strong, Pinterest worthy, and, really, she should stop being creepy and staring at him while he was sleeping.

You do not want to be with Jake. That would just complicate things.

She peered over at him again. Tattoos swirled around his biceps, cutting off at his elbows. My, her tongue could be kept busy for hours.

Are you sure, little voice in my head? Are you really sure that it's a bad idea?

She'd like to say she had an angel on one shoulder and a devil on the other, but really it was more of a pair of wishy-washy horny cupids shouting, *You can do it!*

Jake moved around on the couch and finally sat up, grabbing the blanket and quickly throwing it over himself. She averted her eyes, pretending that she hadn't just been watching him.

"Morning," he said. His voice was deeper, laced with sleep, and it hit her square between the thighs. Thoughts of last night whispered back into her mind—the way his fingers had stroked between her thighs, the way his beard had scraped against her skin as he bit her neck.

She swallowed hard. "Hey."

Nothing to see here. Just the friendly neighborhood peeping tom. She went back to looking at her phone, glancing at her friends' status updates. A bunch of staff members from her middle school had gone out last night to the local karaoke bar. She frowned, the sadness of losing her job sweeping back in like a tidal wave. She should have been out with them singing Bon Jovi. During a normal summer, she'd use these days off to grab coffee with the other science teacher, Sarah Morgansen, to coordinate their curriculum for the year. A sigh rushed past her lips. She clicked out of the app and slipped out of the bed, beelining it for the bathroom.

By the time she'd finished in the shower, Jake was dressed and already packed. His duffel bag sat on the coffee table, zipped, his suit flopped over the top.

"I didn't know how you liked your coffee, so I got one with cream and one without." He didn't look at her. Really, he was looking everywhere in the room *but* her. This trip was quite possibly the worst morale booster of all time.

"Cream, please." He handed her the cup, and she pressed it to her lips, taking a deep pull. Oh, sweet, glorious caffeine. It could solve most of her problems, but not six foot one standing in front of her.

"About what happened last night . . ." He trailed off, still not looking at her.

"What about it?" Really, what was there to say? Besides, maybe, *Oh hey, thank you for the first orgasm in over a year that wasn't because of something battery operated.* Somehow she didn't think that comment would go over very well, especially with how skittish he was acting.

"I was caught up in the moment. I didn't mean for any of that to happen. I don't want to lead you on or anything," he said, frowning.

And there came the one-two punch to her ego. She knew this was coming, but it didn't take the sting away. Not that Jake needed to know that. So she busted out her favorite tool in her self-preservation arsenal—she faked it.

She squared her shoulders and caught his gaze. "I was your wedding date, Jake. Nothing more." She ignored the deflating bubble in her chest. Yes, she wanted to save a horse and ride this man like a bona fide cowgirl, but apparently last night was her Cinderella-at-the-ball moment, and the clock had chimed past midnight. The guy obviously had a lot on his plate. It didn't help ease the burn to her ego, though. Because that was true regret in his eyes. "Don't worry about it. Let's just pretend like last night never happened."

Even though every single nerve in her body screamed otherwise.

Chapter Nine

"So let me get this straight. You went to a wedding, and you didn't get laid. How have we led you so astray?" Hollywood gave Jake a pitying glance and took a swig of his beer.

Jake clenched his teeth and continued to man his station at the barbecue. Failed wedding date was one thing, but burning a burger was sacrilege.

"You'd better watch out. If Reece hears you talking about his little sister like that, he'll kick that pretty-boy ass of yours," Scotty said. He'd been on A shift for years, but with the shuffling of a few people, he'd be joining them on B shift next month.

Hollywood flipped Scotty the bird and continued doing something on his phone.

As if on cue, Reece came out of the house with a beer.

The four of them had started the weekly BBQ tradition a few years back. They'd added Hollywood to the mix when he had joined their unit.

"You have fun at the wedding?" Reece asked.

"Yeah." He used the burgers as an excuse and kept his gaze focused on the flipper.

"Erin have a good time?"

Oh, you mean when she rode my hand and cried out my name? Yup. A good time was had by all, and now he was going to hell for it. "I think so."

Bailey peeked her head out the patio door and called, "Dad, I'm going over to Amber's."

She'd been scarce all day. Unease twisted in his gut. His baby would be gone for three weeks at computer-coding camp. Proud didn't even begin to describe what he felt for his daughter, but he was scared as hell to have her a state away for that long.

"Be back by nine. We still need to make sure you're all packed."

He still couldn't believe his daughter had gotten into an elite computer-programming camp in California. She'd earned her spot by leading her middle-school robotics team to the state championship. The price tag attached to the camp was cringe-worthy. But a couple of extra zeros weren't going to keep his daughter away from chasing her dreams.

"Right." She scoffed at him. Another *Duh, Dad* in the books. They seemed to be multiplying lately, and the once-great relationship they had was now becoming strained. He knew it was normal for kids to pull away once they reached middle school, but he'd always hoped that they'd be above that. That he'd always have his little girl who wore cherry ring pops on her finger and was jazzed over getting a new Barbie. One time at the mall, he'd lost her in a rack of clothes in Macy's. Scariest goddamn fifteen minutes of his life. Now, life was feeling a lot like those fifteen minutes of hell on a perpetual loop. The bottom to Jake's carefully crafted life crumbled beneath him.

Maybe the time off would be a good thing. Maybe she'd come back and suddenly lose the ability to roll her eyes. Now that would make every damn penny of that camp worth it.

"Do they always do that?" Reece said.

"What?"

"Emit that cloud of angst and turmoil."

Jake laughed. "That was her in a good mood."

Reece let out a low whistle. "Christ."

Jake flipped one of the burgers, placing it higher up on the grill. Parenting often went from loving certain moments to wanting to put her for sale on Craigslist the next.

"Preaching to the choir, man. I'm turning gray over here." He tugged at the roots of his hair, and a flash of Erin's fingers raking over his scalp, down his neck, played behind his eyes.

"We don't call you Old Man for nothing. What? Are you falling asleep over there now? Need to park your La-Z-Boy by the barbecue from now on," said Hollywood.

Jake's eyes snapped open. When had he shut them? What the hell had this woman done to him? He stretched his neck from side to side and ignored the sudden need pulsing through him.

"I hope you like your burger charred, because I can arrange that," Jake said.

"That's right. Rule number one, Hollywood: never fuck with the person who holds the burger flipper." Reece shot Jake an assessing look, but Jake just shrugged in response. *Nothing to see here. Nobody fantasizing about your sister. Nope.*

Hollywood shook his head. "Man, the both of you are grumpy as hell. You both need to get laid."

Jake pressed the spatula into Hollywood's burger until there was an audible hiss as fat dripped into the flames.

He put his hands up. "Fine. Don't get laid. What do I care?"

Since when had Jake turned into a grumpy old man who argued against having sex? When it came to a certain blonde temptation, he'd keep it in his pants. That was for damn sure. He'd survived this past weekend, so the rest should be cake. Erin would be out of town in a few short weeks, and if Jake played his cards right, he'd do a good job avoiding her until her taillights disappeared in the distance on I-5.

"Did you see they had a sale on St. Croix rods going on? Maybe you could get Bailey into fishing when she gets back from that fancy computer camp," Reece said.

"Dude," Hollywood chimed in, "no novice needs that expensive of a rod. That's like"—he made a show of counting on his fingers—"fifty Chipotle burritos gone to waste."

"Not for Bailey, you idiot." Reece shook his head. "Jake can give her his old rod and get a new one. Then let me borrow it when he's not using it." He grinned. Reece was such a cheap ass.

"And you wonder why chicks don't like your apartment. Cheap as hell," said Scotty, taking a pull from his beer.

"I'm economical. And how did this turn into picking apart my place?"

Good. Keep the focus on Reece. Maybe Jake wouldn't be struck down by the guilt that had plagued him ever since he had returned to Portland. What made it worse was that everything reminded him of Erin. The clear sky was the same color as the dress she'd worn on the drive home. Hell, the beer he'd been sipping on reminded him of Erin's lips. How she'd wrapped them around her own beer bottle. Beer, damn it. He couldn't even drink in peace without a reminder of her.

He scooped the burgers off the grill and placed them on a plate.

No problem here. His daughter was leaving in the morning. He'd spend the next few weeks keeping himself too busy to think about Erin. He'd managed twelve years without any attachments. What was a handful of days?

"By the way," Reece said, "my mom insisted all of you come to Erin's welcome-home party. She's hell-bent on trying to keep her in town. It's tomorrow—think you guys can make it?"

Shit.

Chapter Ten

"Wow. I don't know what to say." Erin stared at the new comforter in the freshly painted room of her mom's house. Her old room, she reminded herself. When she'd left for the weekend, it'd been an early-2000s time-capsule oasis, complete with Beyoncé posters, old movie stubs, and concert tickets pinned to the wall. Now? It was painted over with a shade of pale lavender that matched the ruffled edges of the equally prim-and-proper bedspread. It was all wrong.

"What happened to all my stuff?"

Her mother, at least, had the sense to look a little sheepish. "I put it in boxes," she said.

Why did this bother her so much? This should be a slam dunk. Now it was portable. She could ship it back to California and keep it in her own place. But just the thought of her mom riffling through all her memories struck something deep within her, rankled her like a cat being rubbed from tail to head with a wet hand.

"I just want you to be comfortable while you're home. Something more mature. You know, in case you decide to stay longer."

All she needed was a bed and four walls, she supposed.

Nope. Still didn't curb the unease stirring in her gut.

An ache started in her jaw, and she rubbed at it, willing the muscles to relax. Ever since she had moved out of the house at eighteen, she'd developed this twitch in her jaw anytime her stress level went into the red. Usually that included occasions such as the first day of school and especially bad Tinder dates. Right now her muscle was hammering out a drum solo to a death-metal song.

You love her. She loves you.

That was the problem. The Jenkins family had a lot of love. And it was spread around as thick as their famous peanut butter. Her dad had been out of the picture for most of her life. He'd divorced her mom when Erin was really young, right after Andie had been born. Their mom had been *invested* in their personal lives ever since. The kind of devotion and passion saved for fantasy-football leagues and which Hollywood Chris was the swooniest (Chris Evans, because, c'mon, Captain America).

"Mom—" This weekend had completely drained her, leaving her with zero fight. Jake's face as he'd dropped her off, that distant, far-off look, had been enough to darken the edges of what had been a fantastic weekend.

"Don't you worry about a thing. I've gotten everything taken care of." She pulled out a list from her purse. "I even printed off a list of jobs around here. The ones highlighted in pink are within a three-mile radius of the house." She pointed farther down the list. "And the ones in yellow are within ten miles, but I think that's acceptable since you've been so far away for the last decade."

Had she also put prison bars on Erin's window? Or would the installation be happening next week? "Gee, Mom. I don't know what to say."

Her mother gave her a quick pat on the leg. "Just looking out for my baby girl."

Erin pasted on a smile. Her mom meant well. She really did, which was why Erin didn't have the heart to feel anything more than slight annoyance. But she had to know the chances of her moving home and being subjected to this all the time were about as good as seeing snow on the Fourth of July.

She wrapped an arm around her mom. "I'm supposed to be taking care of you, remember?"

Her mother waved a hand. "The doctor said I'm fine. I just can't lift heavy things. Plus, what else am I supposed to do all day around the house?" She pointed to the list in Erin's hand. "Just think on it, sweetie. One of those might be your forever job."

Erin jiggled the pages. "Sure thing."

As soon as her mom left her room, Erin sat down on the bed and blew out a sigh. She thumbed through the papers and frowned. There were quite a few opportunities here in town, much more than the suck-tastic hiring freeze going on in California.

She shucked the list to the side and pulled out her laptop. When in doubt, overuse the good old clicker finger by hitting the "Refresh" button on her go-to job sites. A few clicks later, she was in her bookmarked Education Opportunities tab. A whopping one new job posting in the past seven days. She scanned through it. A middle-school position for social studies. Not even in her realm of qualifications. She always preferred beakers and meter sticks to dead kings. Desperate times called for one more click of the "Refresh" button. Nope. Still nothing.

Her phone buzzed on the nightstand, pulling her out of her job-despair spiral.

Her old roommate, Alexis. They'd taught together at Stephens Middle School. She was the seventh-grade math teacher, and they had lived together for the past couple of years.

ALEXIS: Miss my beach buddy.

With the text came a selfie of Alexis, lying on a beach blanket.

Erin frowned. This summer they'd had plans to lounge on the beach down in Southern California, drink way too much iced coffee, and buy planner stickers at Michael's. Okay, the last two were happening regardless of her current situation, because what was life without caffeine and structure?

ERIN: Miss you, too.

ALEXIS: Anything new? When are you coming home? Your boxes are looking awfully lonely.

She stared at the text, debating whether to tell Alexis about her weekend with Jake. Erin hadn't even mentioned him to Alexis. And telling her that she'd gone on a whirlwind wedding weekend that involved finger banging in the ice room at the reception? Yeah, that was a lot to explain over a text. Sloane and Madison would understand, though.

ERIN: Hopefully home soon.

Her mom popped her head back in the room. "Party starts in a few. Come on down when you're ready."

She blew her bangs out of her face as sweat slicked her body. She'd positioned herself in front of the oscillating fan set in the doorway of her room. With every rotation, it ruffled the frilly edges of the comforter. Even after twenty years of living in the same bungalow, her mom still hadn't splurged for central air-conditioning. She had one measly window unit in the living room. Erin had been spoiled these past few years, her apartment cranked to a chilly sixty-eight. Right now, she was fifteen degrees past comfortable.

Thirty minutes from now, people would be arriving for her welcome-home party. The last party she'd been to was her goodbye party at her middle school. Every bite of that WE'LL MISS YOU, ERIN Costco cake burned like hydrochloric acid on the way down. She hated these types of parties. They brought way too much attention, when all she really wanted to do was slip out unnoticed.

Her brother appeared in her doorway, carrying a bright pink box. "Well, look who it is! How long will it take Erin to skip town?" Her brother gave her a wry smile.

Andie joined him, both of them taking up the doorway, blocking her delicious slice of breeze from the fan. "I give her at least till Mom starts going all emo at the party."

"Nah. I'll give her until Mom starts rearranging her sock drawer."

"Can't do that if I'm living out of a suitcase." Erin closed her computer and jumped off the bed.

"So predictable. Let me guess—there's an emergency escape hatch to the roof somewhere here." He winked.

"Why do that when there's a window?" She smiled sweetly. "And no, I won't be making any unannounced escapes." Ten years later and she still hadn't lived down the whole "You thought I was going to a local college, and I snuck out and moved to California overnight" bit. Okay, maybe it had been a bit rash, but she had been eighteen and stupid.

"That's right. Hotshot teacher of the year is going to be back in California before we know it." Reece clapped her on the shoulder.

Those words added salt to the gaping wound in her pride. Just weeks before she'd been given the good old pink slip, she'd been named Teacher of the Year for her school district. A lot of good that title did when she didn't have a classroom to teach in.

It wasn't that she hated Portland. It was just . . . everyone here expected her to be something she wasn't. She wasn't going to take over the family business. She wasn't going to be settling down and having kids anytime soon. Sometimes, it was best to leave the past in the past. And being in this house opened up a lot of feelings she'd long since buried.

"Come on. Let's head downstairs," she said.

In the time she'd been up in her newly converted princess cave, someone had decorated the entire downstairs in streamers and a banner spanning the fireplace that read WELCOME BACK, ERIN!

A cold sweat broke out on the small of her back, and the tiny voice in her head yelled at her like she was a character in a slasher film who was just about to get torn to ribbons by a knife-wielding psycho. *Run, girl! Get out while you can!*

The front door burst open, and one of her best friends stood in the doorway. "Where's my girl?" Sloane took one look at Reece and then scanned the room. Erin didn't fail to notice the quick glare she sent his way. Before she had time to contemplate that, a whir of blue hair raced across the hardwood floors.

Sloane let out a squeal and flung her arms around Erin. "I can't believe it. I get to see my best friend in the flesh. I think the world is ending."

"It'll be ending a lot sooner for me if you keep squeezing like that," Erin managed to get out while her best friend strangled her.

"Shit. Sorry." She loosened her grip. "I'm never letting go. You'll have to take me everywhere."

"That'll get a little awkward with the whole bathroom situation."

"True." Sloane let go completely and settled for an uncomfortably close distance. "I'll accept a courtesy text while you're in there to make sure you didn't fall in."

"I appreciate the concern, but I think I got it covered."

She didn't like this. Everyone making a big deal that she was home. She had emphasized when she'd wheeled her suitcase through the door that this was *temporary*. Why did everyone seem to be treating it otherwise?

"Who else is coming?"

"Just Madison, I think. Unless your bozo brother decided to invite his crew." Sloane sent another glare his way.

Huh. She'd apparently missed quite a bit since she'd been gone.

"Yeah, that's not happening." She doubted Jake would be coming. He'd practically peeled out of the driveway when he'd dropped her off the other day. Also, what was up with the hostility toward Reece? Sure, she found her brother insufferable on the best of days, but that was because he was her brother, and he used to fart in her face. But he'd always been well liked by everyone else. Before she could ask Sloane what was up between them, a knock came from the front door.

She moved toward the front entrance, ready to be reunited with her other best friend. All three of them hadn't been in the same room together since last Christmas when she'd barely gotten to see them because of the holiday weekend.

She grabbed the glass doorknob and twisted. The distressed red door creaked on its hinges as it swung open, and spit went down the wrong pipe when she saw Jake on the other side of the threshold.

She sputtered, trying to catch her breath. How graceful.

"You okay?" he asked. He put his hand on her shoulder, and moments from last weekend played like a highlight reel behind her eyes. *Just choking on my pride. No biggie.*

"Yeah," she wheezed. She wiped at the tears and spotted another guy beside Jake, who was maybe a couple of years younger than Erin, who reminded her of the lead actor on one of her favorite crime-fighting shows.

She worked to calm her racing pulse now that the coughing had subsided. *Seriously? You spent all weekend with him. Act like a normal, functioning adult.*

Although her students would beg to differ that she was anything but normal. She was more the stand-on-the-desk type, shouting, "O Captain! My Captain!"

Jake had the nerve to look even more amazing than he had on Saturday. His blue T-shirt strained against his biceps as he crossed his arms. The same ones she'd grabbed when he'd pinned her against the hallway wall.

The same ones that want nothing to do with you, chica.

It was a harsh reminder but a necessary one. She had no clue what he was doing here, but it sure wasn't because he'd somehow realized he needed more from last weekend.

"What are you doing here?" she asked.

His eyes widened a fraction. Even she was surprised by how rude that had come out. But really, what the hell? "I mean, not that you're not welcome, of course you're welcome to come. My mom's probably made enough chip dip for the whole neighborhood." And she was babbling. She turned to Mr. Abercrombie model, purposefully keeping her attention off Jake. "I'm sorry. I don't think we've met."

Pretty boy stuck his hand out for her to shake. "I'm Cole. I've heard great things about this chip dip." Jake elbowed him in the side. "Oh, and welcome home." He shrugged. He was cute in the same way the guys were down in the city. Carefully coiffed hair. Immaculate button-up and khaki shorts. An ego that might need a shoehorn to fit through the doorway.

Sloane sidled up next to her and wrapped her arm around Erin's shoulder. "What she means to say is thanks for coming." She stuck out her hand to Cole. "I'm Sloane, by the way."

She glanced over at her best friend. *Yep.* She was busy making eyes at the new guy.

"Your brother invited us over. If you'd like me to leave, I can." Jake stood there with a case of beer from a local brewery. His lips curved into a shy smile, and then the dimple appeared. That damn dimple that made Erin's knees buckle.

Even she wasn't a big enough jerk to send them packing.

"The more, the merrier." Her voice pitched, and she quickly cleared her throat. "Come on in."

She moved to the left to let the men in at the same time Jake moved to his right, and they bumped into each other. His body was solid and warm, and Erin was not noticing this one bit.

They both let out a nervous laugh.

Erin went to move to the right, and Jake moved to his left, again putting them right in front of each other.

"Oh, this is ridiculous," she said.

"You." He placed his one hand on her shoulder, his thumb lightly grazing her collarbone. "Stay here."

He brushed by her, his shirt coming inches from her nose.

Don't do it. Don't do it. You're not creepy. You have years of honing your chill factor.

She inhaled.

Okay, yep, she was creepy. And was about as discreet as one of her students trying to text in class.

Visions of Saturday came flooding back to her. The way his teeth had raked across his bottom lip as she'd stroked him. Her body was on edge, wanting to finish what they had started. She was in so much trouble.

♥ ♥ ♥

It had been a mistake coming here. He knew that the second Erin opened the door. Jake was way out of his depths on this one.

Somehow he still had his hand on Erin's shoulder. Because, as it seemed for the past week, his body and his mind had come to two different conclusions when it came to her. The logical one wanted to slide back into his truck and go home. The rest of him wanted to show her just how much he missed her touch. His fingers on his other hand were killing him, digging into the beer carrier like it was his one last shred of resistance.

Someone behind them cleared their throat. Erin quickly spun around, breaking the grip he had on her shoulder, and came face-to-face with her brother. Reece was staring at both of them, his arms crossed.

Erin mirrored her brother's position, while Jake took a sudden interest the Jenkinses' living room. Couch, fireplace, pictures above the mantel. Yep, all there. The last thing he wanted to do was piss off his buddy.

"Oh, I'm sorry. Was I getting in the way of your bromance? Don't be so jealous, Reece." She gave a playful slap to his cheek.

Reece's gaze shifted from his sister to Jake, clearly assessing the situation. Jake lifted a brow, trying his damnedest to convey, *No, dude, I didn't bang your sister.* Technicalities. Back in middle school, they'd read "The Tell-Tale Heart." Even listened to a narrated version. Then, Jake thought the guy was just a bit off and maybe high on drugs. But now, he swore he could hear a heartbeat under the floorboards of the house. Maybe he was finally starting to crack. The back of his neck burned, and he contemplated coming clean to the guy right there in the middle of the Jenkinses' entryway.

He exchanged another look with Reece. Something seemed to placate his friend, though, because his shoulders relaxed. "You kidding me? I've seen enough of this asshole to last me another forty hours."

Crisis averted. For now. The thought of keeping anything from him didn't sit well. And he knew he'd need to come clean sooner or later. Right now, he'd settle for later. Much later.

"Good to see you, too, buddy." Jake turned to Erin. "Beverage for the party girl?" She looked up at him with wide hazel eyes. He'd felt like such a prick showing up here, especially after how he'd acted when he'd dropped her off on Sunday. Pulling up into the driveway and not even walking her to the door. His mother would definitely be warranted in her use of the wooden spoon for that one. But if he'd walked her to the door, he would have definitely done something stupid, like ask her out. No doubt in his mind he'd made the right decision.

"Sure," she said.

He pulled one of the beers from the six-pack carrier, twisted the cap off, and handed it to her. She watched his arms the entire time, her teeth raking over her bottom lip.

Damn it, he couldn't think when she looked at him that way.

"Thanks," she said. And then she brought the beer to her lips, and Jake's heart flatlined. And he realized that not once the entire weekend had he kissed Erin.

Smart move. He had a hard enough time trying not to think about her. About the tiny sounds that came out of her mouth as his fingers slicked over her. The taste of her lips would do him in, he decided.

"So you're all on the same shift together? Like work wives," Erin's friend Sloane said. There was something going on between her and Reece because they kept glancing over at each other every few seconds, looking like they each might be trying to burn holes into the other's head. Which was weird, because as far as Jake knew, they'd always been on good terms.

Erin took another sip of beer, and Jake had to tear his gaze away to answer Sloane's question.

Before he could answer, Reece said, "Hollywood's the work wife since he's the prettiest."

"You're not my type. You snore," Hollywood said.

"I told you that was allergies," Reece retorted.

"Those two bicker like spouses. I stay clear of the drama," Jake added, but his mind was other places, namely the storage room in the barn. Her legs wrapped around his waist. Those damn moans coming from her mouth.

"That's because you have your own drama magnet at home," Reece added.

"I'll drink to that." He took a deep swig of the beer. He'd dropped his daughter off at the airport earlier today. His heart had lodged in his throat for a solid thirty minutes after he'd watched her walk through TSA. He'd been home for only the amount of time it took to change into a clean shirt for the party, and the house had already felt empty. He missed Bailey's heavy footfall along the hardwoods, her punk music blaring from her room. It was going to be a long three weeks.

"I'll be right back." He didn't know where he was heading, just that he needed to get some air. He made his way through the living room, the kitchen, and out into the backyard. The wooden deck led to lush green grass, all blocked in by a white picket fence. He'd shot rockets off in this yard, kicked back in the hammock, and camped out in tents here. All that seemed like a different life.

He sat in one of the Adirondack chairs and leaned his head back against the wood. The air was crisp, the smell of the flowers and tomato plants from the Jenkinses' garden potent in the light breeze. He could breathe out here. Being outdoors always helped clear the mind, even when his problem was less than twenty feet away.

"Didn't expect to see you here tonight." Erin stood in the doorway to the house, still nursing her beer. She moved onto the deck and shut the sliding door behind her, then took a seat in the chair next to Jake.

"Neither did I," he admitted. But if he hadn't shown up, he would've had Reece to answer to.

"Just wanted to say thank you for taking me to Josie's wedding last weekend. It was fun." Her cheeks flushed. "I mean, the wedding was fun. Although other parts were fun, too."

"Erin." He couldn't do this. Not here.

"Oh my God, I just can't shut up around you. One finger-bang session and I'm ruined." She put her head in her hands.

Damn it, he needed her to stop being so . . . Erin. That bumbliness was fucking endearing. More than it would be on anyone else.

"Erin," he warned. He needed to stop her before she said anything else. First, because Reece would murder him if he overheard. And second, the urge to stop her rambling with a kiss was quickly becoming a viable option the longer he was around her.

"Yeah?" She pulled her hands away from her face and took a sip of beer.

"Thanks for being my date. You're a really good friend." Why was this so hard? He shoved his hands in his pockets, and his fingers found the familiar coin. *You can't be with her. You have Bailey to think about.* Just being around her messed with his resolve. "Sorry, I have to head out early, but it was really nice seeing you." He stood and clapped her on the back. Like he would have when they were kids.

Wrong. That felt so wrong.

She looked up at him, those hazel eyes full of hurt, and he knew that he'd made a mistake. Her lips pulled into a tight smile. "Thanks for stopping by. Maybe I'll see you around."

"I don't know if that'd be a good idea." He hated himself for saying that. But he'd laid the foundation. The damage was done. He strode back through the house. He told Hollywood he'd need to get a ride home from Reece, and then he made his way out to the truck.

Jake may not have known what tomorrow would bring, but he was sure of one thing. There was no chance he was seeing her again before she left. He'd make sure of it.

Chapter Eleven

Erin sat at the corner table in Polly's Café, her earbuds in, coffee to the left of her laptop, and blueberry scone to her right. If this didn't scream "I'm hunkered down and ready to kick some job-hunting booty today," she didn't know what did. Two deep sips of her dark roast and she stretched her neck from side to side, preparing herself for filling out another twenty applications today. Or maybe one, if she was lucky.

Forget about the hiring freeze. There had to be *a* position for her. Right? The thought of putting her name in the substitute-teacher pool sent a shiver up her spine. If it was anything like student teaching, where the kids tried to duct-tape her to the chair because she was new, she wanted nothing to do with that. While at Stephens, she'd walked into the teachers' lounge and found subs crying into their packed lunches more than a few times. Yeah, no thanks.

Once she had her country-music station situated, she clicked into the job page for the California school districts. Erin groaned and swiped her thumb over her brow, staring at the page. One new position open at an elementary school. Zero for middle school.

Just for kicks, she opened up Craigslist and searched for teaching jobs. A few preschool jobs popped up, but they were all positions she was overqualified for.

"Any luck over there?" Sloane sat across from her, wiping bagel crumbs from her Smurf scrubs. The Smurfs matched the exact shade of her hair.

"Maybe if I want to be a plumber or nuclear engineer."

She fisted her hands through her hair. "I think it'd probably be easier for me to go back to school and get a new degree than find a job now."

"Yes, we all know the job market is crap." Sloane plopped an extra scone onto Erin's plate. She shifted in her chair, leaning in toward Erin. "But if anyone can find a job, it's you. Hell, you made it out of Portland, even though your mom tried to chain you to the house. You have will-power for miles," she said.

Erin swallowed past the lump in her throat. It wasn't that the statement wasn't true—because she had always wanted out of Portland—but there was more to it. She would have stuck it out here if her mom hadn't been so suffocating.

But when she'd found "Erin's Ten-Year Plan"—filled out not by her, she might add—she had realized her mom would have never let her out of her clutches if she'd stayed. So she'd bolted, racing down the I-5 corridor to Stanford faster than she could say, "Go Cardinals."

"This is just all I've known." She swallowed hard. Even if she'd been in different cities, her career had always been a constant. The thought of doing anything else was terrifying. "What am I supposed to do if I fail?"

"You do what everyone else does. Pick yourself up, binge-watch Netflix, and then make something else work." Her cheek hollowed as she bit the inside of it. "When Brian and I broke up, I thought I'd never date again. I thought he was it for me, ya know?"

Erin nodded. Sloane hadn't talked about Brian in more than a year. They'd dated from Erin's freshman year of college up until last year when Sloane had found him in bed with another woman.

"Well, I'm sick of spending my Friday nights with *Jane the Virgin*."

"Does that mean you found someone?"

"Not yet. I joined one of those dating apps."

Erin raised a brow. "You mean the ones where you have to swipe left or right? Or the kind with the sappy bios that sound like an erectile-dysfunction commercial?" she asked.

"Swiping. I wasn't about to spend thirty minutes on a bio no one reads." Sloane flicked a crumb at Erin. "And for your information, I have a blind date set up next week."

"Just have mace ready in case he's a total creep."

"Girl, you're getting a call if that happens." She took another bite of scone, talking with her mouth full. "How was the wedding?"

"Eventful." Flashes of Jake's fingers sliding up her thigh had her sputtering on her coffee.

"Does this mean you've finally bagged the illustrious Jake Bennett?"

Erin flung her sugar packet at Sloane. "It's not like that. We've been friends for so long, I honestly don't think he'd ever see me that way." Even if there were flashes. "It's probably for the best anyway." At least that was what she was telling herself. "Now if only there'd be some damn job openings."

"Seriously, why don't you look here? I know Portland is *such a horrible place to live*"—sarcasm dripped off her words—"but I'd love to have my best friend back."

"I'm not meant for Portland life. I need the sun and to be a couple of hours from nice, warm beaches." The beaches in San Francisco were a lot like the Oregon coast. She wasn't going to step foot in there without a wet suit. But from Santa Cruz south, she'd lie out and enjoy the white sand and the sun's rays.

"What is this sun you speak of?"

"Your vitamin-D deficiency has clouded your judgment." She looked down at the coffee. "Plus, I applied to a school the other day that could be *the one*. It's a prep school, downtown in the city. I looked at their website, and it seems like a really good fit. If they decide to interview me."

Sloane eyed her over her coffee cup. "This is a job and not an arranged marriage, right?"

"Shut it." There was nothing wrong with taking job prospects seriously. She had to if she wanted her damn apartment back.

"I'm just saying you could get a teaching job anywhere."

"Not anywhere. Just the state of California, unless I wanted to drop a ton of money on licensure tests."

Sure, she could pay the extra money, but what would be the point? She didn't *want* to live here. Not that she didn't love her mom, but Erin had been independent for years. Her mom had finally taken the hint that she was somewhat proficient in adulting. Mostly. The occasional "Here's a few twenties to pad your bank account" came in the mail, sure, but she stashed the money away in a rainy-day fund.

"I'm sure your mom is in mourning."

"She's come to terms." Although, by the way she had decorated her room . . . maybe not so much.

Madison slid in moments later, tossing her purse over Erin to the spot between her and the wall.

"What did I miss?" Her red curls were piled in frizzy disarray on top of her head. Madison was the embodiment of boho chic. She'd been wearing peasant tops and flowy skirts long before they had come in style, and she was the type who would keep wearing them, even when the fad wore off. "I just had one hell of a shoot at the waterfront. Caught the perfect window of the sunrise."

Madison had started her own photography business three years ago, and just last year she had been named the top wedding photographer in Portland.

The three of them had been friends ever since kindergarten. They met up at least twice a year to rent a house on Lake Tahoe. Social media, group texting, and Skype dates were an essential part of their friendship.

"Just the fact that Erin still vehemently denies her Portland heritage," Sloane said.

"Do not." Okay, that was exactly what she was doing. She *really* liked that she was a three-hour flight away.

"I want to hear about the wedding," Madison said. "We barely got to talk last night."

Thoughts of Jake's hands flickered in Erin's mind. "It was pretty. Josie made a beautiful bride."

Sloane snapped her fingers. "Details, woman. You gave us nothing at the party. What's the deal with Jake?"

"Yeah, why was he so spooked at the party?" Madison chimed in, stealing a piece of bagel off Sloane's plate and plopping it into her mouth.

What was this? Interrogation hour?

"Ugh. Can we not mention that?" Her face fell in her hands, and she let out a sigh. "It was the most awkward situation ever." Maybe she was destined to use a dating service. She couldn't even get the proper reaction out of a man she was trying to bed. Jesus, did people even talk like that? Maybe she needed more help than she thought.

"Because you guys hooked up?" Sloane asked.

"No!"

"Liar."

"Why does everyone think I'm lying?"

"Because Jake is . . . well, Jake, and you look like you walked off the set of *The O.C.*"

"I can't tell if you're saying my style is outdated or if I should take that as a compliment."

Madison shrugged. "You could stand to lose the cardigans."

"Seriously, why does everyone hate on the cardigans so much?"

"Because you're twenty-eight, not eighty." Madison tore off a piece of Erin's scone and plopped it in her mouth. "So back to Jake. What happened?"

"I don't know. I thought we were getting somewhere, and then—" She waved her hand and sighed. "Then I was me, and things got weird." She decided to leave out the awkward porn station.

"Are you going to see him again?"

After their cringe-worthy encounter last night? Seeing him again was at a firm 0 percent. "Probably not. It's for the best anyway. I'm leaving in a few weeks."

Madison frowned. "Don't remind us. I want to be in my delusional bubble that you're staying forever."

"I say you call him. He's obviously into you. Why not capitalize on that while you have the chance?" Sloane said.

"And say what?" She brought her fingers up to her ear, miming a telephone. "Hey, Jake, so nice chatting with you. I know you said you didn't want to see me again, but would you like to bone me in my old bedroom right down the hall from my mom's room?"

Sloane placed her hand over Erin's. "Honey, we might need an intervention on your flirting skills if that's all you got."

"I know how to flirt." She flicked a crumb at Sloane. Normally when it came to men, this wouldn't be an issue—whether it was because she didn't have time for dating or the fact that she didn't feel the ticking time clock that her mom so often brought up. She was happy being single. She'd had a few long-term relationships since college, but Erin always found some glaring issue.

"Yeah, we know. It's landed you Tom the Tax Man and Drinking Fountain Dude."

"Can't forget Taco Bell Dude."

"In-N-Out," Erin corrected.

"Whatever. Just as bad. You don't make someone pay for their meal on their birthday," Sloane said.

So what if a couple of her previous boyfriends had either zero humor or an irrational fear of public drinking fountains? Everyone had issues. Hers came in the form of planner stickers and washi tape. And spiral notebooks. Her office-supply love was strong.

"In-N-Out guy aside, Tom had really nice calves. He went mountain biking on the weekends. And we all know that drinking fountains are gross."

They both looked at her.

She groaned. Since when did she advocate for complete duds? "Oh God, I totally suck at dating."

"I mean, you could say your house is on fire, and you need a big, strong firefighter to help put it out," Sloane suggested.

Erin snorted. "Yeah, somehow I don't think that'd work." Knowing her luck, the whole fire department would be knocking down her door. On second thought, that wasn't a half-bad idea . . .

"Don't listen to Sloane," Madison said. "Why don't you just text him to hang out?"

"You guys were at the same party as me, right? The one where he said it'd be best to stay away from me and left within five minutes of being there?"

"I don't know. Some guys are clueless."

But Jake wasn't clueless. He'd been straightforward in explaining that he felt awkward around her and didn't want to ruin his friendship with Reece. And she wasn't going to come between a bromance. Time to turn this interrogation in another direction.

"Well, Sloane's going on a blind date." Bomb dropped. And now the attention could be taken off her for a millisecond.

Madison's head reared back as she regarded Sloane. "It isn't from that hookup app, is it?"

"You act like this isn't the twenty-first century. I'm allowed to be okay with hookups."

"Yeah, but you really want to pick from the general pool of guys who send unsolicited dick pics?" Erin asked.

"I'm one dick pic away from giving up men completely," Madison said.

"Preach." Maybe once she moved back to California, she'd find a nice guy there. Someone like Jake.

Chapter Twelve

Jake shuffled the deck of cards and stared at the men sitting around the table in the break room. It felt good to be back on duty after five days away. If there was one thing Jake loved, besides his daughter, it was his job. Nothing beat a good shift, and every day was a new challenge. They'd just finished checking the gear on the truck, placing their turnouts near the apparatus, and had spent the last thirty minutes brushing up on a page out of the EMT protocol book.

"Twos and sevens are wild. Pennets count as eighty points today." A Pennet, which was a four of a kind named after the highest honored firefighter at Station 11 in the past sixty years, was the most sought-after card hand in their morning game of rummy. A hand of cards served as a chore divider. Specifically, whoever had the worst cards got stuck with duties such as cooking dinner and cleaning toilets. Jake had managed to avoid bathroom duty for the past three shifts.

"I got a question for you," Reece said.

"That's a statement, dipshit," said Hollywood, staring at his cards.

"If you'd let me finish, I'd get to my question," Reece said.

"Well, go on." Hollywood waved his hand dramatically. "Don't let me get in the way."

"You know Yanni?"

"The keyboardist?" Hollywood asked.

"Jesus, dude, you're like twelve. How do you even know who that is?"

Hollywood just chuckled. "I'm a cultured man, asshole."

"Sure you are. Maybe once you graduate from a pacifier." Reece shook his head and smiled. "Anyway, I'm talking about Yanni who used to work at the district office. The one who chewed through toothpicks like he was a damn beaver."

"Oh yeah, I remember him."

"He sold his Jeep." Reece's brows furrowed. If the man was serious about one thing, it was cars.

Reece had been obsessed with Jeeps ever since they were kids. Even had a pic of one in his locker in high school. Jake bet if he peeked into this locker at the station, he'd see one pasted there, too.

"Let me guess—he didn't sell it to you," Jake said. Yanni didn't come across as the type that valued camaraderie. He was a mopey dude who liked to keep to himself. Jake was starting to understand how the guy felt. After the way Erin's homecoming party had gone, his mood was somewhere between general annoyance and wanting to punch himself in the face. Instead of telling her the truth about how he couldn't keep her out of his mind, he had let her believe that he thought that weekend was a mistake.

"No. The asshole sold it to a stranger. Who probably won't give the proper attention to that gorgeous specimen," Reece said.

Hollywood let out a snort. "We are talking about a car, right?"

"It's a lifestyle, Hollywood."

"Right." He laid out a three of a kind and four hearts. "Can't you just buy your own Jeep?"

Jake tried to focus on the conversation, but his mind kept wandering back to Erin. Her laugh. The way her lips pulled over that mouth he so desperately wanted to kiss last weekend. He knew it was wrong, but he couldn't get her out of his head. And with Bailey gone at camp, and the house too empty, he prowled around it like a caged tiger, willing thoughts of Erin to vanish from his mind. Instead, he'd used his hand in the shower, needing release like he was a goddamn teenager again.

"That's not the point. He *knew* I wanted it. Aw, shit." Reece threw down a crap pair of twos.

"Should know better than to trust a guy who hangs tiny air fresheners in his cubicle," Jake added, realizing he hadn't been interacting at all with his men.

"He speaks! And here I thought you'd gone mute today. What's up with you?" Hollywood asked.

"Nothing." But Jake couldn't stop thinking about the frown that had cut across Erin's face yesterday, the instant stab to his gut when he realized he was the one who put it there. *This was a mistake. Let's pretend it never happened.*

What was wrong with him? On most days, he claimed to be a smart guy. He'd done a bang-up job fighting the attraction all weekend. He was the first to admit that. But he had somehow managed to get through it mostly unscathed. And yet, he couldn't let it go. The damn blood humming in his veins pulsed at the very thought of when he'd get to see her again. Which, if he was smart, would be never.

"Here, take a brownie. Lexi made them." Hollywood shoved the plate of baked goods across the table.

Lexi was Hollywood's sister. She was a nursing student at the university in town and loved to bring over baked goods for the guys. He glanced at the plate full of brownies, GOODIES FROM YOUR FAVORITE NURSE scrawled in her curly handwriting in Sharpie.

"Your sister is too good to us."

"Sure as shit, she is."

He snagged one and took a bite, then took a card from the top of the pile. He'd throw down his cards in the death round.

The guys gave him a funny look when he didn't throw down his cards but continued playing, the turn going to Reece.

He threw down a Pennet and two hearts. "Looks like Jake is on bathroom duty today."

"What? We have the death round still."

Both of them gawked at him. Reece said, "Brother. We were just in the death round. Where's your head today?"

Not here, apparently. No, it had been on Erin's lips. The way her dress hugged every curve. How he was going out of his goddamn mind.

"Well, hell." He slammed his cards on the table and shoved another piece of brownie in his mouth. He needed to cool it, especially since he was at work.

The other guys laughed. "Looks like you're on dinner duty, Hollywood."

"Again?" he groaned.

Reece slid his cards across the table toward him. "Remember, we put out fires, not start them. No more grill use for you."

"It was one time."

Just then, the tones went off. They all shoved back from the table, their good-natured joking sliding off them like a discarded shirt as they made their way to the apparatus and into their boots and pants. This one was a medical call, so they wouldn't need to put on their full turnout gear, just their Class Bs. Jake hopped into the passenger seat in the engine and scanned the computer mounted to the dash.

Medical call. Thirty-two-year-old man who needed immediate attention. The dispatcher couldn't get a reason out of him of what exactly was hurt, which either meant the guy was on some type of drugs or hiding something. Nothing good ever came from a patient refusing to divulge information.

They parked the engine in front of the dilapidated apartment complex, and Jake took a quick scan of his surroundings. A few people roamed down the sidewalk toward the far end of the complex. Nothing suspicious. He hopped out of the engine and grabbed the monitor and med box, while Hollywood grabbed the air kit.

They ran up the three flights to apartment 341. There was no need to knock on the door because it was already wide open.

Normally, if there was any form of threat, they'd wait for the police to clear the area and then proceed. Jake guessed he and Reece had come to the same conclusion that there was no immediate threat.

"Hello?" Jake called out.

A faint "Help me" echoed back at him.

They looked at each other and nodded in silent deliberation, all three moving forward.

Stale pizza boxes, takeout containers, and trash littered the floor. Hollywood was the paramedic on their shift, even though they were all technically EMT trained. He moved forward first, his boots shuffling through the deluge of discarded items.

"In here," cried the person.

They waded through the hallway and into the equally trashed living room. Some sort of racing game was on the big screen, and a guy was sunken into the couch, wielding a controller.

"What's your name, sir?" Hollywood asked. He may have been a jokester at the station and prone to being a big flirt at public events, but he was a damn good firefighter and took his job seriously. Someone Jake would want by his side fighting a box alarm fire.

Jake scanned the room. No potential threats. If the guy pulled a knife or a gun, he had two choices. Either he was taking his crew out the sliding glass door on this third-story balcony or he was tackling the guy. As of right now, the guy looked drugged out of his mind, so he didn't look like he posed too much of a threat.

"Anthony."

"Anthony, I'm going to take your vitals and see how you're doing, man," Hollywood said, setting his gear on the ground next to Anthony's feet.

"Can I just finish this up real quick?" He jutted his chin toward the TV.

Jake exchanged a "Are you fucking kidding me?" glance with Reece.

"You take anything lately?" Hollywood asked, ignoring Anthony and digging into his gear.

"Just some hash and a few beers." It was nice when people were honest about what they'd smoked. Better than twenty minutes beating around the bush until they were hauled off in an ambulance.

Hollywood nodded, grabbing the blood-pressure cuff from the med kit and securing it around Anthony's rail-thin arm.

"Blood pressure one twenty over seventy." He procured a flashlight and continued to check his eyes. "Slight nystagmus in the pupils, which would be consistent with alcohol and drug use."

Jake's adrenaline began to fade as he realized this call was a waste of their time. Working with the public was great, but he actually wanted to *help* people.

"Sir, why did you call us?" Reece asked.

They saw a lot of calls like this—people too high to function, people out of their minds from a bad trip. But this guy just looked . . . comfortable.

The sports car on the screen crashed into a lake, and Anthony glanced up at them for the first time since they'd arrived. "I ordered Chinese food."

"What kind?" Reece asked.

"Chow mein, lo mein. Every type of mein, man." The guy chuckled to himself. "But I realized I don't have any money to pay the guy. But then I thought," he said, slurring and pointing a finger to his forehead. "Figured firefighters like to eat." He shrugged.

"Sir, you called us to pay for your food?" Jake asked.

"Didn't want it to go to waste," Anthony said.

Christ. This man was the same age as he was. Except this guy's life was held together by four paper-thin walls and takeout food. "You know who loves food more than us?" Jake said.

"Who?" he asked.

"The police," Jake said.

"I'm sure whichever officer that shows up would love to eat your Chinese food," Reece added.

Anthony threw up his arms. "Man, you are so smart. That's a great idea."

Jake chuckled under his breath. The guy was too high to realize he was going to be booked. It'd almost be worth it to stick around long enough for the cops to show up. They all grabbed their gear, and just as they were passing into the kitchen, the guy shouted, "Can one of you throw me the remote?"

"Sure, man." Jake grabbed it off the counter and tossed it onto the couch next to the guy. "Have a nice day."

Jake shook off his annoyance as he walked out of the apartment. Sure, he was happy the guy was fine, but this wasn't the best way to start his shift. The adrenaline that kicked in at the start of every call hardened into a solid brick in his stomach.

Once they got out to the engine and deposited their gear, Reece said, "I could have gone for lo mein."

"Same." Jake cracked a smile and chuckled. With these types of situations, they had two choices: get pissed or laugh it off. For the sake of Jake's sanity, he chose the latter.

They made it back to the station, everything just the way they'd left it. While Reece and Hollywood made their way to the weight room, Jake headed to the bathroom to get his cleaning duties out of the way. He was busy scrubbing the toilet bowl when Reece walked in.

He leaned against the door frame, watching.

Jake kept his gaze trained to the task at hand, but he could feel Reece's stare burning into the back of his head.

"You know, if you're just going to stand there and watch, by all means make use of the extra scrubber." Jake jutted his chin toward cleaning kit.

"You gonna tell me what's up with my sister?"

Jake scrubbed harder, focusing on a spot in the center of the bowl. "What are you talking about?"

"She got weird at the party. And you left like your ass was on fire."

"Didn't notice." Hell, someone without eyes and ears could probably feel the awkwardness at that party.

"Bullshit. Did something happen between you two?"

"Aw, man. I'm thirty-two, not senile. I know how you feel about me even looking at your sister wrong." He didn't like omitting some facts, but it was better this way.

Jake's cheeks burned, and he cleared his throat, keeping his eyes on the toilet. He liked that about Reece. No bullshitting. They said what they meant and put it all out there. No guesswork. Nothing like how he'd felt this past weekend with Erin.

"You're a grown-ass man. You can do what you want."

"Well, you don't have anything to worry about. Nothing's going to happen." Again.

He could still feel the weight of her palm slicking across the top of his dress pants. The way her red nails bit into the fabric, driving him wild.

"You know, Jake, you are allowed to have fun once in a while." He sighed and tapped his hand against the door frame. "I don't know the first thing about parenting, but I'm sure there's something in the handbook that says you don't need to take a vow to priesthood or anything." He lifted a finger. "I'm not saying to break that vow with my sister, though."

"I have fun."

Reece raised a brow. "When was the last time you went out?"

He shook out the toilet brush and chucked it back into the container. "We barbecued the other week."

"I'm not talking about with the guys."

Jake shook his head. "I don't know. And since when are you so interested in my love life?"

"When you look like you're so wound up you're going to burst a vessel in that pretty face of yours."

"Don't let Hollywood hear you say that. He might get jealous." He was wound tight. Enough that just the damn thought of Erin got him hard.

"Just saying, it'd do you some good to get out there. Bailey's gone for a few weeks. Take advantage." He shrugged.

There were a lot of factors keeping him from dating. His job, mainly. He worked crazy hours nonconducive to relationships. He worked holidays, weekends, you name it. The only reason his family put up with it was because they had to. He'd never ask that of anyone else. And then there was Bailey. He'd been down this road before and wouldn't let her get hurt.

"Just go out and have some fun. Something other than barbecues with us."

Jake nodded. Maybe Reece was right.

He hadn't wanted someone so bad in a long time, not like the way he throbbed for Erin. His daughter was gone for three weeks. What would one date hurt? He'd use this opportunity to get her out of his system. For good.

Before he had more time to think about it, the tones went off again. And like everything else, he dropped everything to do his job.

Chapter Thirteen

Erin wiped the sweat beading on her brow and snuck to the back of the Airstream for a quick break. Even after her coffee date with her friends yesterday, she still felt on edge about this past weekend. Her sister had taken over the register and food prep since there was a lull in customers. With a quick glance to make sure no one was looking, she pulled out her own homemade sandwich. Except hers didn't contain their mom's perfected recipe that had earned them celebrity status in the downtown food-truck community. No, this one was slathered with layer upon layer of Jif. Yes, Erin was a traitor to her own flesh and blood. The guilt-trip ship had sailed years ago, and now she was left with a vessel named the *Zero-Shits-Given*. She'd captained this boat for years. No chance in trading her in now.

She sat on a crate, letting the oscillating fan ruffle her matted bangs. To think, just last weekend, she'd been with Jake. All over him. *Stupid, stupid, stupid.* What had she been thinking? She still couldn't get their cringe-worthy conversation out of her head.

This is for the best. She had to believe that because it meant that a new job was just around the corner, and she'd be out of here and never have to live through the embarrassment of seeing him again.

Andie finished washing a knife in the wash bin, dropped it onto the drying rack, and wiped her hands on a fresh towel. "Can you hand these flyers out to some of the local businesses? Mom asked me to do that yesterday, but we got swamped." She pointed to the stack of pink flyers that advertised a buy-one-get-one-free event for all the food carts in Periwinkle Circle. The food-cart community was a tight-knit group of people who worked together to make sure people continued to come to their end of Twenty-Third. Her mom often headed the fund-raisers and was basically the matriarch in the community.

"Sure." She snatched the flyers off the counter. Anything to get herself out of her head for a few minutes.

Erin made her way down the bustling streets of the Northwest District. Twenty-Third Avenue was a gem in downtown. Tearoom windows displaying decadent macarons, the smell of berry jams and Nutella crepes wafting out of bakery-shop doors, you name it. She stretched her neck, tilting her face toward the early-morning sun peeking over the buildings. Indie music wafted out of open storefront doors, tunes that beckoned customers to take a look at eclectic pieces.

Downtown Portland in the morning had been one of Erin's favorite things as a kid. Store owners setting up shop, watering plants on the sidewalk, everyone waving a cheery hello. They might have been doing it with two-inch plugs in their ears and full-sleeve tattoos, but this was about as *Brady Bunch*–esque as a city could get without being on a film set. She had to admit that this city did hold a certain amount of charm.

She crossed the street, and a unicyclist walking his Chihuahua whizzed by, going in the other direction. Traffic was light this morning. Most of the rush would take place an hour from now. After making her way past her favorite lunch spot, Papa Giermo's, she opened the door to Olivia's, Portland's best baked-goods shop, nestled between a coffee roaster and a bicycle-repair place.

The bell above the door dinged as she entered the shop. The smell of dough, sugar, and fruit hugged her like a warm blanket the second her feet hit the checkered black-and-white tile floor. She inhaled deeply, savoring the scent. *Heaven,* she thought.

"Oh my goodness. Erin? Is that you?"

Olivia, the shop owner, dropped a piece of dough she'd been kneading and sped around the glass display cases, wrapping her arms around her.

"Hi, Olivia." Olivia smelled just like her sweets. A hint of cherry and vanilla, sugar, and something that Erin could describe only as love. She was in her midfifties and, last Erin knew, moonlighted in a band called the Purple Eggplants. Basically, Olivia was a badass Betty Crocker. "It's been too long."

For the first time since she'd been in town, she actually meant it.

"Come. Sit down. Tell me what you've been up to." She motioned toward a set of ice-cream-parlor chairs set up in the corner of the store. Nothing in here had changed since she'd last seen it, which suited this place just fine. Olivia's held a timeless facade that promised handmade pastries and hardworking people.

She took a seat in one of the chairs across from Olivia, who looked at her expectantly.

"What have I been up to . . ." She trailed off, buying herself some time to think. She thumbed the flyers, staring at the awards lining the bakery wall.

What had she been up to since she'd been gone? All she could really come up with was teaching. And a lot of boxed wine. Which tended to go hand in hand. But had that really been all she'd done? Ten years gone and she had nothing to show for herself.

"Just working. Job hunting now."

Olivia's face brightened. "Here in Portland?"

"As of now, no." Whoa, what was with the wishy-washy answer? If anyone else had asked her, it was always a firm "Hell no." "I'm home for the summer," she amended. "Helping out my mom. Oh, that reminds me." She held up the flyer. "The food carts in Periwinkle Circle are all having a sale this weekend. Can I put a poster up in your shop?"

"Of course. Always happy to help out the other local businesses." Olivia grabbed one of the posters and stuck it to the corkboard at the entrance to the shop. Then she nabbed a cherry tart from the display case, plopped it onto a pristine white plate, and placed it in front of Erin. "I've been keeping up with your mom's escapades online. Such a hoot."

Say what? "Huh, yeah." She must have meant whatever her brother posted. Sometimes she'd see the occasional post about something funny her mom had done.

She took a bite of the tart, and her eyes rolled back into her head. Just as good as she remembered. Reece and Erin used to go to Olivia's almost daily when they were kids. She would load them up on sugar and then let them read their library books at the very table she was sitting at now. How many Baby-Sitters Club books had she devoured while eating Olivia's baked goods? For the first time that day, she smiled. "Oh my God. Still amazing. Thank you."

"Cherry tarts are always on the house for a Jenkins."

It feels good to be back.

Whoa. Where had that thought come from? All these childhood memories getting stirred up were obviously messing with her head. Is that why Andie had sent her out here? Did she know she'd feel this overwhelming sense of homesickness as she passed each shop? She shook off that thought. Andie probably just didn't want to walk around, passing out flyers.

"I should get going. Lots of flyers to pass out." She stood and gave Olivia a hug.

"Don't be a stranger. It's good to see your face around here."

Erin nodded, feeling suddenly nostalgic. Everything in this town seemed to have stayed the same over the years.

Walking down these streets brought back so many memories. This town was such a big part of her childhood. And yet, now she was an outsider. Someone who didn't belong in either place at the moment.

She shook off that feeling and took the last bite of her cherry tart. Her phone buzzed in her pocket, and she quickly chewed and swallowed before answering.

"Hello?"

"Is this Erin Jenkins?" Her pulse ticked in her ears. Only three types of people called her. Red Cross, telemarketers, and job interviewers.

If it was the first two, she was going to get really stabby. And possibly need more sweets.

"Yes."

"I'm Brenda from Highland Prep. We've reviewed your application and résumé and were wondering if you'd be interested in coming in for an interview this week."

She frowned. "I'd love to, but I'm visiting family in Oregon." Seriously, that'd be her luck to land an interview and not be able to catch a flight down to California to be there.

"No problem. We can do a video chat. How does tomorrow sound?"

How did that sound? The patrons walking down Twenty-Third Avenue were currently getting a glimpse of Erin's happy dance, complete with "Walk Like an Egyptian" moves. Surprisingly, there was no side-eye action from anyone.

"I appreciate the opportunity," she said. They exchanged contact information, and Erin hung up.

She let out a squeal, clutching her phone.

See? All that weirdness was for nothing. She'd rock the interview tomorrow, spend some more time with her best friends, and in a few weeks, still be on track to moving back home. Whatever fondness she felt for staying here was obviously just the fact that she missed her friends. That was it.

Forty minutes and a whole block later, Erin had passed out the majority of the flyers. Andie could do the rest on her next break. She didn't care if her sister gave her the stink eye. Nothing could bring her down from cloud nine. Because she was going to make this interview work. No matter what.

She made her way back to the food truck, and in the distance, her sister's blonde head poked out of the window, chatting up a customer. Andie had always been a little prickly around the edges, but from the already-full tip jar sitting to the side of the window before the major lunch rush, she was doing just fine with the customers. She handed the guy a sandwich, and he turned around.

Erin's stomach clenched at the sight of Jake.

The euphoria from the job-interview high came to a crashing halt. Those extra posters? Now would be a great time to hand them out. No need to have Andie do it. That idea was in full motion, until Jake spotted Erin and waved.

Damn. There went the escape plan.

Had their awkward interaction at her party not been enough? He really must be a glutton for punishment. She squared her shoulders and walked up to where he stood near a bench. "What are you doing here?"

"If you keep asking that, I'm going to get a complex." He smiled. "I was in the neighborhood."

She shot him a look. The only things to see this far down Twenty-Third were the food trucks. After that, it was all residential. And unless he was rolling in Scrooge McMoneybags type of dough, he wasn't living on this side of town.

He shook his head. "That was a lie. I wanted to see you."

"Yeah?" Her heart raced in her chest. *Stop it. Jake is just like every other guy. No need for the palpitations.* Her body wasn't getting the memo.

He nodded, and for a second, he looked like the shy boy she'd known back in elementary school. Before he'd gone from sweet guy to heartbreaker. He swallowed hard and stared at the sandwich in his hands. "Bailey left for camp yesterday."

"How's that going?" So they were going to play the small-talk game. She'd go along with it. But it still didn't explain why he was here.

"She made it to Stanford safe and sound." His thumbs dug at the foil sandwich wrapper.

"You don't seem convinced."

"This is the first time she's been away for so long," he said, his gaze unfocused.

"I can't imagine." And it was true. Although she worked with kids on a daily basis, she saw each of them for only an hour a day, and then they were gone. A full-time gig seemed like . . . an insane amount of work she was nowhere near ready to handle.

"I didn't just come here to get a peanut-butter sandwich." He quickly added, "Although this really is amazing." He held up their signature peanut-butter-and-bacon sandwich, by far the most popular item on the menu.

"Then why did you come?" That damn shudder in her chest turned to a full gallop again. It seemed to do an awful lot of that when she was around Jake.

"Can I take you out?"

Her breath fizzled out of her lungs. "Out?" No way she'd heard him right.

"I think we started things off a little backward. I'd like to take you on a date. A proper one. With no porn in sight."

Holy crap. An actual date? "I was beginning to warm up to those videos. Harry Twatter was a personal favorite."

He chuckled, his mouth pulling into a smile. "Is that a yes?"

"You don't think this is a mistake? You made that loud and clear at the party." What the heck was wrong with her? Was she actually arguing her way out of a date?

"Of course I think it's a mistake. The way you make me feel—" He dragged a hand through his hair. "I've never felt more out of control. I'm sorry that I acted weird at the party. It's just, Reece was there . . ." He shook his head again. "No, that's a terrible excuse. I was an asshole, and I own up to that."

Her body was about to break out into a football victory-touchdown dance, but her mind was going, *Sloooow down there, Speed Racer.*

"What changed your mind?"

"Your brother, actually."

"My brother." She laughed. "He told you to ask me out?" She would have loved to have been a fly on the wall during that conversation.

"No. But he did tell me I needed to have a little more fun in my life."

"I see."

"I've been thinking about you. At the station. Driving. In the shower. Everywhere." He took a deep breath and gave that damn smile that showcased the dimple in his left cheek. Charge the paddles because she was going to need a shock to the system with the way he looked at her, both shy and so damn sexy. "I haven't done this in a really long time, so I might be a little rusty, but if you're still interested, I'd really like to take you out. Properly."

Bad idea. Alert. Alert. He's too nice—and you know where that leads. The good ol' f-word. And she didn't mean the fun one. No, this was the one that promised attachments. Ones that she couldn't afford to have, not when she was leaving soon.

If she valued her sanity, she'd use her damn head and give him a polite no.

She never claimed to make great use of intellect when it came to men, though. Really, what was there to lose? It was a date with Jake. One single night to finally get him out of her system. That was all this was.

"Yes," she said.

"Great. I'll pick you up at eight on Friday if that works for you."

Chapter Fourteen

"Have you seen my pants?" Erin riffled through her dresser drawers, then sprinted to the closet. None of her dress slacks were in there. Had she left them all in California? "I have an interview with Highland in five minutes."

"What's wrong with what you're wearing?" Andie stood in the doorway with a bag of gummy worms in one hand, her phone in the other. A green-and-yellow one hung out of her mouth as she tapped out a message to someone.

"What's wrong with this?" She'd picked out her favorite black top and covered it with one of the cardigans Andie had made fun of the other day. That wasn't the problem. It was the pants situation. "Unicorn leggings aren't professional."

"It's Skype, Erin. They'll only be able to see your top half."

Of course she'd just thrown all her jeans in the wash, or she'd pull on a pair.

"You think so?" She'd done this a few times when she'd taped videos for class. Why not sit in comfort while she got grilled about lesson planning and her ability to collaborate with other teachers? But this was different. It was a job interview. The admin probably had some super-spidey sense that would be able to tell she was wearing unprofessional attire off-camera. Or maybe going through too many interviews in a matter of weeks had somehow made her paranoid.

"Trust me. Just make sure you're sitting and you'll be fine," Andie said, shoving another worm into her mouth.

Erin took a deep breath. Okay, she could do that. She had a good feeling about this interview, especially after she had done a little Internet sleuthing last night. Highland Prep had been named the top private school in the city for the past three years. They catered to families who wanted a more hands-on approach to learning. From the pictures, they'd done projects in Africa, South America, and Asia, helping problem-solve world issues.

In terms of classroom management, this job would be cake. Dealing with the parents would be a whole other issue, but honestly, she'd take a job just about anywhere right now, and she felt particularly lucky this one had fallen into her lap.

She glanced at her closet mirror, fluffed her hair, and tapped a pencil on her desk, waiting for the call. A few seconds later, the video call function on her computer dinged.

You got this. You're going to kill it. She gave herself one last reassuring nod and then clicked into the chat.

On her screen, three people sat huddled together at what seemed to be a boardroom table. All were wearing nice tailored blazers. Behind them hung the school crest along with their slogan: EXPANDING HORIZONS, EDUCATING YOUNG MINDS.

"Ms. Jenkins. Thank you for interviewing with us today. I'm Brenda Johnson, vice principal. We know this is a bit unorthodox, but we didn't want you to have to fly down."

"I appreciate it." But she also didn't like the sentiment behind it. *We didn't want you wasting your money on a flight.* She shook off that thought and also the one about how many people they were interviewing. Glass half-full. *They wouldn't have interviewed you to waste your time.*

The man in the middle said, "I'm Jeremy Tyler, the principal of Highland." He gestured to his left. "This is Steve Rogers, head of the science department."

"I didn't know that I'd be interviewed by Captain America today," Erin joked. She also could have busted out a Mister Rogers "Won't you be my neighbor?" but refrained.

All three remained straight-faced. Her own laughter faded. She shifted in her chair, crossing her legs, making sure to keep her leggings offscreen. Well, okay, then. Tough crowd. Maybe pretentious schools sucked the humor out of people. She cleared her throat after another awkward beat of silence. "It is very nice to meet all of you."

"I've just gotten off the phone with your previous principal. He speaks quite fondly of you. We also see on your résumé that you received Teacher of the Year for your school district. That's very impressive."

Heat filled her cheeks. Compliments weren't really her strong suit. She never knew how to act. But she had to admit that the award ceremony where she'd received that placard had been one of the highlights of her career so far. All the late-night lesson planning. All the strategizing over seating charts, creating assignments that engaged her students—now that was worth everything. She may have let a whole lot of other people down in her life, but at the very least, she had her students.

"Thank you." She'd miss Stephens. Three years in the same place was a record for her. Stupid budget cuts.

"We're just going to cut to the chase here," said the principal. This didn't surprise her. Erin didn't normally judge right off the bat, but they struck her as people who didn't congregate in the halls of their school to talk about the latest TV shows or chat about the best Thai food in town. They were probably the type to always eat dinner before dessert. She didn't need dessert-first people (although she was definitely one of them). She only needed a job.

"Why do you think you'd make a valuable addition to our staff?" he continued.

Erin launched into her canned spiel that she'd given in every other interview, describing how well she worked with other teachers, making sure to use key words like *collaboration* and *inquiry-based learning*.

Forget the fact that she'd worked her ass off to get to know students on a personal level and that she was one of the few who actually enjoyed working with her age group.

All nodded along at her response. She couldn't tell by their reactions if they were impressed or bored. A chill ran through her at the thought of working with people so . . . uncharismatic as an admin. All her other principals had joked around with her, keeping a lighthearted feel in the school.

It's a job, she reminded herself.

"Did you get the lesson plan sheet that I e-mailed to you?" Jeremy asked.

"Yes. I filled it out with a lesson on mass and density." She'd stayed up past midnight making sure the plan was both educational and engaging.

He nodded. "Do you mind sharing with us?"

"Sure." She reached for it, in the spot she'd left it two nights ago when she'd been working on it. Her hand hit empty space. *Shit.* A quick glance around her desk, and nope, no lesson plan. Then she cut her gaze to the nightstand by her table, across the room. Perched next to her lamp was her lesson plan.

No. Why, why, why did she have to go and make last-minute tweaks?

"Um, yes, I seem to have misplaced them in the other room—" She was about to tell them that she could recite the lesson to them. She'd done it dozens of times with her students.

"We'll wait. Go ahead and get them," the principal prompted. The other two just stared at her, expectant.

Okay. She could get up and go across the room. But . . . she was wearing unicorn leggings. Either way she cut it, if she got up from her chair, those uptight blazer-wearing dudes would know just how much of a fraud she was. Damn it, why did she have to go and listen to her sister? Those wet jeans from the laundry were looking awfully appealing right about now.

She weighed her options. Nothing good came to mind, and she wasn't about to argue with her future employer. If she shut off the camera for a minute, they'd question why, and she didn't want to have to deal with that either. Being on the other end, helping hire staff before, she knew any negative mark was pretty much a *no* in terms of getting the job. Unicorns screamed a big, fat "Hide your impressionable children."

She glanced at the camera again. No, she could totally move out of the frame and get away with this. Her fingers clutched the edge of her desk, nails digging into the wood. Okay, do-or-die time. She braced herself and tried to scoot offscreen to the best of her ability. Maybe if she was quick enough, they wouldn't notice the bright pink unicorns with the sparkly horns.

One, two, three—go. She shot up at Flash speed. Looked like Steve Rogers wasn't the only superhero in the house today. She quickly walked to the edge of the room. Maybe, just maybe—

A sharp intake of breath speared through her computer speaker, followed by a sputtering cough. Yep, there went her chance of not being noticed. Her face burned, and she cursed under her breath. *You got yourself into this mess. Own up to it and get this job.* Erin grabbed the papers, squared her shoulders, and held her head high as she walked back to her chair. She'd own this unicorn outfit.

To the credit of Jeremy, Brenda, and Steve, they didn't mention her outfit. That didn't mean she didn't realize the interview was over before she was even able to talk about her lesson. But she explained her density and mass lecture and did it with a smile.

"Thank you, Erin. That was very impressive."

She nodded. "I appreciate you taking the time to interview me." At least she could say that she gave it her all.

And with that, they signed off. Erin had done enough interviews to know this was the worst of them yet. Which meant there was zero chance of her getting this job. She plunked her head on the desk and groaned.

Moments later, someone knocked on her door.

"What?" she called out.

Andie cracked open the door. "How did the interview go?"

"You were wrong about the outfit," she said, her voice muffled in the crook of her arm.

What was she going to do? That was the last interview she had lined up for the foreseeable future. There was no way she could move back to the city if she was a substitute. There'd be no health insurance, and rent was already ridiculous. She could look in other parts of California, but the farther away she got from the city, the less chance she had. Not only was there a teaching-job shortage, but a lot of hires were also based off connections. She needed to come up with a plan B. And fast.

Chapter Fifteen

"So let me get this straight." Jake's tongue swirled around his scoop of double-chocolate-chunk ice cream. "You wore unicorn pajamas to a job interview."

"Leggings," Erin groaned. Not even a sea-salt-and-caramel ice-cream cone from Salt and Straw could lift her spirits after how badly she'd bombed that interview. "And they weren't supposed to *see* them."

His tongue gave another swirl around the ice cream, and her stomach bottomed out as she watched. She didn't know if he was doing it on purpose, but with every flick, all she could think about was how that would feel between her thighs. She crossed her legs, and the fabric of her underwear brushed against her sensitive flesh, amplifying the low throb that settled between her legs. Ever since the other weekend, she'd been thrown off-kilter. She blamed it on a major case of female blue balls. That shit was real and painful.

The sun hovered above the waterfront, deep shades of pinks and purples melting into the horizon as they walked together.

"It's their loss if they can't look past that."

"Somehow I don't think that's their mind-set."

"If you're even half the teacher I think you are, they'd be stupid not to hire you," he said.

"For all you know, I could duct-tape my students to their chairs and put on Bill Nye every single class."

"I think you'd be fulfilling some of those teenage boys' fantasies with that."

She swatted his chest. "Sicko."

He grabbed her hand before she could drop it from his pec and gently squeezed. "Something will work out. Even if it's not this job, there'll be something else."

"How are you so sure?" When it came out of his mouth, she almost believed it. She *wanted* to believe it. Badly. But something about Jake's sure-and-steady tone calmed the chaos swirling like an EF5 tornado in her head.

"Because life has sucker-punched me in the face a hell of a lot of times, and I'm still standing."

They walked in the section where there was a large fountain with a sculpture of a metal fish jumping high in the air. Behind it was a tall metal fence with locks hooked through almost every available space. This place was called Wishing Corner, where all wishes were supposed to come true. Messages threaded through the holes, dreams waiting to be fulfilled. Hopes bound tightly to this city.

It was a hokey spot tourists usually traveled to because it was in the guidebook. Much like they went to Voodoo instead of the local favorite, Blue Star. Madison and Sloane both had locks here somewhere. Erin didn't believe in luck. She'd worked too damn hard her whole life to leave things up to chance.

"Do you think any of these wishes have come true?" she asked, staring at the thousands of pieces of silver glinting in the remnants of the sunset.

"I'm sure they have. They say that if you wish for something hard enough, then it'll happen."

"If that's the case, wouldn't everyone be asking for chocolate and six million dollars?"

"No. Deep down, everyone wants something deeper than what money can buy. Craves it." He swallowed hard. And for a moment, Jake looked just like the wild boy she'd loved when she was a kid. "When I first found out Maisey was pregnant with Bailey, I came down here."

They moved to the bench that sat directly across from the fence. The moonlight shone on his profile, his hair glossy and looking completely touchable. He leaned back into the seat, resting his arms on the top of the bench. The tips of his fingers caressed her shoulder, and a wave of goose bumps cascaded over her skin from the simple touch. She still couldn't believe she was here with him. So many times in high school, she'd lie in her bed, spoon peanut butter out of the jar, and dream up dates she'd go on with Jake. Sometimes he took her to the movies. Sometimes he took her to the local make-out spot in the West Hills area. None of those compared to actually being near him, feeling the warmth of his skin, and being his entire focus at the moment.

"At first, I just wanted to blow off some steam and take a run along the river," he said. "And then I saw the fountain. For some reason, I liked it better than the big fence with locks. Reece and I would sometimes come down here and pocket some of the change."

"You know that's illegal, right?" She might drive five miles over the speed limit and fudge the truth a little when she talked with her mother, but half the stuff Jake and Reece had done as kids would have had her rocking in a corner if she'd participated.

"Hey, I didn't claim to be a good kid." He smirked.

But damn, did he grow up to be a fine man. Which was more important.

"That morning, I'd just been accepted into an elite training for a hotshot crew. And then Maisey dropped the bomb. So I threw out my one wish to the universe."

"What did you wish for?" she asked.

The muscle in his jaw feathered as he stared at the fountain. "I hoped I'd be good enough for my kid."

Erin swallowed hard. She realized that this was probably the day that Jake had turned from a bad boy into a good man. And she felt slightly guilty because the first thing she'd wish for—if she did believe in wishes—would not be something so altruistic. Maybe she'd save that for the third or fourth penny.

"I never looked back. She's always come first."

"I think you're doing a great job," Erin said, suddenly feeling out of her depths. Jake had a whole life here, a daughter who depended on him. She'd always claimed to have a responsibility with her students, but she saw them for fifty minutes at a time. This man had raised a human. And somehow being a good dad was sexier than any firefighter outfit.

He smiled. "I'm trying, and that's half the battle."

Jake's heart threatened to beat out of his chest. Which was ridiculous. He was eating ice cream in a public place. But just being around Erin stirred up something inside of him like a brushfire during a windy day. Embers on dry leaves. It was only a matter of time before Jake's carefully cultivated forest of solitude burned to the damn ground.

A gust of wind kissed her shoulders, and Erin shivered. The night was cooling down much faster than Jake had anticipated. He shucked off his jacket and wrapped it around her shoulders.

"Thank you," she said, pulling it closer to her body. She looked sexy in it, her hair a little windblown, her cheeks blooming a deep pink.

He stared at this fountain. He'd come here thirteen years ago feeling so goddamn helpless. His gaze shifted across the courtyard, scanning over the families, couples, and runners slowly making their way through the perfect July night. Anywhere but at the woman who put that same fear in him. Back at nineteen, he'd been an idiot. Naive. He had thought sheer determination would solve everything. Determination did jack shit when left with a goodbye note and a crying baby. From that day forward, he'd decided to put all those feelings into raising his daughter.

He pulled a coin out of his pocket. The old quarter was covered in black Sharpie and had been since it had come into his possession twelve years ago. He'd kept this quarter since the day Maisey had disappeared. She'd left money—two twenties and some change, including the blackened coin. Said that Jake should use it for formula and diapers. He'd deposited the cash into Bailey's princess piggy bank and pocketed the quarter.

The coin served as a reminder of why he did this, why, he now realized, he'd been so lonely. He'd carried it around in his wallet for more than a decade to remind him that people leave. But he'd be a constant in Bailey's life. Because no matter how out of control he felt his life was sometimes with the whole parenting gig, he made damn sure that he was there for her.

Enough.

He'd been carrying around this weight for long enough.

"Give me a second," he said, taking his arm from around Erin's shoulder.

He palmed the coin, rubbing his finger along the grooved perimeter. If there was ever a night for wishing, this one was it. He flicked the coin into the fountain, and it hit the water with a gratifying *plop*.

Erin's blonde hair ruffled in the breeze. His jacket ended at her knees, looking so damn adorable and sexy at the same time. When she looked up at him with those big hazel eyes, his fingers itched to run through her hair and pull her to him until their lips met.

"What did you wish for?" she asked.

"If I told you, then it wouldn't come true."

She slid her gaze to him. "You really believe in that?"

He didn't know what he believed in, but hell, anything was worth a shot.

"And birthday-candle wishes. Every one of them has come true." To make it another year, to be the father Bailey deserved.

"I wouldn't have pegged you for the superstitious type," she mused. Damn, that smile made his chest squeeze. What was it about her that had turned him into a total sap? He'd never noticed things like the way a woman's eyes crinkled or the soft curve of her neck. Something about Erin sparked something inside Jake, something that wouldn't quiet down.

"Nothing wrong with putting a wish out to the universe. Sometimes the universe delivers." It'd given him a supportive family, a tight group of buddies, and a daughter who still managed to melt his heart. When she wasn't rolling her eyes.

He might have been dealt a rough hand, but as cliché as it sounded, he got the best thing in his life because of it.

She shook her head. "I don't think I believe that."

"Then what do you believe in?"

"I don't know. I just know that things aren't going to happen by putting something out in the universe. Like with the whole teaching thing—me filling out a million job applications, going to interviews, showing my skill set. Those are going to be the things that get me a job."

"That'd probably go a lot better without unicorn pants."

She screwed her face. "You think you're so funny."

Erin's eyes tracked the movement of his mouth as he took another lick of his ice cream. Her eyes dilated, and her teeth raked over her bottom lip. It was clear what she wanted. He'd happily use his tongue on her. Every damn inch. "On occasion."

He walked closer to her, pulling her into his chest as they walked down the waterfront. This felt good. Right. He liked the way she fit under his arm.

"Do you like having your family close?"

"My family is nosy as hell, but I couldn't imagine living far away from them. It'd be lonely without them." Not to mention there'd been a lot of choices when it came to babysitters when Jake was on shift. He'd never had to put Bailey in day care when she was younger because of his family. "Why? Changing your mind about California?"

"What? No." Her response was quick, almost rehearsed. "It's been my home for the past ten years. It'd be leaving a piece of me behind."

"That's not how you felt with Portland?"

Her brows furrowed as she seemed to contemplate this. "I don't know. There were just so many things that drove me away."

Her lips pressed together in a thin line. He was desperate to kiss her, to finally know what those lips felt like against his own, but he was finally getting somewhere with her and didn't want to spoil the moment.

"Running from problems never helped anything." He glanced over at Erin. Her posture had changed since the sudden shift in questions. Give her a pair of tennis shoes and she'd be ready to run.

Chapter Sixteen

Running. He had to bring up her past. But if there was one thing Erin was good at, that was it. The "13.1" and "26.2" stickers on the back of her car were testaments to this. "It's worked for me so far."

"Were you happy in California?" His solid gaze slid over her, watching her so carefully.

"I loved my job." The other stuff? She realized it was disposable. She thought she'd miss her downtown apartment. Or the fact that she had the best takeout options known to mankind. But when was the last time she'd had a real honest-to-goodness conversation with her old roommate? She didn't count their conversation earlier this week, when she'd pointedly left out key information about the wedding. And she could get takeout food anywhere.

"What about the rest of it? Friends? Dating?" he asked.

She blew out a sigh and shoved the rest of her cone in her mouth, giving herself an extra few seconds to think about how to respond. "I had a couple of good friends." She shrugged. Her dating life had been a disaster. First there was Dean with the good hair. That was about all he had going for him. Erin now knew better than to date men prettier than she was. Then there was Jared, occupier of best friends' beds. And you couldn't forget Michael, who was actually married with two kids. Yeah, Erin hadn't found that out until she'd shown up at his house as a surprise.

Okay, so maybe she did have a crappy track record with dating. That didn't mean she was running because of it. "Dating . . . well, you know how it goes."

"Not really. I haven't been on a date in a long time."

The thought boggled her mind. All her friends in California would take a ticket and line up like they were in the DMV to get a chance with him. There might even be some catfights.

"I'd give you an A plus."

His brows raised, and that dimple made an appearance. "Impressive. Especially coming from a teacher."

She wagged a finger at him. "Jobless teacher."

"It'll happen, shortcake."

She smiled. When Jake said it, it made it sound possible. Maybe he was right. That tiny little sliver of hope she'd been holding out glimmered under all the angst and despair she'd been feeling ever since that "Sorry, your position has been cut" e-mail had landed in her in-box. "Maybe I should try out that wishing well."

"Couldn't hurt."

She shoved her hand in her purse and dug around, coming up empty. "Uh, I don't carry cash on me."

"First you steal my bagel, and now you want my cash. You know, I'm beginning to see a pattern here." He pulled out his wallet, searching in the billfold.

"The bagel was purely coincidence. The cash, not so much. I mean, I'll take a twenty along with the penny if you have one in there."

"Can't blame a woman for knowing what she wants." He chuckled and then produced a penny. As he placed the coin in her hand, his fingers lingered, his strong hand encasing hers. Just that simple touch spread heat from her ears to her toes. "It'll happen, Erin. You'll be back in California before the school year starts and have your own class again." His Adam's apple bobbed, and his smile didn't quite meet his eyes.

A wave of goose bumps cascaded down Erin's arms, and she hugged Jake's jacket tighter to her body. It was so easy to talk to him. To tell him exactly what she felt. Which scared the crap out of her. Why was it that she couldn't find anyone in San Francisco to connect with? What made him so different?

Because he's Jake, a little voice whispered in her head.

He'd always been in the back of her mind, even when she lived so far away. And now he was dangling this perfect date in front of her even though she knew that her time here was slipping through her fingers like sand? She didn't know whether to be elated or bummed. Was there a word in the dictionary that combined the two emotions? She'd just made one:

Bumated: (adj.) The act of feeling both overwhelming happiness and soul suckage simultaneously. *Also see:* Date with Jake Bennett.

His gaze lingered on hers and then traveled south to her lips.

She swallowed hard. "Thanks." She closed her eyes tightly, and for the first time in years, she let herself wish. She didn't know if it went against wishing-well-penny protocol, but she packed in an extra two wishes just in case the well was feeling especially nice.

"Let's get you home. I have to wake up early for my shift tomorrow."

They'd made their way out of the riverfront and back to Jake's truck. Silence settled into the truck cab on their way home.

Before it had the chance to get awkward, he pulled into her mother's driveway. How funny that the one true date she'd been on in a long time happened to end at her childhood home. It seemed like a time warp really had happened. Add in Jake feeding Erin gummy bears while watching *The Notebook* together, and the transformation of high school fantasy would be complete.

They both got out of the truck and he led her to the front porch, his arm wrapped protectively around her hip.

"I had a really good time tonight," she said.

He nodded. "Me, too."

She shrugged her shoulders, the weight of Jake's jacket a comforting reminder. "Oh, here. I should give this back to you." She went to slip it off when his hand came to rest on her arm.

"Keep it. It looks better on you."

He smoothed his hand over her cheek. Those hands that had so skillfully worked over her body were kind and tender as they brushed along her jawline. She bent her head back, leaning into his touch.

"I'd really like to kiss you now," he said.

She let out a shaky breath. She'd wanted this since she'd seen him at the bakery. No, since before she was even of age to drive. She'd wanted Jake Bennett for *years*.

She swallowed hard, trying to keep her voice level. "I'd like that."

Both hands came to rest on her cheeks. His lips met hers in a soft brush. A tentative taste. Smooth, silky lips parted way to his tongue, playfully teasing at the entrance of her mouth. A warmth rushed over her cheeks, her whole body tingling. *This* was happening. He'd had his hands on her before. All over. And yet this simple touch felt more intimate than his fingers stroking her most private places. His lips reminded her of warm honey, of being cocooned in an angora blanket. Soft. Warm. Comforting. Their tongues tested, toyed with each other, as the kiss deepened. Erin felt herself slipping away, every swipe of Jake's lips pulling her under the current.

She liked how Jake kissed her, like he was savoring every swirl, every brush of their lips. Her lips sizzled from the touch, sending a blast of liquid heat straight to her core.

"Good night, Erin." He kissed the top of her head, and the skin on her face tingled. How could he make the simplest gesture seem so important? But that was Jake. He moved with importance. Everything he did was concise, straight to the point.

"Good night," she breathed.

And with that, he took a step off the porch and made his way to his truck.

What if you could have this every night? The thought was fleeting, disappearing faster than a shooting star across the sky. She didn't have the luxury to wonder such things.

Erin shuddered and reached for the doorknob, her mind still foggy from Jake's lips. She entered the darkened room and locked the door.

"That's my girl," came from the darkened corner.

"What the—? Oh my God." Erin's heart pounded in her chest, and she fell against the side of the couch, trying to catch herself. Her arms flailed, and she landed butt first on the hardwood floor. Her mother sat on the bench under the bay window, beaming ear to ear.

"Were you watching me?" This crossed so many lines. Which didn't surprise her one bit.

"What else is there to do? I have to get my entertainment somehow. I will say, Jake is a nice catch. I was serious about a man who can cook."

"Mom," she warned.

"Maybe he can come over here for dinner sometime this week."

"Absolutely not." And there her mother went again, overstepping. *Ignore. Smile. Move on.*

"Why not?"

"Because—Mom. Please." She didn't want to get into it now. Not when she'd had the best night in . . . well, since the wedding, she supposed.

"Wait till Sadie hears about this." Her mother disappeared to her bedroom, doing a little victory dance before shutting the door.

Never a dull moment in this house.

And, even though this totally violated her privacy and made her want to bang her head against a desk a few times, there was a pang deep in her chest at the thought of how much she'd miss all this when she moved back to California.

Chapter Seventeen

ALEXIS: Hey girl! Miss u.

ALEXIS: Going out tonight with Chloe and James. I'll have a glass of rosé in your honor.

ALEXIS: Been a few days. Lose your phone?

Erin was a crappy friend. Alexis had left more than a dozen texts over the past week, and she hadn't returned one. First, because she was trying everything in her power to close herself off from the painful realization that she very well might not be going back to California if she didn't get her ass into gear. Second, her fear of missing out was strong. And it got only worse when Alexis texted her about all the awesome things she was doing without her.

She sat at her usual spot at Patsy's. The tufted chair had practically formed a permanent indent of her ass. Madison and Sloane had joined her, both done with work for the day.

"I need your opinion on which shot you like better. I'm entering it into *Career World*," Madison said, swiveling her laptop around.

"You're serious about entering that?" A reality show didn't seem like Madison's sort of gig. Especially one that matched people up based on job compatibility.

"If it gets me more clients, then yes. I look at this as a promotional opportunity."

Savvy. Madison had always been that way. Back in elementary school, they'd put a lemonade stand up in front of Erin's house. While Erin had been worried about the sugar-to-lemon ratio, Madison had been coming up with ways to tack on extra fees for cups, and manpower to stir the ingredients.

Erin glanced at the black-and-white photo of the bride throwing her bouquet into the air. It was an artful shot where the bride was bent backward, the jewels in her corseted top gleaming. The second photo was of the groom seeing the bride for the first time. Tears welled in his eyes—love, kindness, and tenderness shining in them. The bride was a soft blur in the background. Erin hoped that a man would look at her like that one day, with so much tenderness it would be a kick in the gut.

"I like the second one."

"Same. The dude is absolutely gaga over that woman," Sloane added.

Madison smiled, apparently pleased with their answers. "I like that one, too." She went back to typing on her laptop.

"How was the hospital, Sloane?"

She shoved a piece of scone in her mouth and then took a sip of coffee, her eyes lacking their usual shine. "My shift was brutal last night. So many codes."

Erin frowned. She hated to think about all those little kids in pain. She didn't know how her best friend did it. She'd crumble if she lost anyone that she loved that much. The realization of that statement hit her like a ton of bricks.

"Only thing that brightened my shift was hearing about your date," she said.

"Let me guess. My mom informed on me." She knew her mom liked to hover, but this was an all-time low, even for her.

"Actually, yeah."

She choked on her coffee. "What do you mean? She actually called you guys?" Okay, this was taking it too far.

"She posted about it."

"What do you mean? I follow her account and didn't see anything." The woman had this horrible habit of posting updates about the family on other people's posts tagged to Erin's account. Her mom didn't quite understand the concept of posting on someone's wall. Or using private messaging instead.

Sloane pulled up the app on her phone and clicked into a profile: @hotmamajenkins.

What? A completely different account? What was her mom? Some undercover *Real Housewives of Portland* star?

"Dear God." She looked at her follower number, and her eyes bugged. "She has more followers than me." And Olivia's comment made so much sense now.

"She's popular. And funny, too. There's apparently this hot tatted dude that's been coming around the food truck when Andie is on shift. Their interactions are so cu—" Sloane stopped once she realized Erin's glare. "Okay, I'll shut up now."

"How did I not know about this?" It was like she had just been informed she'd been mispronouncing a student's name for the entire year (which she had done once and felt awful).

Sloane and Madison shrugged like this was common knowledge. How much had she missed since she'd been gone? She did the weekly phone calls with them. Okay, maybe that had fallen to the wayside during the school year and became every other week, but still. It felt like she didn't know anyone anymore.

She looked at the description below her mother's picture. "Avid reader of the smutty stuff. Mama of three. I don't mess around about peanut butter." Erin put down the phone. "I've seen enough."

"She was live tweeting from when you pulled into the driveway." Sloane put her hands up as if saying, *Just putting that information out there 'cause I know you can't resist.*

"Fine. Give it back to me." She grabbed the phone and scrolled down.

> Here my girl comes. It's been a while since she's
> been on a date, you know.

> Oh, he's getting out of the car. Opened the door for
> her. Good move, Jake! I like a man with manners.

> Plus, for all you reading this: he can cook, too!
> Swoonage factor at a ten, ladies.

> Bow chicka wow wow. I haven't been kissed like
> that since . . . maybe I need to try that online dat-
> ing thing.

> Hey, you'd better watch where those hands go,
> mister! That's second date material.

The last tweet was followed by a GIF of a little girl giving the stink eye while crushing a soda can.

"Oh my God. My mom's GIF game is strong." Which was impressive, since she thought her mom barely knew how to text. She scrolled down farther, to a few days before she'd come back home.

> So excited to have my baby girl come home. Been
> gone for way too long. Miss her terribly. Off to BBB
> to spruce up her room.

She shoved the phone back at Sloane. Guilt was a common emotion that spread through the Jenkins household faster than a case of norovirus. They'd been brought up Catholic, after all. But the healthy amount that had been instilled since childhood, one that urged her to dial her mom weekly and donate a few bucks toward people's GoFundMe accounts, now bloomed in her stomach, churning the croissant and coffee from earlier.

She glanced down at her computer screen and muttered under her breath.

"What's up?" Madison asked.

"Need to head to my house for family dinner." Maybe she'd talk to her mom about the social media posts. Maybe not.

She hated that her relationship with her mother had become so strained. They used to be close.

"*Your* house?" Madison quirked a brow.

"It was a slip." She focused her gaze on her coffee cup and took a sip. The longer she played the avoidance game with everyone, the better. At least until she figured out her whole life situation.

"We'll wear you down eventually," said Sloane.

Erin's coffee bliss lasted all the way until she walked in the front door to her mom's place. Now that Erin was home, her mother insisted that they start up their Thursday-night dinner tradition. Mandatory under penalty of being crushed under an ungodly amount of guilt.

Her mother went balls to the wall for this dinner, even going so far as to using the table in the dining room reserved only for holidays. Never-used crystal glasses shimmered in the light behind the glass doors of the china cabinet, along with fine silver tucked away in pockets of velvet in the oak drawers. Nothing had changed in their home. The same painting of a sunset hung between the two windows, and a dent from when Reece had thrown Erin headfirst into the wall still marred the spot near the light switch. It was like this room was a time capsule, preserving everything from Erin's childhood.

Her mother rubbed her hands together, looking from Erin to Reece to Andie. "Three kids under one roof again and it's not even a holiday. Dreams really do come true."

"Don't lead poor Andie and Erin on, Mom. We all know I'm the favorite." Reece took his place across from Erin.

Her mom patted Reece on the shoulder as she sat down beside him. "Whatever you have to keep telling yourself so you can sleep at night."

Reece choked on his water. Erin hid her smile behind her napkin.

"Oh, you just got burned by Mom!" Andie said.

Her mom continued, a smirk twitching at her lips. "Just letting you all know that the doctor cleared me for work. I can go back to the truck starting tomorrow."

Happy dance for Erin. "I'll still help out if you need me." Plus, she wouldn't turn her nose up at money.

"I appreciate that." Her mother speared a pea on her plate. "Have you talked to Jake since the other night?"

Reece's fork clattered to his plate. "Why would she be talking to Jake?"

"They went on a date. If you would read my posts."

Picking up his fork, Reece sawed his piece of chicken Parmesan like the caveman he was and then brought a piece to his mouth. "Ma. Your posts traumatize the general public."

"Do not. People were really rooting for Erin and Jake."

"About that . . ." Erin trailed off. God, she hated confrontation with her family. She could think all the stabby thoughts and perfectly worded arguments she wanted, but when it came to the whole execution thing, it fizzled out before it could reach her tongue.

"Just a word of advice—be careful with him," Reece said.

"The protective-brother thing has an age limit, ya know." She twirled a forkful of spaghetti on her plate. She was just having a good time with him. Two people who could talk to each other. And yes, kiss.

"Expires upon death." Reece speared a piece of asparagus on his plate and scowled. Which wasn't very different from his normal expression. He'd been especially grumpy lately after the bad breakup he'd had with Amber.

"Yeah, I don't think I'll be taking advice from someone whose bachelor pad is stocked solely with ketchup and beer."

He pointed his fork at her. "Ketchup is child's play. I've upgraded to Frank's."

"Let Erin have her fun. She'll only be in town for a few more weeks," her mother said.

"The guy has a kid, Erin," Reece said.

"Yeah, so? Do kids suddenly make you undateable?" Erin asked.

"Ruined my dateability," Erin's mom muttered.

"Heard that!" all three said in unison.

"It was one date. No need for anyone to freak out." Erin definitely wasn't freaking out. Nope. Not one bit. "Don't worry, Reece. I'll be out of your hair in no time."

"What if you took a year off? You and Andie could work the truck," her mom said. "And did you happen to apply to any of those schools I researched for you?"

When Erin was in fifth grade, she'd needed a palatal separator because her mouth didn't have enough space to fit all her adult teeth. Each morning, her mom would use a key to twist the lock in the middle, slowly widening her palate. Still one of the most painful things she'd ever experienced. Every time her mother asked her about her job, about staying here, about anything to do with home in general, it felt like it was just another turn of the key. Except this time, Erin didn't have any space to spread out. She needed a place to fly.

"I've got things handled on my own," her sister bit out. Andie stuck out her tongue, but Erin didn't miss the venom in her words. She'd been in a particularly bad mood this whole week.

Their relationship hadn't always been solid, but it seemed more strained than normal since she'd been home.

"Maybe you could learn a thing or two from her." Her mother's normally cheery composure slipped, and she regarded Andie with a look of pure irritation.

Whoa. What the heck was going on here?

Andie's shoulders curled, and she jabbed her fork into a pea. "I know. Erin is just so perfect. Maybe I should be just like her when I grow up." She flipped her hair and pulled her lips into a fake smile.

"That's not what Mom meant, Andie," Reece chimed in. "It's hard to do anything without a degree nowadays."

Erin glanced from her mom to Andie, whose cheeks were flame red. She felt for her. When her family steamrolled like this, it solidified her reason for leaving. They were hurricane-force winds barreling through a city made out of sand.

Andie's gaze lasered in on Reece. "What a hypocrite. You don't have a degree." She turned her glare on her mother. "I don't see you hounding him."

"That's right. Reece is a lost cause. Mom's come to terms," Erin joked, trying to relieve some of the tension in the room. This was not how she'd expected their first dinner back together to go. She'd hoped that everyone would have waited to draw their mental daggers until *after* dessert.

"Reece has picked his career. You're nineteen. You have so much potential," her mom said, ignoring Erin's comment.

"Right. I'm sorry I'm not living up to your expectations. I'm sorry I'm not Teacher Barbie or Firefighter Ken." She flicked her hands, motioning to her body. "I'm just Screwup Andie. And for my next act,

I'll manage to disappoint the whole family from my room." She pushed back from the table and threw her napkin on the table.

Holy drama llama.

Moments later, the door upstairs slammed. Her mom flinched. Reece stared at his plate.

"I'm guessing the whole college discussion isn't going the best?" Erin felt a little selfish but was glad the attention was finally off her for a moment.

"I just don't understand," her mom said. "She had a full ride with the track scholarship."

It did seem odd that Andie would give that up, but she'd been so adamant her freshman year that she didn't want to go to college, and then before she could even compete in the season opener for her track team, she'd packed up her bags and moved back home.

"Who knows? We all do stupid stuff." And she wasn't so sure if getting involved with Jake crossed into that territory or not.

They managed to make it through the rest of dinner without any theatrics, and after they were finished, she helped her mother with the dishes and crept to her room. Erin lay on her bed, staring up at the ceiling. But instead of being greeted with Justin Timberlake's poster, it was the damn purple walls. She shouldn't be irked about it. It wasn't her room anymore. A piece of her childhood had been cut out and replaced by something out of a friggen Pottery Barn ad.

A knock came from the other side of her door, and moments later, her mom slid into the room, clothes draped over her arm. "I did a little shopping and thought you could use some new outfits."

"Mom."

Another twist of the key. Except this one was around her neck, cutting off her air supply.

"Just a few things. Some skirts, blouses. Stuff you'll need for interviews around here," she continued, oblivious to the inner freak-out going on in Erin's head.

"What do you mean, 'around here'?" she asked.

"Aren't you going to apply to any of the ones I printed out for you?"

"Wasn't planning on it." Erin had heard of white-coat syndrome, where patients' blood pressures skyrocketed just by being around medical professionals. She wondered if there was a documented syndrome like that for nosy parents.

She pushed herself up to her elbows. "I already have a wardrobe. One that's suited me for the past few years. I appreciate what you're doing, but this isn't going to make me stay." That nauseating feeling swept over her again. She hated disappointing her mom. She really did. Which was why she'd never confronted her, just kinda slipped away, hoping to go unnoticed. Not that that had worked very well when she'd gotten several frantic calls after she'd left a note that said she was moving to California. That certainly wouldn't work now that she was under the same roof.

"I just want you to know that we care about you so much. Sometimes I feel like I don't even know how to talk to you anymore." Her voice wobbled. She sat down at the foot of Erin's bed and gave her calf a light squeeze.

"Mom."

"We've missed you. And I'm sorry if we've done something to push you away. That's not what we wanted."

"I moved away because I needed to find myself." She really didn't want to admit that she'd moved away because of her family because that made her sound like a monster, and she couldn't bear to hurt her mom in that way.

"Did you?"

"I don't know." Had she really found herself? Sure, she had her shit together, mostly. She'd held a steady job, had a master's degree. On paper, she had it all. But something had been missing lately. Every time she went out with Alexis, it seemed more like a chore. She didn't want to go to the same bars. She didn't want to keep meeting the same type of guys.

"You're still young. I didn't know what I wanted until I was thirty."

"Didn't you have Reece and me by twenty-five?"

She shrugged. "Sometimes when you have kids, you lose sight of who you are."

She wondered if Jake felt the same way. He'd changed so much from the time she'd been away, and she wondered if that was just him maturing or having the weight of Bailey on his shoulders.

As if her mother could sense her thoughts, she added, "Jake's a good man."

"How did you know I was thinking about him?"

"Because you've always thought about him, even when you were younger. I saw the way you looked at him," her mother said.

"I just don't know if I can be what he needs me to be," she admitted. She didn't know if she *wanted* to be that.

"What do you think he needs?"

"I don't know. But I'm not sure that I'm ready to settle down. Jake and Bailey need stability."

"I think Jake knows better than anyone what he wants and needs."

Erin felt so small. She never thought she'd be back here coming to her mother for advice. At almost thirty, she thought that she was long past the age of needing this. And yet here she was, tears blurring her vision. "How am I even supposed to find a place to live if I can't find a job?"

Maybe that was her problem. She'd placed so much emphasis on being a teacher that that was an integral part of her personality. Without her job, she was missing a chunk of herself.

"You stop that thinking right now. You're my baby girl." She grabbed Erin's hand. "Just because you've been knocked back a step doesn't mean your whole plan is crumbling. You'll find something.

There will be jobs. But maybe you need to focus on doing a little soul searching in the meantime."

Erin nodded. The lump in her throat grew, and her eyes burned.

"But just know I have never been prouder. And you can stay here as long as you want."

"On one condition. No more clothes."

She lifted up her fingers. "Scout's honor."

"And no more live tweeting about my dates."

Her mother smirked. "People love your romance. They keep asking for updates."

"Do you even know these people?" She didn't like the thought of her love life out there for the rest of the world to see.

"Sure. I blog with a lot of them."

"You blog?" Erin's cheeks heated. She was so out of touch with her family. Something was definitely up with her sister. Her brother was . . . well, Reece. And her mother had an alternate life she didn't even know about.

Maybe this trip home hadn't been a bad thing. Maybe this was the opportunity she needed to mend things with her family. To prove that she wasn't the same person she'd been when she sped off in her Jetta at eighteen.

Chapter Eighteen

Jake scanned the contents of the Intimidator, checking that all the equipment was put back in its proper place from A shift.

Blood kit.

Air kit.

Monitor.

Simple tasks. He liked those. They droned out the shit storm that had been pouring down on his thoughts ever since he'd taken Erin out.

He checked the chart on the wall by the door to the rec room. All the meds used last shift had been replaced. He double-checked. Never could be too sure.

His mind started to slip back to Friday. The softness of Erin's lips. The sounds she'd made, similar to when his fingers had been inside her. He fumbled with a vial of insulin.

Three days later and he still hadn't texted her back. Didn't know if he *should* text her back. He didn't like this, the whole overthinking thing. That was why he'd sworn off dating in the first place. It was just too damn confusing.

He glanced at the med box one last time, silently inventorying everything.

A hand clapped on his shoulder, and Jake gritted his teeth, trying not to lose count with his task.

"Missed you the other night for burgers. Where were you? And don't give that lame excuse that you were busy. We all know you just sit at home and watch your *Matlock*, old man," Hollywood said.

"That's *Murder, She Wrote* to you, asshole. And no, I was out with a friend." So he didn't actually watch the show, but if this asshole was going to treat him like an old man, he'd play it up. Even if Jake was only a few years older than Cole was.

"Your friend. She happen to have the same last name as another one of our firefighters?"

That title—friend—sounded so wrong to Jake's ears. Sure, they'd kissed. And talked. Hell, he'd done more talking in one night than he had in an entire month.

Keep yourself guarded. You have more than yourself to think about.
Jake nodded.

"Bring her over," Hollywood said.

"Over where?"

"To the lake this Friday."

He huffed out a laugh. Erin at the lake with his men? This screamed *bad idea*. "And subject her to your heathen ways? Not happening."

"What? You nervous we'll steal her away?"

"More like scare her away." The guys were great to shoot the shit with, but he didn't know how they'd be around Erin. Reece and Erin barely got along to begin with. Add in the whole gang? Probably not a good idea.

"Nobody but you would be stupid enough to fuck with Reece's sister," Hollywood said.

Right. Jake had apparently been whacked over the head with a stupid stick.

His gut told him this would end badly, and his gut hadn't been wrong yet. And yet he couldn't get Erin off his mind. "We're just keeping it casual. It's not like that." If he said it enough times, it'd be true.

"Who's this prick talking about?" Reece strode in from the kitchen, stopping to lean against the door frame to the garage.

"Don't you see how he's going all googly-eyed? Who do you think?"

Reece cut his glance to Jake. He was majorly fucking up bro code by talking about Reece's sister, but Jake hadn't been using much of his head lately.

"Who?" Reece asked again.

Jake cleared his throat. *Damn.* He really didn't want to do this at work. It'd be much easier with a beer and a burger. "Erin."

"My sister, Erin? Is that the one you're referring to?"

"There's a brownie in the kitchen with my name on it. I'll just leave you two to work this out," Hollywood said. He disappeared into the station, the metal door shutting with a loud *clunk.*

"Hey, man, I'm sorry—"

Reece put his hands up, stopping him. "You don't need to explain anything to me. You're a grown-ass man. It's weird—I'll admit that."

"It's weird for me, too," Jake admitted. "We cool?"

"Always," Reece said as he checked out the contents of the med kit, even though he'd just seen Jake do this. "Just remember she's leaving." He gave him a knowing look.

Yeah. Something that he knew but was choosing to ignore at the moment. His thoughts were interrupted when the alarm beeped, and a message came over the intercom. "Station Eleven, all units needed for a child trapped in a burning residential structure." A child in a fire. Anytime kids were involved, there was an unspoken understanding that they picked up the pace, got out of the station a little quicker. Each and every one of these calls made Jake's stomach clench. He didn't know if it was a parent thing, but every time there was a kid in need, he saw Bailey's face.

Jake quickly put all his tools back into the apparatus and pulled on his turnout gear, making it in the truck in less than a minute. He pulled up the address on the navigation system as Reece started the engine. By the time they hit the main road, they all had their headsets on.

"Make a right here. Showing higher traffic level on Brooks Road," Jake told Reece, his throat tight.

"Roger."

They were all quiet for a minute, and Jake guessed that the other two were mentally categorizing the tasks that needed to be done to get this kid out safe, like he was.

Two minutes later, they pulled up to a three-alarm blaze. Flames licked out of the open windows upstairs. Jake's pulse ticked in his neck. *Go time.*

Most of his calls were medical, so to get a call for something that was the very reason he became a firefighter to begin with amped his adrenaline until his heart rate gushed in his ears. Sweat beaded at the top of his lip, and he hadn't even made it into the fire yet.

He was already out and making his way to the house while Reece secured the hose to a hydrant across the street.

"My baby!" a woman screamed, her clothes all askew. She clutched an infant to her chest, rushing to Jake. "Isaiah is in there," her voice wobbled, sending another kick to Jake's gut.

"How old, ma'am?"

"Six." Young enough that he might not know what to do in a situation like this.

"What floor?" The more information he knew, the better the chance to get the kid out. He knew one thing for sure: he wasn't leaving that house without that boy.

"His bedroom. Second floor. My husband went in to grab him, and that was before I called you guys."

Shit.

"I'll be back." He didn't want to make the woman any promises. The flames out the windows were evidence enough that this might be a recovery mission instead of a rescue. He relayed the information over the headset.

He rushed to the front door beside Hollywood. A wall of heat hit him as soon as he ran across the threshold. A flood of smoke floated around them, making for zero visibility. Hollywood had already kicked open the door in search of people while Reece was hopefully well on his way to creating an opening in the roof. Jake's pulse hammered in his ears, and the sound of his breathing was the only thing he could hear over the crackling of the flames around him.

His suit was meant to withstand hundreds of degrees, but with how hot this fire was burning, it was as if he didn't have any protective gear on at all.

Jake tested out the stability of the stairs, making sure the integrity hadn't been compromised yet.

A beam collapsed in the hallway as he approached the second floor. He scanned both ends, two doors on the left, four on the right. The flames roared up the walls from baseboard to ceiling, the sound almost deafening. Embers rained down above, the floor burning hot beneath his boots. Once he had been in a training exercise where the fire had burned too hot, and the magnetic name badge on his helmet had melted into the material. A few of his men had nearly passed out. Give it another few minutes and this house might be in a similar situation.

Jake looked up and down the hallway again. He'd start on the right first, Hollywood following close behind. The door was already open, smoke pummeling out of it. Any minute now, Reece would create an opening in the roof, hopefully give them a little more breathing room, a place for the smoke to escape.

Jake rushed through and found a man on his hands and knees, coughing and sputtering. Sweat soaked his white T-shirt, and soot covered his arms and face. Hollywood broke out from behind him, rushing to the man's side, giving him the spare oxygen mask. Jake scanned the room. No sign of the little boy. Most likely, the dad had been disoriented and ended up in this room. Lack of oxygen to the brain would do that.

"Do you know where your son is?" he asked the man, though he wasn't expecting much of an answer.

The man's eyelids drooped closed as his body slumped against Hollywood's, but he managed to shake his head no.

Jake turned to Hollywood. "Get him out. I'll find him."

Hollywood hesitated, his brows pinching together. It was protocol to stick together, being within either touching distance or earshot. But any longer in this inferno and the dad wouldn't make it.

"Go," Jake repeated.

Hollywood nodded and rushed the father down the stairs.

Jake turned to the hallway, the thick smoke impossible to see through. He made his way into the second room, a nursery, the crib charred, the walls smoldering. Another few minutes and the structure would be compromised. A total loss. Something that wasn't typical nowadays with everything covered in fire retardant.

He got down on all fours, the heat blooming across his gloves and the turnout gear. Sweat trickled down his back as he peeked under the crib. All clear.

He shoved himself up to a standing position and made his way to the next room. The smoke was too thick to see through at this point, and Jake walked the perimeter of the room, keeping his hand on the wall for reference. When his knees brushed what appeared to be a race-car bed, he crouched down. His heart tripled in pace when he saw a large lump in the corner. The lump moved and let out a whimper, barely audible among the hiss of the burning house.

Fuck yes. It was a good sign the boy was still able to make sounds.

His gloved hands grabbed the boy around his middle and dragged him from where he'd been hiding. The boy's shirt was soaked through with sweat, and he was limp in his arms. Jake pushed down the dread that prickled at his scalp. *Too hot. The boy was too clammy.* He cradled him in his arms and sprinted for the hallway.

Embers rained down on them as Jake raced for the stairs. So close. Just a few more steps and he'd be on the main floor. Jake's breath echoed loudly in his mask, the oxygen warm and muggy. His skin felt sticky in his suit. One foot in front of the other, he booked it down the stairs, the heat pressing on them from all directions. *Please stay with me, buddy.* He cradled the kid closer to his body. Four steps to go and he'd be a couple of yards from the entrance. Then he could get the kid some proper medical attention. Jake's foot hit the third step, and sparks of pain shot up his leg as it crashed through the wood. Sharp splinters gashed his shin, and a guttural sound ripped out of his throat as his unoccupied arm flailed, fighting to keep upright. With one hand, he gripped the handrail, the other still holding the boy firmly to his chest.

No. He would not get trapped in here—he'd seen it before. Firefighters getting split up and then trapped, unable to get out of a situation before it was too late. Any moment now, the whole second floor could collapse. He didn't want to be a fucking pancake today. Not like this, when they were so close to the entrance.

Jake gnashed his teeth together, the pain searing up his leg. "Shit." Every muscle in his body coiled tightly as he used every bit of strength to haul himself and the boy up on his other leg. He wouldn't let him down. Isaiah was going to live.

His leg wobbled as he managed to right himself, and his whole back jarred as he hopped down the last two stairs and hobbled to the entrance. Air gusted behind him, and a loud crash echoed through the house as a support beam fell on the stairs, right where Jake and Isaiah had been moments before.

Close call. Too close.

Hollywood met him at the front door when he emerged from the house. He had a gurney and oxygen at the ready when Jake cradled the boy and set him down.

He tore off his mask and swore under his breath, praying that the kid would respond to Hollywood's compressions.

One. Two. Three. Four. The compressions continued while oxygen was fed through the mask.

"You need to get that leg checked out," Reece said, shaking Jake's shoulder.

Jake waved him off. His leg could wait. He needed to make sure the kid was all right.

C'mon, kid. Pull through. His mother wailed along with her baby on the sidewalk. He was thankful she was giving them space to do their work, especially when these seconds were critical. The father was on another gurney, being examined by an EMT who'd come on the scene while Jake was inside.

Station Three had joined them, their men at the hose, trying to slow the burn.

The compressions continued . . . and nothing. Isaiah's chest remained still, no sign of life.

No. This couldn't be happening. He'd been on the force for ten years, and he hadn't lost a single kid to a fire. Bailey's smile flashed in his mind. All the birthday parties. Movie nights. Kissing her good night even though she claimed she was too old for him to check up on her now. *Come the fuck on.* This little boy's parents couldn't be robbed of this. Not so young.

Hollywood's composure seemed to fray at the edges with each failed compression. His breathing turned heavy, and the crease in his forehead deepened. Knowing Hollywood, they were both coming to the same conclusion.

"Come on, little dude," Hollywood said, his voice cracking.

"Where's my son? Oh God, please let me just see him."

The dad pushed off the gurney and sprinted to his son's side. "Oh, Isaiah. Buddy, please," the dad pleaded.

That uptick in the guy's voice turned Jake's throat to its own inferno. He clenched his jaw. He would not lose his shit in front of the parents. No matter what happened to the kid.

"Sir, you need to get more oxygen," he said.

The guy fell to his knees, coughing, tears rolling down his ashen face.

"My son. Please. Save him." The wife came to join him, the husband wrapping a protective arm around her. Both watched their son, completely helpless.

He knew Hollywood was doing everything he could. Jake took a moment to check himself. There was nothing he could do to secure the house. The two crews were already hosing down the perimeter. Jake always tried to distance himself from these situations, because if he didn't, the what-ifs would come pouring in faster than a fully opened fire hydrant. Things like: *What if this was my house? What if it was Bailey lying lifeless on the ground? Or Erin?* His throat constricted.

A tiny cough tore his attention away from the house and back to the kid. Another cough ignited a swell of hope. And then the boy was moving, sputtering, taking huge gulps of air.

Yes.

He looked around wildly as his parents descended upon him, wrapping their arms around him.

This was what he lived for. Why he trained so hard. For moments just like this. He held back a whoop. That'd be saved for beers tonight with the guys after their shift. After he checked in on Bailey—because, holy hell, was that a reality check.

"Thank you," the dad said, now taking the air that an EMT was pushing at him insistently.

This call put everything into perspective. What was most important in his life. He definitely needed a beer tonight. Or three.

He'd decided that as soon as that boy took that lifesaving breath of air, he wasn't going to piss away his own shot at a good life. And if that meant setting himself up for failure by seeing someone who was leaving, well, then so be it. But there was a tiny part of Jake that held out hope. Hope for what, he didn't know. This thing with Erin was too fragile to think about too seriously just yet.

One of the EMTs took the family to the hospital while a medic bandaged Jake's leg. And then he loaded up his gear and got back in the apparatus.

He turned to face Hollywood. "You were good out there today."

The whole goddamn spectrum of emotions morphed across his features. "For a minute there, I thought that was going a different direction."

"That's why you never give up, brother." He turned back around and rested his head against the seat, grabbing his phone from the cup holder. Bailey was in class at the moment, so he shot her a quick Love you, kid text and would settle for calling her later.

They pulled into the engine bay, and Jake's heart nearly flatlined when he spotted a familiar blonde in cutoffs and a tank top leaning against the wall.

Erin's heart picked up to a gallop when Jake opened the door to the fire engine. He was covered in soot, sweat paving a path of tan skin over his cheeks and forehead. And he was limping. Why was he limping?

She clutched the tray of cookies to her chest, the lip of the metal digging into her stomach.

"Bad call?" The words barely made it past her tight throat. Seeing him like this reminded her that Jake wasn't bulletproof. Or fireproof.

"Could have been."

"What happened to your leg?" She noted the tear in his turnouts and the blood speckling the material.

Jake shrugged. "Just a little cut. Nothing to worry about."

She eyed him. It looked like more than that, but if he wanted to play it off like it was nothing, then so be it. She wasn't going to mom him.

Honestly, though, it was freaking her out a little bit that he was hurt. Jake and her brother had been invincible as kids, impervious to injury. It seemed like they were always getting themselves into sticky situations—jumping off roofs, nearly getting trampled by horses—and yet they'd always managed to come out unscathed. She swallowed back the thick lump in her throat. How much luck could two guys have?

"If you were a steak, you'd be well done," she said, trying to keep her tone light, even if she felt anything but.

"Comparing me to a piece of meat. A little cliché there, Heron, don't you think?"

At least he was in good spirits. That was one thing she could always count on with Jake. The apocalypse could descend upon them, and he'd still crack a joke. The yin to her neurotic yang.

Her gaze wandered over his sooty clothes again.

Okay, it should be a sin to look this gorgeous when he looked like a toasted marshmallow. She didn't even know how she'd ended up here. One minute she was banging her head on her desk filling out yet another job application, the next she was stress baking, and then her car magically made its way across town. She could play it off like she wanted to see her brother, but she was never good at lying.

"What's up?" he asked. "Everything okay?"

He'd just gotten back from a gruesome fire. By comparison, her day had been cake.

She couldn't help it, though. Ever since the night of their date, that kiss replayed over. And over. And over in her head.

"I needed to see you." Why was her heart beating so fast? And why was it so important that she see him right now, while he was on his shift?

Those were two questions she couldn't answer. Or wouldn't let herself answer.

"Give me a second." He peeled off his turnout gear and placed it by the passenger side of the fire engine. Sweat soaked through his navy shirt and his basketball shorts. A bandage was wrapped around his right leg, blood already soaking through the gauze.

"Hello, Erin Jenkins, wonderful human being." Cole walked around the truck and leaned against the side, looking like he was ready for a photo shoot.

"Just give him the cookies and he'll leave you alone," Jake said.

"Hi, Cole." She handed him the tray, and he gave her a smile that would make most women drop to the floor.

"Goodbye, *Cole*," Jake said, his voice strained.

Reece gave her a cool nod before heading into the station with Cole.

"I thought you guys might like some treats." She couldn't stop staring at the sweat, the smoky skin. How hot did it get in those suits?

She'd always thought firefighting was a safe profession. Sure, there were issues with getting hurt by lifting heavy objects—at least according to Reece—but she never really thought her brother's life, or Jake's, would be on the line. But one look at his ash-covered face said otherwise.

"Buttering me up with sweets. I like this deal. Listen, I'm sorry I haven't called. It's been a little hectic." He rubbed the back of his neck and frowned.

"It's okay. I've been dealing with family stuff." Or figuring out how to. Interactions with her sister had been icy at best this morning. "I came because I have news."

He lifted a brow.

"I made it to the second round of interviews with the middle school."

A smile spread across his face. "That's awesome."

His sincerity and support eased the tightness in her chest a fraction. Her teeth raked against her bottom lip as she regarded him. So damn sexy.

He backed her up against the wall until his chest was pressed against hers. His hands slid down her waist and curved to cup her ass, hoisting her up until she wrapped her legs around him.

"We should go out and celebrate," he murmured against her lips.

His pulse ticked in the vein in his neck, and Erin wanted to run her tongue along it. His lips moved from hers to her cheek to the curve of her neck, gently nipping at her sensitive flesh. Her eyes fluttered shut, and a groan slipped past her lips.

If someone would have told her two months ago that she'd be spending her summer in Oregon, jobless, with her mouth on Jake Bennett, she didn't know which part she'd find most unbelievable. They all were, to some degree, she supposed.

"I can't think when you do that," she said.

"I don't know what you're talking about." His lips ghosted over the shell of her ear, and a shiver worked from the top of her spine to her toes.

"Yeah, that. I won't get a word in edgewise if you keep doing that," she said.

"Good. Then you'll hear out my proposition."

"Yes?" Please let it involve a hot tub, a can of whipped cream, and Jason Momoa as a tap-in alternate. A girl could dream, right?

"The crew is going to the lake on Friday. I know it's last minute, but the guys wanted you to come along."

"They want me to come along, or you do?"

"Yes, I do." He smoothed his thumb down her cheek, and she leaned into his touch. "So what do you say? Come with me?"

She'd agree to just about anything when he used his lips. "See you on Friday."

Chapter Nineteen

Jake pulled his truck into the gravel lot of Three Pools, the prime section to go floating down the Santiam River at the North Fork Park. He cut the engine and wrung his hands on the steering wheel, hoping that today would go smoothly with Erin and the guys. His gaze met Erin's, and she gave him a megawatt smile. Yeah, today would be just fine.

"Ready for this?"

She raised a brow, her smile turning impish. "Are you?"

Hell. Probably not.

He watched as Erin slid out of the truck, her shorts clinging to her thighs. He swallowed hard and slipped out of his side, keeping his eyes on her the second he made it past the cab.

Erin sauntered around the truck like she owned the river. With the way her hips swayed in those cutoff blue jeans, she could own the whole goddamn world for all Jake cared.

He rounded the tailgate to find Hollywood at the other end of the gravel parking lot that led to the river and hiking trails, throwing his arms out dramatically. "I put my Cheetos in your truck. Where the hell are they?" Hollywood said. The guys had ridden in Reece's truck, and Jake had driven Erin in his.

The late July air was muggy with the promise of another hot, blue-skied day. Their hour-and-a-half ride had been filled with conversations about Erin's potential new school and about her roommate.

"Reece probably ate them," Erin said. "I'd check his hands."

Hollywood trudged over to where Reece sat in a lawn chair and lifted his hands. Even from the tailgate, he could see they were stained orange.

"Traitor!"

"You were taking too long with unloading all the floats." He tossed the remnants of the Cheetos bag at Hollywood.

Both Reece and Hollywood had brought women with them, both of whom Jake had never met before. Amy and Lea. They were both sitting in lawn chairs next to his friends, sunning themselves in their bikinis.

The place they'd parked at had quite a few trails jutting from the main area that led to small, secluded sections with high rocks to jump into deep pools of water. The water was moving at a good clip today, which would make for some great floating down the river.

"Ready, ladies?" Reece said, brushing off his hands and then grabbing a blue-and-white inner tube.

"We're not going to hit any rapids, are we?" Amy said, clutching at her tube.

"Nah. This river doesn't have any," Reece said.

Reece and Jake came down here every summer to float. Jake's aunt used to own property up here, and they'd stay at the tiny double-wide, partying, riding the horses on the property next to theirs, and sneaking into the neighbor's hot tub. All that seemed like a lifetime ago.

"You coming, Jake?" Reece called, already knee-deep in the water.

He turned to Erin, who was still sitting on the tailgate, feet dangling, her head tilted to the sun.

"You ready?" Jake asked.

"Would you be cool if we went hiking first?" she said. She still had her eyes closed, and it looked like she was trying to soak up every drop of sun. Maybe she was.

He turned to Reece. "We'll catch up in a few." But Reece and the crew were already in the water and floating down the bank.

Once the group was out of sight, Erin hopped down from the tailgate. "That trail looks good." She pointed.

Jake tried to keep his expression neutral as Erin pulled her tank top over her head, exposing tanned skin and a barely there bikini top. She tossed it in the truck and then made her way to the trail-post sign. The red ties dangled down the center of her back, and Jake wondered how long it'd take to yank those and fling the scrap of material to the ground. It wouldn't take much, he decided.

Torture. Why did he think this was a good idea to bring her up here? He could barely keep his hands off her with her clothes on.

"I've been thinking a lot about what you said the other week," she said as they disappeared into the forested area. Their tread emitted a light *clomp* as their feet hit pine needles and earth, and the scent of tree sap made him think of long summers spent in the woods.

"There were many thought-provoking things said. You'll have to be more clear," he joked.

"You're right up there with Gandhi, Galileo, and Oprah."

"Really, out of all the people to pick from, you choose Oprah?"

"Um, yeah, did you not watch her show after school every day?"

"Can't say I did." He chuckled. It was easy talking to Erin. He'd never had that with anybody but his friends.

"I was talking about you calling me out on my bullshit. About me running."

Had he really been that harsh? "I didn't mean to offend you."

They came to a fork in the trail, the left going deeper into the woods, the right sticking closer to the water. They veered to the right. "The way I see it—I get a fresh start. A chance for a do-over, to try something new."

"What about the people in your life? Don't you miss them?" He couldn't imagine just packing up his life and leaving his friends and family.

She shrugged. "Sometimes."

Red flags waved in a frantic SOS call in the back of his head. *Shouldn't be messing around with someone like this. Not safe for your sanity.* But there was more to Erin than she was letting on. He'd known her when she was younger. Knew just how caring she was, how she was still close to Sloane and Madison. Even someone so transient had to put roots somewhere.

She's leaving, asshole. The logical part of his brain was still trying to decide why he'd even asked her to come today. Whatever this was between them was damned before it even started.

"I don't know. I think that sounds lonely."

"Lonely is being stuck in the same routine every single day. I can't imagine a life like that."

I can, he thought. His routine was what kept him functioning. What got Bailey to practice on time. What put dinner on the table. "Here, let's cut this way." He knew these woods like the back of a fire truck.

They passed a clearing that gave way to columns of gray rocks and trees. Below them was a pool of deep, glistening water. "I've never been to this spot before," Erin admitted.

"My aunt showed me this place when I was younger." It was a little-known secret, the swimming hole filled with crystal-blue water that wasn't overrun by tourists. Only the locals around North Fork ventured here, and they were all either sleeping off a hangover from the night before or back at it at the local bar.

"Have you ever jumped off there?" Erin pointed to the large rock jutting out over the lake. He'd jumped off it quite a few times when he was younger. Before Bailey, he realized.

"Yeah. Back in high school. Reece used to come here with me. Made sure I didn't do anything to break my neck."

"Man, you guys got to do all the cool stuff in high school. I was stuck manning the food truck."

He gave a sheepish grin, but he didn't fail to notice the hardened edges of her eyes.

"Last one up there buys dinner." She pulled her hair out of her ponytail, and then she was off, blonde hair whipping behind her.

"I don't know . . ."

Erin glanced behind her, not stopping. "I'd better not hear any excuses, Jake. You run into burning buildings for a living. A rock should be a breeze."

And it should have been. But he'd quit taking risks in every facet of his life ever since his daughter had been born. Sure, there was always a risk running into a burning building or dealing with ornery patients, but he had backup. His team had his back, no matter what.

They continued their ascent up the rocks, Jake staying a close distance behind Erin in case she slipped. Once they reached the top, they both stood a few feet from the edge of the cliff. Her face and body were covered in a light sheen from the exertion, her skin flushed. Jake had the sudden urge to whisk her into the secluded tree line and finish what he'd started three weeks ago. He tore his gaze away from her and looked over the cliff. The water shimmered down below, cool and enticing. Trees encased the whole area, only giving way to the shoreline and the pool.

"When I was little, I used to watch *Carmen Sandiego*." She let out a humorless laugh and sat down on the edge, her feet dangling over the rocks. Jake joined her.

"I thought it was so cool, how she would disappear, go to all these cool places. I thought that's what I wanted, to float around. Now I don't know what I want anymore."

"Nothing wrong with not knowing what you want." Jake was the last person who should be giving advice. He played it safe.

She turned to him, expression unreadable. "Do you ever think about the what-ifs?"

He shook his head. He didn't know how to answer this. Or . . . maybe he did, but he didn't want to admit it to himself. What if Erin didn't get the job in California? What if she stayed here? He didn't like all those variables. Fires. Medical emergencies. That was the stuff he understood. "I think that's a dangerous way of thinking."

"Says the person who uses wishing fountains."

"Those are scientifically proven effective."

She looked over at him, and those perfectly pink lips pulled into a smile. "You're cute when you're full of crap."

His damn heart pounded. It pumped to the rhythm of Erin's name. It had since the moment he had seen her in Barry's Bakery.

She looked up at him, her gaze raking across his chest before meeting his eyes. "What are we doing, Jake?"

"I have no fucking clue," he admitted.

"Me either."

"All I know is that I can't get you off my mind."

"Then don't." She gave a wry smile, then stood and shimmied out of her cutoffs, tossing them on a nearby rock. "Come on." She started walking toward the edge of the rock.

"We should probably head back. Especially if you want to float the river." It was a cheap response. Because jumping with Erin seemed to mean more than just jumping off a rock. It meant continuing into uncharted territory without a compass or a bag of bread crumbs.

"The Jake I knew wouldn't hesitate for one second."

"I'm not that same guy."

She put her hands on her hips. "Who are you, then?"

What the hell type of question was that? He was Jake Bennett. Had a handful of guys he was lucky enough to call his friends. Had an amazing daughter and supportive family. And yet, if he was going to get all philosophical, things had been off for a while now. Years, maybe.

"You can't spend the rest of your life playing it safe, Jake."

His life was anything but safe, especially with a preteen daughter, but what Erin said shook something inside him. Made him want to roar, beat his fucking chest. Show her that he was damn fine the way he was. "You do realize I run into burning buildings, right?"

"You know that's not what I'm talking about."

Yes, he did realize what she was saying. He knew he was living a shell of a life, and Erin had been the first to point it out. "Then what do you suggest, oh wise one?"

"Take a leap of faith." She gestured to the water below.

"Isn't that meant in more of the metaphorical sense?"

She rolled her eyes and held out her hand. "I'm about to pee my pants over here. If I can do it, so can you."

Erin's hair tumbled over her shoulders as she shook her head. The afternoon sun shone on her deep honey skin, highlighting the freckles splashed across her nose and cheeks.

For her, he'd do this. And as soon as he grabbed her hand, he realized he'd do just about anything for Erin Jenkins. "I'm done playing it safe."

They both took a running start and jumped off the rock.

Chapter Twenty

Erin hit the water with her toes pointed and her free hand plugging her nose. The chilly water shocked her system and left her breathless as she surfaced for air.

What the hell had happened between them up on that rock? She'd shared things about herself that nobody knew. Not even Sloane and Madison.

Jake surfaced next to her, swiping a hand over his face to push back his hair.

She treaded water, staring. "See? Just needed a little bit of encouragement."

"I think that was peer pressure." He shook his head, spraying water in her direction.

She laughed. "Poor Jake Bennett, getting bullied by a mean woman."

Water beaded down his neck, his chest. The water in this part of the pool was crystal clear, giving Erin a direct view of Jake's broad chest and abs. His swim trunks were plastered to him as he treaded water, outlining a certain part of Jake that Erin had fantasized about for the past few weeks.

"It really is a tragedy. I think my pride might be a little wounded." Every word he said, that deep voice called to her, stirred up feelings, made her whole body tingle. She needed him. Needed to be close to him. They'd kept a safe distance since the wedding, but she was done holding back.

She swam to him until they were inches apart. And every bit of tension that had been between them snapped like a rubber band. He pulled her to him, her body flush with his. Rough hands encompassed her waist as she wrapped her legs around him. Skin pressed to skin. Her hands tangled in his hair. Everything about him felt so good. So right. His fingers dug into her side, while his other hand cupped her ass as she rocked into him.

"I can't quit you," he growled. His lips met hers, the kiss frenzied, their teeth clicking together, tongues devouring. Her brain turned to static, everything around them going blissfully blank. Just his lips, the way he kissed her like she was his lifeline—that was all that mattered right now.

He managed to get them to shore and carried her to a secluded spot, hidden from the main trail. A jagged rock dug into her back as he set her down. They both watched each other. Water droplets beaded down his chest, his stomach. She swallowed hard as he dropped to his knees.

Erin shuddered beneath Jake's intent gaze. As soon as his knees hit the dirt, everything in her tightened. His lips met the inside of her thigh, and her head knocked back.

"I'm done holding back, Erin. I've wanted you for so damn long."

Holy hell. The floodgates to the lady bits yelled, *Release the kraken!* Erin's bare feet dug into the dirt and gravel on the ground as Jake used both hands to part her thighs. This was it. What she'd ached for. Every night she'd lie awake in her bed, thinking of Jake, wondering what he would feel like between her thighs. Whether she would ever recover after giving this piece of herself to him.

"I want you. More than I've wanted anything in a very long time," he said, his warm breath whispering over her skin.

Erin's legs shook under Jake's perusal. His blue eyes washed over her—fierce, wild.

His knuckle grazed down her thigh to the edge of her swimsuit. "This right here. I've been thinking about it for a solid week."

"If you wanted to borrow my bikini, you could have asked," she joked. While inside she was one of those cartoon characters breathing into a paper bag.

"I don't want your bikini, Erin. I want my tongue between your thighs." His mouth glided across the top of her knee and lightly skimmed to the middle of her thigh. Featherlight touches of his fingers caressed down her other leg, teasing the line of her bathing suit, dipping under the fabric, and then traveling back up her leg.

Her breath turned shallow as his mouth moved closer to her center, then moving to the other leg.

"Please," she pleaded. She'd never come from kisses alone, but at the rate this was going, her body keyed up to the point where one touch might do her in, this might be a first.

His mouth stilled on her thigh, and he looked up at her through long lashes. "Please what?"

"Please do whatever it is you're going to with your tongue."

He chuckled, his breath ghosting over her skin. "Are you this bossy with your students?"

"More so." Her hips bucked against him. A little bit of encouragement.

His chuckle vibrated deep in her belly, and everything in her clenched.

His fingers twined around the ties of her bathing suit, and he looked up at her once more, seeking approval. She nodded, and he pulled at the strings to her bikini bottom. Both ends untied, and the suit fell to the rock, exposing her. Erin's pulse beat rapidly in her temples, and every inch of her skin felt like it might combust at any second.

Her eyes drifted to Jake's, searching for any type of reaction, good or bad. His pupils dilated, and his jaw dropped a fraction. His fingers worked their way up to her bikini top, and his deft fingers worked at the ties, and moments later, the top hit the ground with a *thwap*.

Jake blew out a low whistle. "Shit, Erin. Look at you." His lips met the spot where her jaw met her neck, and her eyes fluttered shut. "Absolutely gorgeous."

What was so different about Jake that he could make her feel so comfortable? She was spread out before him, completely bare, and all she could think was, *More, more, more. Faster.*

Was it the fact that she'd known him her whole life? Or the fact that the guy could make her forget her name with just a smile? Call her Betty because she didn't care who she was as long as she was underneath those carved-out biceps.

Within seconds, he lowered himself, his mouth working down the column of her throat. The warmth of his lips on her skin sent a ripple of goose bumps skittering across her arms and legs. His tongue circled over her collarbone, only to be replaced by the gentle brush of his teeth. Jake had changed so much from the daredevil boy she'd crushed on throughout her childhood. Sexy. Steady. This man had the same intensity, but it was focused. Right now, his complete attention was on her, and she might melt into the ground, given another ten minutes.

His mouth moved to close around her nipple, his tongue flicking over the peaked bud. She let out a cry, raking her fingers down his back, her own back levitating off the rock.

"You sure you want this?"

She nodded. Right about now, she'd say yes to just about anything he suggested. Is this what being drunk on lust was? Her body blazed, her skin feeling tight, too hot.

"Spread for me."

So she did. The cold surface bit into her bare skin as her legs fell open for him, exposing herself.

"Gorgeous," he said, his eyes hooded. He lowered down, his tongue tracing the seam between her thighs.

Sparks blasted behind her eyes as his tongue swirled and flicked. She rocked her hips into him, the sensation prickling over her skin, igniting liquid heat in her veins. She'd burn for him. She'd burn until there was nothing but embers and ashes left.

"Please, Jake. I need you." She pushed him away, immediately mourning the loss of his tongue. But she wanted to feel all of him. His powerful hips thrusting into her. The fullness that only he could provide.

He moved to his feet, tugging down his swim trunks, every inch of his skin on full display.

Erin's mouth went dry.

Broad shoulders covered in ink. Lean abs still glistening with water. Lines cutting from his hips, leading to the swell of his cock. She swallowed hard.

He prowled over to her and sank to his knees.

"Mine," he growled. Something feral crossed his gaze, like he'd finally let that last bit of control slip away.

His cock teased her entrance, and her head knocked back into the rock. He slicked his length against her, coating his arousal.

"Please." Her legs shook. She needed him inside her. She needed to feel him on every level.

Jake let out a deep, shuddering breath and then sank into her.

She cried out, wrapping her legs around his waist, anchoring herself to him. Because if she didn't, she might float away.

"Shit, Erin." His voice came out strained as he thrust into her again.

This right here. This was the wind, the sea, the sun, everything she'd ever desired, everything that kept her moving from town to town. Being in Jake's arms, feeling the weight of him, and being filled by him captured everything she'd been searching for. He could fuck her until her back was raw, and she'd still ask for more.

His hand moved between them, his fingers finding the spot needed to find release. She closed her eyes, drifting, drifting, drifting until her back arched, and she spiraled, Jake following shortly after.

And she decided she'd make this moment worth it. For whatever potential heartache there would inevitably be, Jake Bennett would be worth every tear.

Chapter Twenty-One

After forty-eight hours of rest, Jake should have been bright-eyed and bushy-tailed for his next shift, but all he could focus on was the crust in his eyes and his bed beckoning him back. He smiled, thinking about yesterday. He hadn't felt this happy in years. Another thing that made him happy? His daughter would be home in just three short days.

He glanced at the clock on the microwave and picked up his phone, dialing Bailey's number. This was the only time he'd been able to connect with her on a consistent basis, because she was in classes most of the day and hanging out with her friends in the evening.

She picked up right before it hit voice mail. "Hey, Dad."

"Hey, princess. How are you doing?"

"Oh my God, I'm having so much fun, and there was this girl Christina, you remember her, the one who thinks she's the shit with her PLC programming skills. Newsflash: She's not."

Jake *mmhmm*ed and *right*ed as his daughter gushed about how her computer code won that day's competition over the girl who'd been rude to her from day one. He liked that his daughter was having a good time, but he was ready to have her home. An empty house just felt wrong. He stared over at her place at the kitchen table. If it was a typical morning, he'd be reading the news on his phone, and she'd have her nose in a book. A pang hit him square in the chest at the thought that he didn't have much longer before she'd be out of the house for good.

Don't get ahead of yourself. He had years. He still had a lot to teach his daughter.

"I can't believe I only have a few more days. I want to stay here forever."

He focused back on the conversation. No need to let her know that her old man had turned into such a sap since she'd left. "I tried to get them to sign the adoption papers, but it was a no-go, kid."

"Yeah, your jokes still aren't funny."

"Does that mean I have to stop renting out your room when you come home? Or are you okay with sleeping on the couch?"

Bailey scoffed, but then said, "Dad?"

"Yeah, sweetie?"

"I love you. Be safe today."

"I will. Love you, too."

He ended the call and made his way to the bathroom to finish getting ready for his shift.

Thirty minutes later, he slumped into the chair in the conference room and waited for Hollywood and Reece to join him, along with the battalion chief for the morning meeting.

Chief Richards was a gruff man who liked his coffee black and a cigarette the minute he stepped outside. He clicked on the TV and started up the presentation on the flat screen. Most of the time, he couldn't be bothered with pleasantries. Jake attributed that to the fact he was a year from retirement.

He started the meeting without even looking at the men. "We're getting ready for Brew Fest, which starts up this Thursday." He pulled up a slide that had a map of all the parking zones and where their rigs would be parked during their next shift. They participated in all the local events, making sure civilians were safe, setting up first-aid stations wherever needed.

"We'll also be partnering up with PD to get some good PR."

"You mean get *them* some good PR," Hollywood said.

Station Eleven was attached to the local PD. They'd razz each other every chance they got, but it was all in good fun. They were all on the same team. Even if firefighters got the better end of the deal in terms of PR with civilians.

"So what are you suggesting? We make balloon animals with them?" Reece asked.

Richards stroked his fingers over his chin, contemplating. "I am fond of the dog ones." He slammed his hand down on the table, rattling his cup of coffee, some of the liquid spilling over the edge. "No, you assholes. Hand out stickers together. Show your rigs to the kids."

Jake and Reece exchanged glances. Right. Richards had been up Reece's ass since the moment Richards had transferred to their station. He didn't know if it was because their senses of humor clashed or what, but he'd taken a personal interest in shitting on anything Reece had to say.

After being briefed completely about the Brew Fest plans, Hollywood took another page out of their EMT book and gave a short refresher on EpiPens. Richards disappeared outside for what Jake assumed was a smoke break.

"How about a round of rummy to decide who has to be stuck on sticker duty?" Hollywood procured a deck from his pocket.

"Works for me," said Reece.

Cards slid his way, and Jake collected them, putting them in order. He stared at his phone. He hadn't heard from Erin since last night, since he'd dropped her off. He shot her a quick text.

JAKE: What are you up to?

ERIN: Running along the riverfront.

JAKE: Didn't you hear that texting while running is dangerous?

ERIN: Maybe you should stop texting me then.

He smiled and stared at the message.

Reece tapped the edge of the table near him, snapping him out of his stupor. "Hey, asshole, it's your turn."

Jake turned his attention back toward the card game and threw out a couple of cards.

"Who are you texting, anyway?" Reece took a bite of a brownie. "Also, whoever made these is my new wife."

"Erin's friend Sloane made them," Jake said. "She and Erin baked yesterday and sent me home with the leftovers."

Reece choked. "Never mind. They're probably poisoned."

Jake tossed a card into the discard pile. "What the hell is going on there?"

"Nothing. She's always had it out for me ever since I dated Annie. They work together in the ped unit," Reece said.

"Well, you never did call the woman back. People tend to take offense to that."

Jake and Reece may have been the same age, but they went about dating completely differently. Reece dated everyone with a heartbeat, and Jake . . . didn't. There'd been a few of Reece's past flings who'd shown up while he was on shift at the station, trying for a second chance. He felt bad for all those women. Reece never seemed to commit, not since his high school sweetheart, Beth, had ended things and married some dude in the navy a few months later.

"Unless they're addressed directly to you, I think they're safe."

Reece made a show of pushing the brownie farther up the napkin.

The tones went off, and they all shoved back from the table, flopping the cards facedown before they made their way to the engine. Once they heard it wasn't a fire call, Jake remained in his class Bs and booked it to the engine.

"We've got a female in her late twenties. She collapsed while out on a run. Isn't responding."

Jake's heart rate sped up. He thought of Erin and how she said she was going for a run around the same location the operator had given.

Reece stretched his neck from side to side, steering his way downtown. Jake shoved on his headset out of instinct, but everything that

Reece and Hollywood were saying slipped to the back of his mind. At the forefront was *Please don't be her. It can't be her.*

Reece took a sharp right down Third Avenue, snaking his way through traffic. Jake knew Reece was driving as fast as he could to the call, but that didn't help the pounding in his chest.

As soon as Reece parked the Intimidator, Jake booked it out of the truck. *Need to get to her. Need to make sure she's okay.* His feet pounded against the pavement to the same beat of his heart, until he was at a full-out sprint.

It didn't take long to find her. A crowd of people circled around someone on the ground, a couple of people motioning him over.

He advanced on the woman lying lifeless on the concrete, several people surrounding her. His heart lurched.

"Move out of the way," he called, dropping to his knees in front of the woman.

The woman lay clutching her chest, rolled to the side. Brown curls. Not blonde. A woman with a larger build than Erin. The knot in his chest loosened. He put his fingers on her wrist, leaning down to her face to listen for any sign of breathing. There was a faint pulse, and her breathing was shallow.

Hollywood and Reece flanked him seconds later. With Jake's airway bag he'd forgotten in the truck.

"She's got a pulse," he said, forcing down the embarrassment of how he'd just freaked out over nothing. A rookie move, one that had no place during a shift with Reece and Hollywood.

The EMT team followed moments later with a gurney. It was a minor miracle they weren't there to see his blunder. Just the two men that counted on him on a daily basis. The EMTs loaded her onto the gurney and started a line on her.

Jake gave the go-ahead to transport her to the hospital. Reece shot him a look as they walked back to the engine. It wasn't unwarranted.

He'd forgotten his med bag, which was his essential accessory when he went on any call.

Stupid. If Reece hadn't picked it up, if she'd needed it, that could have cost her life if he'd had to run back to the engine.

As soon as they climbed up into the engine and shoved on their headsets, Reece's voice bellowed, "What the hell is wrong with you?"

He shook his head. He'd never felt this way on the job. Not once. Now it was like he was fresh out of training, shaking like a damn newbie. "I don't know. I was distracted."

"Distracted? Are you fucking kidding me?" Reece yelled.

"Hey, he said he was sorry. Let it go, man. Nothing went wrong," Hollywood piped in.

Reece continued, ignoring him. "Shit, man, we need your head in the game. What if it had been something more serious? We rely on each other."

The only time Jake had seen Reece so heated was when he'd spilled half of his cherry Icee on the seat of his car in high school after he'd just gotten the car detailed.

Jake didn't even know why he'd been so spooked. The chances of it being Erin were slim to none. He'd never been flustered on a call, not even as a rookie.

"I don't know what that was, but that can't happen again. That's our lives on the line if you fuck up."

He nodded. Damn it, Jake needed to get his shit together. He knew that adding someone new into his life would cause some waves, but he didn't think it'd get in the way of his job. Firefighting was everything. He wouldn't let that happen again. Reece was right. He'd put his men at risk with his actions. Any added risk and one of them might not be coming home that night to their family. He thought about if it was reversed and one of the guys put him at risk. Bailey being all alone. He couldn't do that to her.

As soon as they reached the station, he pulled out his phone, which he hadn't bothered to check since the incident. Three texts.

Just got back. Crazy hot day out there.
Want to hang out after you get off shift tomorrow?
:-)

He set his phone down, deciding not to respond.

Chapter Twenty-Two

Okay, Erin wasn't one of those people who needed instant gratification. She wouldn't even classify herself as clingy. But Jake hadn't responded to her texts in twenty-four hours. And it showed that he'd viewed them. What the hell was up with that? After their day at the river, she thought things were going well. Obviously, she was a horrible judge of this whole dating thing. Maybe he was just like all the other guys. She hoped he'd prove otherwise by at least bothering to text her back and ask her out again.

She slipped in next to her sister at the dinner table, whose mood seemed to have upgraded from arctic chill to frosty. At this rate, she'd have things smoothed over by Christmas.

"How are things going between you and Jake?" her mother asked.

This was a record. Food hadn't even been scooped onto her plate yet, and she was getting the third degree.

The annoyance that usually followed a question like this from her mother didn't come. Ever since they'd had their heart-to-heart, everything had settled down. They'd fallen into a nice rhythm.

"I don't know. He hasn't texted me back since yesterday." She thought about calling him, but this was supposed to be a fling. No need to rock the boat. He'd call. Eventually. Maybe.

"Good," Reece mumbled. With the way his eyes shifted, not meeting hers, that was a dead giveaway that he knew something.

Oh no. What had he done now?

Potential sibling assholery called for a kitchen interrogation session.

"Reece, do you want to help me get something from the kitchen?" Erin asked.

He speared a forkful of steak, the juices oozing out onto the plate. "Not really."

She gave his shin a swift kick under the table. Ten years later and he still kept his legs in the exact same spot. Some things never changed.

"Ow. Shit."

Erin shot him a glare, and he lifted his hands. "Yes, fine, I'll go to the damn kitchen," he said. He pushed back from the table and tossed his napkin next to his plate. "If Erin bashes my head in, wrap my steak in foil and save it for later, okay?"

"Heck no. If it's a head wound, I'm not letting a perfectly good T-bone go to waste," Andie said.

Erin made her way through the hallway lined with family portraits and artwork, past the den with the untouched furniture, and through the dividing doors, which flapped shut behind her. She tried for her best intimidating pose, but her brother had a full foot on her. Too bad he'd never been scared of her.

"Do you have something to do with Jake not returning my texts?"

His lips pressed together. *Guilty. As. Charged.* He tried to play it off with a shrug. "Maybe he's just come to his senses."

"What the hell is that supposed to mean?"

"I'm looking out for my friend, Erin. I love you. You know I do, but what are you playing at here?"

"What do you mean?" She stared at her brother. Hard. He'd always been on her side. Sure, they fought like any siblings do, but he'd never meddled with her relationship before.

"Jake's getting forgetful on the job. He's distracted. For fuck's sake, he thought the girl we were treating yesterday was going to be you. I've never seen him move so fast." His hands gripped the counter, the color in his knuckles draining to bone white.

Her heart made an unexpected U-turn in her chest. "How does that have anything to do with him ignoring me?" And why had he thought it was her? So many questions, and the one person she wanted answers from wasn't returning her calls.

Reece's hands formed into fists at his side. He looked like he was fighting for some type of control. "Don't you get it, Erin? This is Jake's life. My life is in his hands on these calls."

When they were younger, Reece had always been the sensible one. Overly cautious. The one to remind her to put on sunscreen when they went outside. The one who held her hand to cross the street when they walked to school together. The one that was always in control of a situation. Whatever had happened yesterday had really spooked him.

"You're blaming me for him being distracted?"

"Hell yes. The guy already has enough on his plate. He doesn't need you playing with his feelings."

What the hell? Is that what her brother thought of her? That she was just coming in here to stir up trouble and then leave on her merry way? If she could fight this damn attraction to Jake, she'd stay miles away from him. She'd do anything to avoid the inevitable pain of what the next few weeks would bring. It was looming in the distance, like a storm coming into the bay. What they'd shared at the river was something she'd never experienced before. She didn't know if she'd ever experience it again.

"What is that supposed to mean?"

"You know exactly what I mean. How many relationships have you had, Erin? How many guys did you just string along because you couldn't commit?"

"You're really judging me by my dating history. Get off your patri-archal high horse there, brother." Oh, if she had the proper arm span to reach the giant oaf, she would deck him in the face right now. "I didn't know I needed to submit a curriculum vitae to you before going out with your friend."

"Have you changed? You move every few years. You never stay anywhere for long. Why is that?"

Her brother always did have a knack for sticking his thumb in the exact spot that would elicit the most pain. Right now, it was like he was digging his thumb into her solar plexus. Her breath barely made its way to her lungs.

"I had to move for different jobs," she said.

"That's bullshit. I think you're afraid."

That'll be a yes for $2,000, Alex.

I'm always afraid, she thought. That little voice came out of nowhere, confirming her worst suspicion. The only time that little voice quieted was when she was with Jake. "You think you're so perceptive. Maybe try taking a look in the mirror. I see a man who's afraid to let go." They all saw it. He'd never been the same after his high school girlfriend had left him to marry another man.

His eyes sharpened, and Erin immediately regretted bringing up that subject. It was a low blow, but Reece wasn't exactly playing fair. "This isn't about me, Erin." He let out a frustrated sigh and raked his hand through his hair. "All I'm saying is he deserves better than that. He's been through enough to have you come tearing through his life. You said it yourself. You're leaving in the next few weeks. So do what you do best." He waved his hands dismissively, as if she very well might disappear into a puff of smoke.

Erin had to admit that hearing her words thrown back in her face ranked up there with getting physically slapped.

"It's not like that with Jake." *Then what is it?* the tiny voice in the back of her head asked. She didn't know. There was only one thing she was sure of at this point: she didn't know how she was going to work things out because Jake and California were not synonymous. They were the parts of a Venn diagram that never overlapped. "And anyway, what happened to being the protective older brother in this scenario?"

He scoffed. "You've shown everyone you can take care of yourself."

"I can."

"Then do him a favor and don't get involved unless you intend to stay."

He brushed past her and out of the kitchen, most likely resuming his spot at the table. It'd been foolish to start this with Reece. She was leaving in a few weeks. Why pick a fight with her brother now? But she couldn't let this go. The thought of Jake putting the team in danger because of her. Her stomach turned leaden.

She moved to the center island and picked at the grout in the tiles. No use going back to dinner. She wasn't hungry.

"Mom, I'm heading out for a while," she called. She grabbed her keys and drove.

Jake stared at the empty spot at the dining room table as he ate a bowl of cereal. Parenting had forced him to eat balanced meals, for Bailey's sake. Since she'd been gone, he hadn't cooked anything more complicated than chicken and rice. He couldn't wait to pick her up from the airport tomorrow.

His phone sat next to him, blinking. Possibly another message from Erin.

He'd gone from full throttle, embracing the fling, to questioning everything. He still couldn't believe he had let that interfere with his job, the one thing he held sacred.

Answer her back, asshole. Instead, he shoved the phone aside. Later. He'd figure out what to say to her once he got his shit together. Yesterday had rattled him to the core.

He took the last bite of cereal, pushed back from the table, and deposited the bowl into the sink. As soon as he cleared his place at the table, the doorbell rang. He glanced at the clock on the microwave and frowned. He hadn't been expecting company, and this was getting a little late for solicitors.

He opened the door to find Erin standing on the other side, her arms hugging her body. The air in his lungs evaporated. Just seeing her immediately put his body on high alert.

"Hey." He'd successfully avoided her for the last day, and he was planning on continuing that after the spook he had on his shift yesterday. Zero chance of that now that she was standing here, so damn gorgeous.

"I know you have been avoiding my texts, but I wanted to clear up some things," she said.

Fuck. Leave it to Erin to never hold back. She said what she felt, and he respected that. It was a relief not to have to play mind games like some of his previous girlfriends had.

"Okay." He opened the door wider, letting her inside. He'd been a dick to ignore her, but he didn't want to commit to anything until he had some time to think.

"Reece told me about what happened yesterday."

"Yeah, that wasn't my finest moment on the job." One of the worst, probably. Besides the time he passed out in training and fell down a flight of stairs.

"Want to talk about it?"

"Not really." In fact, if he could just ignore it for the rest of his life, that'd be just fine. "Want to come in?"

Shit. What was wrong with him? He should be distancing himself from her, but there was that damn magnetic pull between them that he couldn't ignore.

She made her way to the kitchen and turned to Jake. "The river was a mistake." She hoisted herself up to sit on the kitchen counter, her legs dangling over the edge. Those damn cutoffs rode high up her thighs, barely covering the spot he'd kissed two days ago.

"A complete mistake." He moved closer to her, his arms resting on the kitchen counter, caging her in, standing between her legs.

Everything inside him roared, *Let her go. Tell her to leave.* But he couldn't. Her breasts brushed against his chest, and she looked up at him with an intensity that turned his insides aflame. Something about her called to him like a damn beacon.

Her legs hugged Jake's sides as he closed the distance between them.

"We can't keep doing this, Erin." The words were hollow. A feeble attempt to save himself. Because Erin was going to wreck him. And he didn't know if he could handle it.

"I know." She hopped off the counter and slid slowly down his body inch by inch. Jake fisted his hands in his jeans as a preventive measure to stop his fingers from tangling in her hair. Every damn cell in his body lit up, his cock swelling against his jeans. She moved past him toward the other end of the kitchen.

Jake walked behind Erin, watching the sway of her hips. Back and forth. Back and forth. The motion was mesmerizing.

She opened the fridge and bent over, rooting around for something, and came up with a beer. *Christ.* He'd take her right here if that didn't sound like a horrible idea. He was supposed to be putting some distance between them.

Erin found the opener mounted to the underside of the counter and cracked open her beer. She took a long pull, her mouth so sweet and delicious the way it curved over the opening. Jake's dick twitched in response.

"Do you have any idea what you do to me?" he rasped.

"Enlighten me." She took another sip and watched him as she lightly trailed her tongue along the edge.

"I have never had an issue with keeping my cool. Ever." He swallowed hard, keeping his gaze on her face. Everything else would just remind him of the day at the river. "But I *need* you, Erin. To the point where you take up every bit of available space in my head. Hell, even when I'm asleep, I'm thinking of you. And then when we got the call yesterday about a female passed out on the riverfront, I lost it. I fucking lost it." He could still feel the remnants of his heart tremoring at the thought of her lying lifeless on the ground. He'd gone through a spectrum of emotions over the past twenty-four hours, but shame remained a steady hum in his veins. He couldn't afford to bring emotion into his job.

"I'm sorry. That must have been really scary."

"You don't get it. I've passed up chances with women for most of Bailey's life. I wanted to protect her. Protect myself."

Her lips quivered in response. And the wall Jake had tried to build to shut her out for good crumbled.

"I can't pass this up with you. I can't stop thinking about you. And I don't want to. I'm sorry I ignored your texts yesterday. I just didn't really know how to handle what was going on." He moved closer to her.

Her chest rose and fell heavily in response. "I like you. A lot," she said.

"I think we can assume the feeling is mutual."

"I don't want to give up what we have just because I'm leaving in a couple of weeks. I want to make the most of our time together. What you said out on the river—you're not living scared anymore. Well, I'm not either," she said.

"Let's make our time count for something." More than he could articulate. More than he wanted to admit. Because what he felt for Erin ran deeper than just liking her, and he wasn't ready for that. At all.

His hands coasted down her waist and hooked under her ass, pulling her up until she wrapped her legs around him. He may not have had the words to show her how he felt, but he had other ways of letting her know.

His lips met hers, and he kissed her slowly, carefully. This was Erin. In his house. And it felt so goddamn right.

He moved past the entryway, up the stairs, and toward the back of his house until he reached his bedroom. His knees hit the edge of his bed, and he laid her down. She looked perfect there, sprawled out on his comforter, gazing up at him with eager eyes.

His heart squeezed in his chest. A few weeks ago, he didn't think it'd be possible to feel *anything* toward someone. Yes, he'd been out with a few people, but none of them had slipped past his walls. Erin obliterated them with the Jaws of Life.

He promised himself he'd take it slow, but everything about Erin told him to move. Fast. To devour every inch of her while he could.

She sat up on her knees, and both hands tugged at the bottom of his shirt, pulling it over his head. His hands glided up her stomach, pulling up the tank top, exposing her breasts. His lips moved from the arc of her neck to the valley between her breasts, finally swirling his tongue around her peaked nipple. Her body ached in response, and she let out a soft moan. He pushed her down until she was flush with the bed.

"I will make every moment with you count."

Chapter Twenty-Three

A shaft of warm, buttery sunlight streamed through the crack in Jake's curtains. Erin shifted in bed, nestling into the cozy down comforter. She could lie here all day, ignoring the call of the outside world if it meant that she could stay in this bubble a little longer.

She turned to where she'd slept next to him, cocooned in his warmth all night. Jake was nowhere to be seen, but there was a note on his pillow, along with a bouquet of wild flowers and a box of cherry tarts in an Olivia's box.

Even a free spirit can enjoy the taste of home. Went out for a run. Be back soon.

Jake freaking Bennett. She knocked her head into the pillow. He was going to be the end of her.

Just as she folded the note, the door downstairs creaked open. Jake appeared in the doorway moments later, earbuds in his ears, a trail of sweat suctioning his T-shirt to his chest, outlining every muscle.

He pulled an earbud out of his ear and smiled at her. "I was hoping I'd be back before you woke up."

"Just woke up." She lifted the box of cherry tarts. "How did you know these were my favorite?"

"You forget. I know a lot about you, Erin. Ten years may change some things, but not when it comes to your home."

Jake was beginning to feel a lot like home. She held the comforter tighter. That thought should scare the living crap out of her. What scared her more was how much it *didn't* make her want to book a flight out of town.

"I know this is kind of sudden, but do you want to come over for dinner tomorrow night? I'm picking up Bailey today and thought maybe we could all get together. If you're interested." He held her gaze, clearly trying to gauge her reaction.

There should be red flags. Warning flares visible from the space station. Erin *should* have wanted to sprint out of the room screaming. Instead, something in her chest fused together. Damn it, she was like the Grinch when his heart grew three sizes on Christmas day. She knew what he'd just asked of her took an enormous amount of faith—to trust her around his daughter. "I'd love to have dinner with you and Bailey."

He nodded, which seemed more for his own benefit than Erin's. "Okay. It's a date."

He pulled his shirt over his head and tossed it into the laundry basket across the room. "I'll be right back."

She joined him in the shower.

Two hours later, Erin made her way home. She grabbed her laptop from her room and headed down to the kitchen, where her sister was making lunch.

"Ah, Teacher Barbie. I was wondering when you were going to show back up," Andie said.

"I'm not here to pick a fight." Why was her sister still so defensive? It wasn't Erin who had brought up college at dinner the other night.

"Good. At least I can eat my lunch in peace," she grumbled.

Where had she gone so wrong that their relationship couldn't even handle a tiny spat? She'd never been that hard to talk to over Skype, but then again, that was because her sister always had something to talk about from school.

She got it. She sucked as a sister. She had a lot of making up to do. Given the limited time frame, she didn't know if that was possible.

"Where's Mom?"

"At the truck." Andie grabbed her ham-and-Swiss sandwich and sat down. Her blonde hair was pulled into a messy bun, putting her tattooed shoulders on display. The ink seemed to sweep deeper down her arms than she last remembered, and she wondered when she'd had the new design done.

Erin slid into the seat at the table across from Andie. "Are your friends back in town on college break?" Friends seemed like a safe topic. One that should get minimal side-eye action.

Andie frowned, putting down her sandwich. "No. Most of them stayed on campus. Since they're sophomores now, they got apartments."

"That sucks." Back when Erin was in college, she always dreaded small holiday breaks where students would go home for the long weekend. Since she'd lived a state away from her family, she'd opted to stay in her dorm and binge-watch TV shows, ignoring the pang of missing her friends. Erin couldn't imagine how Andie felt with her friends suddenly ripped out of her life.

"It does."

"Andie . . ." *Let me in. Let me be the sister you deserve to have.*

"Please don't, Erin. I don't want to talk about it." Tears glistened in her sister's eyes. Her sister may have been a lot of things, but it was rare to see her cry.

"Okay. Well, I'm here if you decide you're ready to." She was about to say more when her phone buzzed on the table. A California number.

Oh gosh. She was not prepared to handle any type of news at the moment, good or bad. She shook out her shoulders and tried to calm her breathing.

"Hello?"

"Ms. Jenkins?"

"Yes."

"This is Brenda from Highland Prep." That tiny thread of hope ballooned in her chest. She'd made it to the second round, which was better than the last few interviews. This could be her lucky break.

"Hi there. Thank you so much for interviewing me last week."

Her sister looked at her, giving a thumbs-up.

C'mon, Job Gods. Work your magic.

"I'm just calling to inform you that we have picked someone else for the position."

That tiny thread, her last real shot at getting a solid work opportunity, snapped.

"Oh, okay." The hot sting of rejection burned at the back of her eyes. Erin may have been an optimist, but she was also a realist. Things weren't looking good for her in terms of having a classroom in the fall. The hope and happiness that had filled her chest deflated like a week-old balloon.

"Thank you for letting me know," she added, her throat thick.

She gave a polite goodbye and hung up the phone.

Andie pushed her food to the side, only one bite taken out of the bread. "What did they say?" Her apparent loathing of Erin had lifted for the moment.

Erin pushed the ceramic chicken pepper shaker around on the table with her finger. She missed *her* table decorations. Missed the feeling of having something that was just hers. "They hired someone else."

Andie scoffed. "Their loss."

"Maybe." She wasn't so sure anymore.

Erin didn't quite believe in signs, but everything was pointing to California not happening. Would being stuck in Portland really be such a bad thing? She had her best friends here. Jake. Her family. Okay, the last one was a stretch, but she was starting to see the appeal of seeing them on a more permanent basis.

"I'm serious, Erin. Any school would be lucky to have you."

She wanted to agree with that statement, but she was having a hard time believing it now with this constant stream of rejection.

"Thanks," she said.

Enough of the complaining. Erin wasn't a wallower. She was a doer.

It was now time to implement stage three of her job-hunting expedition: throw shit at the wall until something stuck. Desperate times called for grasping at anything.

She opened her laptop and pulled up the e-mail that had been sitting in her drafts folder for the past week. It was a Portland private school job application she'd found on the list her mom had given her. She'd included her résumé, her three references, and her teaching credentials. Everything was there, ready for her to send off. An added bonus, the school even seemed to be right up her alley in terms of their curriculum. The only thing holding her back at this point was if it was the right time to be looking in her hometown. And if she was really ready to live this close to family, giving up the buffer of six hundred miles.

She glanced over at her sister, still pushing her sandwich around on her plate. Erin so desperately wanted to work past the barriers Andie had put up.

"I'll be back," Erin said, scooting her chair back.

She stood and stretched out her aching limbs. She made her way out the sliding door into the backyard and sat on the old tire swing hanging from the oak tree. Mount Hood loomed in the background. It was such a clear day that she could see the snow on the top of the mountain. She'd miss this view when she left. She'd miss a lot of things, she realized.

"Would it really be so bad if you lived here?" she said aloud. She leaned her head against the tire, rocking back and forth, back and forth. A warm wind ruffled her hair, and she took a deep breath. That last rejection hadn't hurt as bad as she thought it would, which left her wondering, *What the hell am I supposed to do now?*

She didn't have an answer to that. So, instead, she went back inside to sit with her sister. She needed to try to mend that relationship before she slipped away.

Her sister was still sitting in the same spot she left her, this time, a few more bites had been taken out of the sandwich. Andie wouldn't make eye contact, instead choosing to stare at her plate.

Obviously, Erin had a lot more work ahead of her. She glanced at her computer screen, and her stomach lurched. The e-mail that had been pulled up was no longer in her draft box. She clicked on a few other tabs, looking to find where it had gone. In fact, it looked like a couple of things had been messed with—tabs out of order, pages scrolled down farther than she remembered.

"What happened to my computer?" she asked.

Andie took another bite of her sandwich. "I don't know what you mean."

She shot her sister a look, but Andie still wouldn't look her in the eye. "There was an e-mail up."

"Oh, you mean the one that was an application to a school *here*."

"Yeah, that one." *Crap. Please say you deleted it.* Or that it somehow fell into the Internet abyss. There was a dark side of the Internet, right? One that housed pop-up ads and those stupid chain letters that promised imminent death if you didn't forward to at least fifty friends. Please say that was where her application went.

Andie shrugged. "I sent it."

"You did *what*?" Oh no. And of course it was too late to hit the "Undo" button.

"You needed that extra push. Were you actually going to hit 'Send'?"

Erin crossed her arms. "Maybe." Erring on the side of *maybe not today . . . or the next*, but a *maybe* nonetheless.

"Liar. The worst they can say is no."

What was with her friends and family? Maybe she gravitated toward these types of people.

She snapped her laptop shut. "This is the last time I'm leaving you alone with my computer."

"Would it really be so bad to be back?"

For the first time since she'd stepped foot out of her car, her answer was no. It wouldn't be completely awful to be back here.

Chapter Twenty-Four

Jake paced the airport main entrance, the hum of people bustling around him, and the overhead announcements putting him on edge. His baby had been gone three whole weeks. If this was a taste of what it was going to be like when she went off to college, he was in no way ready.

His breath caught in his chest when he spotted Bailey wheeling a carry-on past the TSA area. As soon as she saw him, she broke out into a sprint and jumped into his arms. He wrapped her in a hug, squeezing her tight. There was a good chance he might never let go.

"I missed you so much!" she squealed.

"Missed you, too, princess." Again, that nagging thought of having only six more years with her until college hit. He pushed it aside. He had his daughter here now. That was all that mattered.

"Okay, too much. You're crushing me," his daughter wheezed.

"Sorry, kiddo." He set her down and looked at her. So vibrant. It was like her skin had captured the sun, completely radiant.

This time he didn't even get a scoff from her.

"What do you say we get your bag and then go get some frozen yogurt?"

"Duh. Like there's any other option but yes. I have so much to tell you. The director asked me to come back next year and said I could even help out with the younger students. Said I'd make a good teacher."

That one word brought images of Erin to mind. She'd texted earlier and said Highland had passed on her. Dumb move on their part, but Jake felt the tiniest bit relieved that she hadn't gotten it. Yeah, he was an asshole.

"That's amazing. There's something I'd like to ask you." This was a risk. Jake didn't like bringing new people into her life. But if things were to somehow work out between him and Erin, he'd need the green light from Bailey. A no from her was a no from all, no matter his feelings toward that person.

Bailey patted Jake on the back. "Yes, I will take a Lexus as a sixteenth-birthday present. Glad you're thinking ahead."

Christ. That was four years away. He still needed to mentally prepare. "But I already got you a Barbie Jeep. That should have enough battery to get you to school and back."

She rolled her eyes. "You're the literal worst."

"It's my job to make you as miserable as possible." He put his arm around Bailey and pulled her close.

"You're doing a great job." She looked up at him. "What was it you wanted to ask me?"

"I'd like to bring Erin over for dinner."

"Your wedding date? The one with the really pretty hair?"

He smirked. "Yeah, that's the one."

Bailey shrugged. "Cool."

"You're okay with that?" Bailey used to beg Jake to go on dates when she was younger. When she was six, she'd tried to play matchmaker with her teacher and had written a note asking her out on a date on Jake's behalf. It had made for a very interesting parent conference. Since then, she'd brought it up only a few times, sometimes saying she wished she had a mom to take her shopping, to get her nails done. Those times especially made Jake's throat feel like he'd swallowed a bucket of nails.

Bailey shrugged. "Yeah." Then her expression changed, and Jake dreaded whatever was going to come out of her mouth. "Okay, it is a little weird, but only because I've never seen you date anyone. I don't have to call her 'Mom' or anything, do I?"

"What? No. Of course not. Things aren't that serious." Were they? He'd never thought about a single woman more than Erin. The way she smiled. The way her fingers tangled in her hair when she was deep in thought. How she made him laugh. Everything about her called to him.

"Earth to Dad. Oh my God, you're thinking about her now, aren't you?" Bailey wrinkled her nose.

His shifted his eyes to his daughter. His number one girl was back today, and he needed to put her first. "Of course not. I'm still thinking about you and your nonexistent Lexus."

She smiled up at him, batting those blue eyes. "So, since you're having Erin over, does this mean I can go out on a date with Zack?"

"Absolutely not."

She scoffed. "Completely unfair."

He ruffled her hair. "Glad to have you home, kiddo."

Jake drove to Bailey's favorite frozen-yogurt place, where she loaded her cup up with vanilla froyo, gummy bears, sprinkles, and raspberries, then took her home where they watched movies the rest of the night. He sat with his arm curled around her shoulder as she snuggled up to him on the couch. He looked over to the other side of him, an empty spot on the large leather sectional. *There's room for one more,* he thought.

Why did the thought of Erin hanging out with Bailey scare the shit out of Jake so much? Yesterday, it had seemed like such a great idea to invite her to dinner. Now, maybe things were going a little too fast. He glanced at the clock. She'd be here in less than an hour, and Jake still hadn't finished cooking. He'd never been one for place settings, but now the forks looked like they were in the wrong place. And why did the napkins not look right?

Bailey walked to the fridge and pulled out a soda. "You really like her, huh?" she said, nudging the door shut with her foot.

"Why do you say that?" Damn it, Jake was freaking the fuck out, and he needed to get a grip. It was dinner. People ate. End of story.

"Because you've been folding and refolding the same napkin for the past five minutes."

"It's nothing. Just a little nervous." He'd always protected Bailey. Done everything in his power to make sure her heart stayed intact. And now what he was doing . . . Well, it was a risk to them both. For Erin, it was worth it.

"If it makes you feel better, I promise not to bring up too many embarrassing things you do."

"Thanks, kiddo." Although he did wonder what info she had in that arsenal of hers.

"Got your back, Dad." She gave him an impish smile.

"That's what I'm afraid of." He gave the napkin one last fold and then set it down, making his way to the pot on the stove. Gumbo, fried chicken, and—shit. He'd forgotten the biscuits. He glanced at the clock again. A little under an hour. He had time to run to the store and get back before she got here.

"I'll be right back, princess." He kissed the top of her head and then grabbed his car keys.

Erin took a steadying breath and glanced at her watch. Fifteen minutes early, because hello first-dinner-with-the-daughter jitters. *Nothing to worry about. It's just a meal.* She squared her shoulders and knocked on the door. She'd ignore the flutter in her stomach, which she only seemed to get when an admin was going to be sitting in her classroom, critiquing her teaching.

Kids were so much scarier than a principal, though. Specifically this one, because it mattered if Bailey liked Erin.

After a few moments, the door swung open. Bailey stood there in jean shorts, Chucks, and an I CODE FOR FOOD tank top.

"Hey there." Erin smiled. *Too big. You're showing all your teeth like a lunatic.* She took the smile down a notch.

"Hi. My dad should be back in a few minutes. He had to run out and get biscuits." She did a once-over of Erin's outfit and then said, "Come on in."

Her gaze took a quick sweep of the family room. The only places she'd really been were the kitchen and Jake's bedroom. Now she noticed all the photos lined along the mantel, Bailey's school pictures, art framed around the room.

Unease settled into her gut.

How do I fit into this equation? Did she even fit in, or even have the right to want to know the answer to that? One day at a time. She didn't even know where she'd be tomorrow, let alone years down the road, so such heavy things shouldn't even be crossing her mind.

She swallowed hard and followed Bailey into the kitchen. "Did you have fun at camp?"

Bailey's blue eyes brightened. "Yeah, I learned a lot about coding. Mostly HTML, which can get a little tricky. Have you ever done that?"

"No. I know how to work the apps on my phone, and that's about it."

"I learned how to make those at camp."

"Holy crap." Er—"I mean, sorry. That's awesome. Was it hard?"

She shrugged. "A little. But once you understand the code, it's not too bad."

A beat of silence passed between them. What was wrong with her? She worked with kids for a living, and she couldn't come up with a single thing to ask. "So . . ."

"Please tell me you're not going to ask me what my favorite subject in school is. Every adult that doesn't know what to say to a kid asks them that."

Yep. That was the exact question that was seconds from popping out of her mouth. Bailey didn't need to know that, though.

"I don't want to know the answer unless it's science." She lowered her voice to a whisper. "And just an FYI—teachers hate to talk about anything school related on summer break."

"I once saw my teacher at the movie theater. It was super creepy."

"Crazy to think teachers have lives outside of school, huh?" They both stood at the stove. Bailey took the lid off a pot of what appeared to be gumbo and gave the soup a stir with a wooden spoon. A long silence spanned between them.

"So are you and my dad, like, dating now?"

How was she supposed to navigate this? She'd never dated anyone with a kid before. If she could even call it dating. She didn't know what it was because everything about what she'd experienced with Jake was so foreign.

"I don't know. I'm probably moving back to California at the end of the summer." Saying those words out loud somehow felt wrong for the first time. She'd been repeating them so often, they'd just flowed off her tongue, even if they now weren't entirely true.

"That sucks," Bailey said, wiping her hands on a dish towel set next to the stove.

"Why?"

"My dad looks a lot happier. He's smiling more."

This kid was perceptive. More so than a lot of her students. "Does he usually not smile?"

"I don't know. He's usually pissed about something I've done." She laughed, and when her lips pulled into a smile, Erin's heart dropped. She looked so much like Jake. Had the same mannerisms. For a fleeting second, she thought Andie would really dig this kid.

"My mom is the same way," Erin said.

"Annoying?"

She bumped her with her elbow. "I wouldn't say your dad is annoying. But hey, at least he didn't make you dress up as a jar of peanut butter and walk around downtown promoting a food truck in front of all your friends." The memory still rang clear. The way her so-called friends had snapped a pic of her and posted it on social media.

"Okay, your family sounds way worse than mine. Although Grandma did buy me Barbie underwear for my birthday last year."

"Smiling and nodding does wonders. It's pretty much the best life skill I've acquired when dealing with family."

Her family had always been a little over the top, but they worked hard and had earned every bit of success they had in the food industry. Even if she didn't want to join in the family business, she was proud of them.

"So your mom really owns Butter Me Up?"

"Yeah."

Her face brightened. And Erin was mentally heaving a sigh of relief that she'd finally found some common ground with the kid. "That's so cool. My friends and I go there sometimes on the weekends."

"I can teach you how to make the peanut butter if you want."

Bailey's eyes widened. "Really? That'd be cool."

Erin had never wanted a kid to like her so much. It seemed like a minor miracle that this was going off relatively well.

Just then Jake walked through the door. His nostrils flared as he looked from Bailey to her.

Seeing Bailey and Erin together honestly freaked Jake the fuck out. Bailey had a lot of positive role models already with his sisters, but he'd never really thought about having anyone there as a mother figure in her life. As a soon-to-be teenage girl, it occurred to Jake that she probably needed one. And the way Bailey was smiling at Erin was a fist to Jake's gut.

This was dangerous thinking because he knew in the back of his mind that Erin could leave at any minute. She'd never wanted to stay in Portland. But he had to admit that he would consider himself lucky to come home to these two women every day. Hell, he'd have to run this by Bailey if things got more serious.

"You two having fun?" He kept his voice neutral, even though his damn hands were shaking as he set down the bag of biscuits.

"Sorry, I know I'm a little early," Erin said. "Your daughter's a great hostess."

"Erin told me the secret ingredients to her mom's peanut butter, and she said she was going to show me how to knit. Last year she knit a unicorn beanie. Isn't that so cool, Dad?"

"Showing your Portland roots there, Erin?"

Erin crossed her arms, leveling him with a look. "Everyone should know how to knit."

Jake smiled and tossed the mail onto the counter. *Hell*. Why couldn't he breathe? He knew she'd be coming over, but to see her in his kitchen looking so gorgeous made his chest hurt. And she was next to the one person he loved more than life itself.

"We can go to the yarn store this weekend, and you can pick out the colors you like," Erin offered.

Bailey's face lit up like Erin had just told her she was going to take her to a Taylor Swift concert. "So cool. I was thinking maybe lime green and black."

"Great color choices. Starting with two is smart. We can always work our way up to more." Erin pulled up something on her phone and showed it to Bailey. "Here are some designs. We don't want to get too intricate for the first one, but you'll get the hang of it."

Jake had no clue his daughter would be remotely interested in knitting. The thought would never have crossed his mind.

"Whoa. I really like the zigzag one."

"That one's a little tricky, but I can show you how."

Showing would take time. That was good. That was what he needed more of.

Jake hated ruining the moment, but he didn't want his gumbo to get cold since Bailey had taken it off the stove. "You guys ready to eat? The gumbo and chicken are ready."

Bailey tore her gaze away from Erin's phone and nodded. "I'll get drinks. What do you want, Erin?"

And so it went. The most domesticated dinner to happen in the Bennett household.

It still was a little awkward to have another woman in the house, but Jake was finally willing to entertain the possibility of this becoming a habit. If Bailey agreed it was okay.

Jake spooned the remainder of the gumbo into a Tupperware container while Erin hand-washed a few things and Bailey dried them. *Holy shit*. This all just felt like he was on an episode of *Leave It to Beaver*.

Bailey dried the cast-iron skillet and placed it in the cupboard next to the oven. Fuck, he didn't know if Erin had crazy voodoo magic, but his daughter hadn't rolled her eyes the entire night.

Bailey's phone buzzed on the counter, and she picked it up, smiling. "Can I please go over to Charlene's tonight? She asked me to sleep over."

Already? "I don't know." He'd just gotten her back. He wanted to keep her home for as long as possible.

"Please, Dad. I haven't seen her in three weeks." She pressed her hands together, jutting out her bottom lip into a pout.

He glanced over at Erin. An empty house meant she could stay the night, which wasn't a bad alternative. "Fine. But this weekend you're going fishing with your old man."

She crossed her arms, debating. Finally, she said, "Fine." She disappeared up the stairs at warp speed.

"I think she's had enough adult time." Erin laughed, her eyes crinkling in the corners.

He moved to her, unable to go without her touch for another damn second. He stood behind her and let his hands slide over her shoulders as he leaned down to kiss her neck. She shuddered beneath his touch, and he was suddenly very thankful that his daughter was spending the night at her friend's house. "Thank you for tonight. I know she doesn't always show it, but she really liked talking to you about the knitting stuff."

"I'm excited to show her. It'll take a while, though." She turned and looked up at him, thoughtful.

He understood what she was getting at, a silent permission asking if she'd gotten the okay to stick around.

"I think she'd like that." He brushed his knuckles across her shoulder. "We both would."

Her cheeks flushed. "I'm glad to hear it."

Bailey bolted down the stairs, her backpack hoisted over her shoulder. "Okay, I'm ready." She shot them both a megawatt smile.

He put his arm around Bailey. "C'mon, kid. Let's get you over there."

Thirty minutes later, Jake and Erin entered his house through the garage. Jake chucked his keys onto the counter and then led Erin over to the couch.

"You're really good with her." She sank down to the couch, straddling Jake.

"She makes it pretty easy. She's a good kid," he said. His hands gripped Erin's hips. He could barely go a minute without touching some part of her. "Do you want to stay the night?"

She smiled. "Yes." That smile pulled the blackout shades wide open, leaving him short of breath.

"Erin. I—"

Her phone buzzed against his hand. "Hold that thought." She pulled her phone out of her back pocket. "Oh, huh, I have a voice mail."

She put the phone to her ear and listened to the message. A smile split across her face as she hung up the phone. "I have an interview here in Portland," she squealed.

"I didn't know you applied."

She nodded, beaming. "I applied to a couple, just to, you know, cast a wider net."

Portland. Not California. This he could deal with. This gave them a shot at testing out whatever this was between them. "That's amazing. Call them back to schedule an interview."

"I will in the morning." She tossed the phone on the couch and kissed down his neck. "Now what was it you were going to tell me?"

What was he going to say? *Please stay. I've never felt this way about anyone before. I love you.*

He pulled her into a kiss.

Chapter Twenty-Five

Erin swatted at her phone as it buzzed on Jake's nightstand. Whatever it was could wait. She nestled into Jake's warm chest as his hand smoothed through her hair and down her body. She let out a contented sigh. Now this she could get used to. Toasty sheets brushed against her skin, and she burrowed her head into the crook of his arm. She didn't know what she expected to happen last night when she came for dinner, but this morning she woke up with the realization that this just might work out. Her phone buzzed again, and she took a quick glance and saw that it was a voice mail.

Another one? But this time it was a California number. A familiar one. Her stomach clenched tight. What could her old principal be calling her for unless it was to chat about the Portland school? Maybe they had called her references already.

Another call came in. Her principal again.

She cleared her throat, so her voice wouldn't sound froggy. "Hello?"

"Erin! So glad I was able to reach you."

Call a person enough times and they're bound to answer. "What's up, Greg?"

The sound of his voice brought back the ache that had hollowed her chest for the past few months. She missed Stephens so much. Wished she'd never lost her position there. Most of her friends had managed to keep their jobs during the massive budget cut because they'd already moved past their probationary period. She was one year away from that. One stinking school year.

"There's been some shuffling around in the budget for next year."

"Yeah?" Maybe they'd take back some of the teachers they'd let go.

"There's an opening for the eighth-grade science position. With your name on it."

She bolted upright in bed and cringed when she realized she'd taken more than her fair share of sheet and comforter with her. She glanced over at Jake, who was still sound asleep. "What?"

"Your job, Erin. It's here if you want it. We'd love for you to come back. It'd be temporary for another year, just until voting for next year's budget, but you could move past your probation period. What do you say?"

The answer slipped out without a second thought. "Yes."

Her school. The school she loved so much was hers again. Her classroom. Her students. She could already picture what she was going to post on her bulletins for the first day of school.

"Thank you so much, Greg."

"There's an in-service day next week I'd really like you to attend. I know you're still in Portland visiting family, but think you can swing it?"

She looked over at Jake and frowned. The man she'd known so well, yet was getting to know in new ways. Erin had Jake's past and present, but she wasn't an idiot. There was no future here if she took her old job. Playing house and building a family with him wasn't in the cards from hundreds of miles away.

She hesitated, a *no* forming on her lips. No to going to the in-service day, no to the job in general.

What she was feeling for Jake went beyond anything she'd experienced with any other guy. Was it because she'd held him on a pedestal her entire life? She had a hunch that added to the equation. Prior raging teenage hormones + adult(ish) wish fulfillment = heart eyes.

Stop. This was her job. She couldn't turn that down because of a man, no matter if it was Jake Bennett.

She was meant to go back to California. Where she belonged. She took a long, steadying breath and said, "Yes, I can make the training."

As soon as she hung up the phone, Jake's eyes opened, and he stretched his arms over his head, the muscles in his abs running taut. She'd miss this. She already missed this, and she hadn't even left yet.

He blinked and then sat up, his expression darkening. "What's up?"

She worried her lip. She'd never had a hard time speaking her mind to him, but the thought of telling him the news was a dropkick to the gut.

"I got another call," she said.

"From the Portland school? Did they already hire you because you're so awesome?" His lips met her neck, slowly working their way down her chest. A calloused hand smoothed across her stomach, and everything south clenched.

No, no, no. If she didn't end this now, she'd never be able to. This job was what she'd wanted the entire summer, what she'd *wished* for. She couldn't waffle now.

"Jake." She put her hand on his shoulder, pushing him away. This was the right thing to do. It had to be. He and Bailey were already functioning well without her. She didn't need to blast into their home like the damn Kool-Aid Man and ruin everything.

"What?" he asked, his eyes searching hers. She didn't know what he'd find because right now it was like she was having an out-of-body experience.

She shook her head. What she was about to do to this man was inexcusable. "I'm sorry."

He kissed her forehead, which sent a tingle from her knees to her toes. "It's okay to not be in the mood, Erin. I can go make us some breakfast."

"No, it's not that." She wanted to jump his bones every damn chance she got. That would never change. That was the problem. She *wanted* to be around Jake. Everything about him, from the way he made her laugh to the way he kissed her until she was breathless. She wanted to stay cocooned in his safe world but knew this wasn't a possibility.

"I got my job back." She chewed the inside of her cheek, bracing for his reaction.

His brows slanted together. "What do you mean?"

"My old principal from Stephens called. There's been a shift in the budget, and my position opened back up."

"That's great." His smile wavered. "But what about the Portland job?"

"I'm not going to take a gamble on a what-if. This is my career. I love that school. This is my chance to put down some more permanent roots."

Why did this all feel so wrong? Every word coming out of her mouth tasted of ash and lies. *This is for the best. You were going to leave anyway.*

"I'm so damn happy for you, Erin." He pressed his lips together, frowning. "Actually, fuck it. I can't lie to you." He shoved a hand through his hair. "I don't want you to go."

"I don't have a choice."

"You *always* have choices, Erin. Don't pull that bullshit line on me."

"This job is really important to me."

"Is it that job, or are you taking the first opportunity to run again?" He scrubbed his hands over his face. "You know, I tried to tell myself not to let you in, that it was a terrible idea."

A lump formed in the back of her throat. "Jake—"

"But I couldn't stay away from you. Trust me. I tried. You know why I couldn't?"

"W-why?" she asked. Maybe she didn't want to know. Right now, she didn't need to hear anything that might change her mind.

"You have something that nobody else does."

Her chest squeezed.

Don't tell me. Please, don't tell me. Because whatever he had to say would absolutely wreck her. She could feel it coming, the calm before a terrible storm.

But she couldn't resist. She had to know.

"What is that?" *Please don't make this hurt any worse.*

"My heart," he said. "I'll lay it out there for you, Erin. I thought I was afraid of being with someone, but I'm not afraid of that with you."

No. No. No.

Her own heart squeezed so tight it sent jolts of pain to every crevice of her body.

"Why would you tell me this?" She needed this to be a clean break. Damn it, they'd been seeing each other for only a few weeks. She'd felt less after a breakup with a guy she'd been dating for a year.

"Because it's true." The hurt in his eyes sparked the rush of hot tears climbing up her throat.

She pushed those tears back down, needing to stay strong. "I'm leaving, Jake. I have the job. What am I supposed to do?"

"I don't know." He threw his hands in the air. "I don't fucking know. I'm not a monster. I'm not going to tell you how to live your life. All I want is for you to be happy. And if this makes you happy, then that's what I want for you." His blue eyes softened. "But all I know is that when I'm with you, that's the only time that my heart races. You're the biggest risk I've ever taken, and I'm not letting you go without you knowing that this past month has been the best I've ever had."

She couldn't leave her job situation up to fate. With how the rest of her interviews had gone, she wasn't sure she could snag the Portland job. And she didn't want to be wishy-washy with her old principal when that position could easily be filled by someone else. No, it was time to go back to California. Back to the life she'd had for the past ten years.

Something that sounded so right on paper felt so wrong.

She pushed back those thoughts and slid out of Jake's bed, pulling on her clothes. "I'm sorry, Jake. I can't stay here." She shook her head, tears stinging her eyes. "This was a fun break, but I have to get back to reality."

Oh God, this hurt so much. She never thought she'd regret getting a job offer, but this felt wrong. What was she supposed to do, though? This was her career. There was nothing here for her. She just had to keep telling herself that in order to get herself out of his house.

"I get it, Erin." His Adam's apple bobbed, and she didn't know how much longer she'd last before breaking down. "You deserve the best."

She slid on her top and allowed herself one more look at Jake. The devastation on his face. The hurt—she'd put it there. She'd done exactly what her brother said she'd do. She needed to get out of town before she had the chance to hurt anyone else. "Goodbye, Jake."

She barely made it up the porch steps and into her mom's house before the waterworks started. She managed to make it to her room and then slid to the floor, tears streaming down her face.

Moments later, a pair of warm arms wrapped around her, pulling her into her sister's body. "What happened?"

"Life," she muttered. Why had this decision been so hard? She loved Stephens. But the look on Jake's face . . . it'd haunt her for the rest of her life. Her friend, her lover, someone who she could tell anything to—she'd hurt him. And she didn't even know if it was for the right reasons.

"You're going to have to be a little more specific. Life is one big shit-flinging monkey," Andie said, rubbing soothing circles on Erin's back.

Erin sobbed into her shoulder. The tears just kept coming. They might never stop. "I got the job."

"The Portland one?" Andie shifted, and then gently placed a tissue in Erin's hand.

"No. My old job," she sniffled, wiping her eyes and nose. *Pull it together. You should be celebrating.*

"And we're not happy about that? I just want to make sure we're on the same page."

"I don't know. I said I wanted to move back to California, but . . ." She swiped at her eyes with her palms. These should be happy tears. Friggen elation at the fact that she didn't have to fill out one more god-damn job application.

"California doesn't have Jake," her sister said, confirming the worst part about her job.

"Nope." Since when did she ever factor in a guy to her decision? She had goals. She went for them. Period. And now, all she could think about was Jake's smile. The way her skin practically tingled whenever he was around her. She'd never had that reaction to a person before. And now it was being torn away because of a job. One that had the possibility of leaving her in the same position she'd been in this entire summer.

"And you don't want to take a chance on the one in town?"

"No." She paused. "I don't know. This is my old school. I love the people there. You know?" She had history there. She had her old students, whom she'd be seeing again. Ones who needed her.

It doesn't have your family or Jake.

Erin extinguished that thought. This was a sure thing, a job. That was what had kept her sane for the past ten years.

"Yeah, I guess," her sister said.

But Andie's frown hit Erin almost as hard as when she'd broken the news to Jake.

"I never understood that quote about getting your heart's desire being a tragedy. Now I get it." She so got it. Because she just got two of the things she desired most, and now she had to make a choice between them. That was an especially deep level of cruelty.

"Why can't you have both?" Andie asked.

"What? A long-distance relationship?"

Andie nodded.

"The chances of that working out are slim. Plus, if I go back, I have no intentions of moving to Portland. I'll have tenure at my school. Jake already has a life. I can't ask him to pick up and move Bailey. She'd hate me forever."

They were at a stalemate. They were on borrowed time to begin with, and the last grain of sand had emptied to the other side of the hourglass.

"Then I think this calls for extra-chunky Jif," her sister said.

"Jif? We don't have Jif in this house."

Andie raised a brow. "You really think your hiding spots are that great?"

Erin knocked her head against the wall. Andie lifted up the loose floorboard and procured the jar of peanut butter with a spoon. *Damn.* She was just starting to get to know her sister. Just starting to come back into her life when it seemed like she needed someone to talk to.

"I'm sorry I'm going so soon." She wished she had more time with her sister. To solidify their relationship. She wished for a lot of things, but as she knew from before, wishing got her nowhere in life.

"You act like you're dying." Her sister rolled her eyes. "You're a state away. We'll still have Skype."

"Yeah." But she could tell her sister's words were forced. She knew it was different—she wasn't an idiot.

"I love you, Erin. And I'm proud of you for living your Teacher Barbie life down in California."

"Love you, too."

Chapter Twenty-Six

Jake scrolled through the news on his tablet and pushed the soggy cereal around in his bowl. If this were any other breakup, he'd be lifting weights with Reece or Hollywood. Or going out for beers with them, getting his mind off Erin. But that was the thing. He didn't want to forget about Erin.

What the hell was wrong with him? He'd broken his cardinal rule of never getting attached, and now here he was nursing wounded pride. And some other stuff he wasn't willing to admit to himself yet. He'd been a fucking chump to lay it all out on the table for her. He had a losing hand and should have known when to fold. Instead, he'd put it out there just for her to trample on.

Bailey bounded down the stairs and skidded to a halt at the kitchen island. Charlene's mom had dropped her off earlier this morning, and he'd managed to avoid seeing her until now. "Whoa, Dad. What's wrong?"

"Nothing, kiddo." He waved a dismissive hand. "What are your plans for today?"

"Well, I was supposed to go shopping with Erin . . . but she just texted me that it probably wouldn't happen today." *Or ever, kid.*

She frowned, and Jake's gut bottomed out. He'd been foolish to bring Erin to the house, to bring her into Bailey's life. Because now Bailey was disappointed.

"I'm sorry, Bailey. I never should have done this." Stupid. He was so damn stupid for bringing Erin into Bailey's life. What was he thinking when he'd decided it'd be a good idea to invite her over? Obviously, he hadn't been.

"Done what, Dad?" She picked at the polish on her nails. She was still that innocent baby girl in his eyes. He wanted to fucking roar for causing any bit of pain to his child.

"Brought Erin over here. She just heard back from her old school—she's moving back to California."

Bailey brows scrunched together. "I'm glad you did. I saw you happy for once. Even if it sucks now."

He pulled her in for a hug, holding her tight. "You're my top priority, kiddo. Always will be." He smoothed a hand over his daughter's back. "Why don't we head to the mall today and get some yarn. I can look up a YouTube tutorial. How hard can knitting be?"

"As much as I love your guilt shopping sprees, I'd rather have you happy. Why didn't you ask her to stay?"

I did. She didn't want to. He'd been such an idiot lately.

"Because she deserves to be happy, too." He believed that with every ounce of his heart. He'd never ask anyone to give up their dreams, but when she'd left, it had made it abundantly clear that they never would have worked in the first place. Their priorities were in different places. He had his family. She was busy finding herself. Or whatever she was doing. He still wasn't even sure what in California had called to her so much.

Bailey shook her head. "Her loss." She grabbed a granola bar from the pantry and said, "Froyo date?"

He took a steadying breath and smiled at his daughter. She was turning into such a great young lady, one who was smart, kind, and thoughtful, and he was so darn proud of her. This was enough. He'd get back to his main priority, and maybe sometime after Bailey left for college, he'd find someone who was ready to stick around on a more permanent basis. He ignored the clench in his gut at the thought of being with anyone but Erin. That'd subside, though. With time.

"Sure, princess." And this time she didn't flinch. Maybe things would go back to normal. At least Jake would be smarter next time.

He put his arm around his girl and kissed the top of her head. Everything would be all right. He just had to keep repeating that to himself until he got the image of Erin out of his head for good.

@hotmamajenkins: So proud of my daughter for getting her old job back! They knew what they were missing.

@hotmamajenkins: But no amount of peanut butter is going to fill the hole that'll be left when she's gone.

Erin tossed her phone on the bed and continued shuffling stuff around in her suitcase. It'd been two days since she'd broken it off with Jake, and she still couldn't get his words out of her head. *You're the biggest risk I've ever taken.*

Erin didn't like to gamble. With her money or her feelings. Was she a chicken for not telling him how she really felt? Hell yes. But what would that have really done? Made things worse, for sure. He hadn't contacted her since she'd left his house, which wasn't surprising. With how she'd acted, she didn't even want to be around herself.

Erin tossed another cardigan into her bag. Maybe this year would be different. Maybe she'd find someone down in California. She shoved another sweater into the suitcase.

"Yeah, you're not going to find anyone, you idiot," she mumbled to herself. A guy like Jake came around only once in a lifetime. Her window had passed. She might as well resign herself to a life of spinster-hood. She wondered if she could Amazon Prime a menagerie of cats.

A knock came from her door, and she turned to find her mom leaning against the door frame.

"I feel like you just got here." Her mom frowned, but as far as guilt trips went, this wasn't even bronze-medal worthy.

Erin shook her head. If her mom pressed any further, she didn't know if she had it in her to put up a fight. She'd been left a husk of a person ever since leaving Jake's house. This honestly wasn't what she had expected when she said yes to the job.

"I can't give up a sure thing," she said.

"I know, sweetie." Her mom came over to sit on the bed, grabbing Erin's hand. "And I'm so proud of you. Those kids need you."

"You're not upset?"

Her mother's expression softened. "I would love nothing more than for you to be in Portland, but you need to spread your wings. If that means you need to go to California, then so be it. But you do this for you. Not because of other people's expectations. We'll always be here for you."

Hot tears formed in Erin's throat and stung her eyes. She didn't expect this summer to change how she felt about her family, but she was going to miss them. She was going to miss everyone.

"Is Jake still not talking to you?"

She blinked back tears. "No. And I don't blame him. I did exactly what Reece said I would." She really was an awful person. Even if she wanted things to work out with him more than anything, she just didn't see a way.

"Stop that line of thinking. Jake is a grown man. A good man. He understands what your career means to you. And if he doesn't, then he didn't deserve you in the first place." Her mother nodded, like her word was gospel.

She wished it were as easy as her mom explained. But somewhere along the way, she'd fallen for the man. And hurt him. There was no coming back from that.

"You will find your happiness, Erin."

"I love you, Mom." And the floodgates released. Tears streamed down her cheeks.

Her mother pulled her into a hug. "Love you, too, sweetie. Always. Now let's get you packed up and ready to teach science."

Two hours later, Erin stared at the packed boxes in the back of her Prius. Her whole life fit inside the back of a car. Granted, she had to use her Tetris skills, but still, what had she accumulated throughout her adult life besides a mild case of anxiety and the start of wrinkles around her eyes?

Call her a romantic. Call her desperate, but she kept looking over her shoulder, expecting Jake's truck to roll up behind her. For him to hop out and wrap his arms around her. For him to beg her not to go. Which was stupid because that wasn't happening. Not because she didn't think Jake wanted her to stay, but because he was a good man. A stable man. The type who wouldn't ever ask her to give up her dreams because, above all else, he respected her.

Madison and Sloane pulled her into a group hug.

"Do you really have to go so soon?" Sloane asked.

Madison shrugged. "We could chain her to the porch."

Erin laughed, hugging her friends tighter. "You guys are the best. I'll be home for Christmas." She pulled back and looked at them. She knew that no matter where she went in the world, these two women would always be there for her.

"Brother alert," Sloane said. She gave her one last hug and shuffled back toward the porch, Madison doing the same.

Did everyone have to make such a big deal out of this? All it did was make the hole in her chest spread.

Reece walked up beside her and stared at her car. "I'll miss you," he said.

"Miss you, too, big bro." Even though he was a huge pain in her ass, she knew what she said was true. She'd miss him. Her mom. Everyone. Because somewhere along the way, Erin had fallen back in love with Portland, and she couldn't do anything about it.

"I don't blame you for wanting to take this job. And I'm sorry for what I said to you the other week. That wasn't right," he said.

Her throat squeezed. She wouldn't cry in front of her brother because she'd never hear the end of it. "Just make sure he's okay."

Reece nodded.

She hugged her sister and mom goodbye, silently reassuring herself that she'd be a better sister, a better daughter. She'd make an effort to keep in touch with them.

As she slid into the driver's seat, she checked her rearview mirror one last time. No Jake. *Stop being delusional, girl.*

She rested back against the headrest, then started the ignition. Her mom, siblings, Madison, and Sloane waved at her from the front porch, and Erin pressed her lips together to keep from crumbling. *Put your car in drive. One step at a time.* She'd get her life back to normal.

What if this is supposed to be your normal? That exact thought had plagued her ever since she'd said yes to her principal. Now with her car packed, her gas tank full and ready to make the ten-hour trip, was this really what she was meant to be doing? At least she had a long car ride to decide this.

She made her way to the end of the block and clicked her blinker. Left to the highway, right to downtown.

One of these destinations was home. One was the unknown, something she'd never been scared of until now. Her gaze swept from left to right. She put her blinker to the left. Then turned it off. Then put her face in her hands.

Was she going home or leaving home? She wasn't so sure anymore.

These past few weeks had stirred things in her, made her realize maybe she'd been running for all the wrong reasons.

A car pulled up behind her, and she had to make a choice. She couldn't just sit at this intersection all day.

Erin took a deep breath. Before she could stop herself, her car turned toward downtown. She needed to see it one last time. Because she didn't know when she'd be back next. She parallel-parked in a spot in front of one of the bakeries and got out of the car.

Savory scents of cinnamon and toasted bread wafted out of storefronts as she made her way down Mississippi. She didn't dare go to Periwinkle Circle, but she walked the same route as she had with Jake on their date, making her way down to the riverfront.

She stared out at the fountain. All the wishes glittering in the morning sun.

She'd give anything for the fountain to actually work magic. Then again, hadn't it? She'd wished for her job that night with Jake. She got it.

A little girl plunked a coin into the fountain and giggled. She grabbed another fistful from her mother and tossed them in. After her mother ran out of coins, she took her hand and went on, strolling along the waterfront.

The water was still rippling from the girl's coin throwing. She stared at the blue water, watching the coins glisten in the light. She should be passing through Salem by now, on her way back to California, and yet here she was, staring at a fountain.

She pulled one strap of her purse over her shoulder and shuffled in the mess of receipts and unearthed a coin at the bottom. One shiny penny. *What the hell? Why not one more wish?* "Come on, universe. Give me this one thing, please." She was pleading with a public fountain. It was okay to assume that she'd gone off the deep end and straight into crazy territory.

It hit the water with a loud plop and sank to the bottom. Right next to one marked with black Sharpie. Oh, give her a break.

"This is what you give me, universe?" she called to the sky.

Of course her coin would land next to Jake's. Of all the places to land, it had to be next to the one reminder she didn't need. But wasn't that why she was down here in the first place, re-creating their first date like a complete psychotic person. Maybe she was experiencing a mental break.

A jogger stared at her as she ran by. Which wasn't uncalled for. She was yelling at a fountain.

She stared at that damn blackened coin. What had he wished for? Did she even have a right to know? No. Not after she'd just run through his life like a tornado.

Why had she hurt him like that? What was she so afraid of by staying here? Damn it, why did she miss Jake so much? This was a fling. Something that had an expiration date. Not something she needed to be angsting about like she was thirteen.

"This is ridiculous." She wasn't one to leave things up to chance. She hadn't made it as far as she had because of luck. No, she'd worked her ass off, and a freaking penny wouldn't matter in the grand scheme of things. She was a woman of science, for heaven's sake.

Erin kicked off her flip-flops onto the brick pavement and rolled up her capris. Damn it all to hell, she was getting that wish back. She plunged one foot into the frigid water and then the other. A shiver ran up her spine, but she was determined. No backing out now. She was in full swing with her crazy and intended to follow through.

There were a few gasps that came from behind her. Whatever. She had a bone to pick with the fountain. She reached down and grabbed her coin. Then she looked at Jake's sitting there. She couldn't get it out of her mind. Why did it matter what he'd wished for? For all she knew, it had everything to do with Bailey. Or staying safe on all his shifts. Which would then make her the worst person in existence, because, damn it, she was grabbing his coin.

She palmed the coin, the weight burning her skin. A piece of Jake. One that he'd carried around for so long. The weight of loss, the weight of the fear of taking chances. He'd shed it for her. And she'd gone and annihilated any hope for a future with him.

What the hell was she doing? She looked around the waterfront, at the fence with the locks, the shops in the distance. *This* was her home. She belonged *here*.

She couldn't leave this city. Not when her family was here. Her friends. Jake. The people who mattered most. She could make the best of any job. And she still had an opportunity.

Why was she running? The answer practically jumped off her tongue on a moment's notice when she rolled into town. And now, what did she have against her city? She had nothing. She loved downtown. She loved the culture. She loved . . . Jake. And that was the one thing that San Francisco would never have.

She pulled out her phone. She had a couple of calls to make.

Chapter Twenty-Seven

It was a well-known fact that when Jake felt guilty, he went to Barry's Bakery to get Bailey a bagel after his shift. This time, he'd said no to a group date with the infamous Zack. He might have been feeling a little bitter about his breakup, but Bailey was still too young to be dating. Right? Sure, he had dated around her age, but he wasn't ready to let her grow up that fast. He also might have been making up for the fact that Erin had backed out of that trip to the yarn store.

Jake cussed under his breath. This was what he got for opening himself back up. He had inadvertently hurt his kid. The one thing he promised himself he wouldn't do. Back to square one. But this time, the hole he'd been filling with work and his daughter was left wide open and gaping, like a damn puncture wound and no sutures in sight.

"Bagel for Jake," the barista called.

But before he could snatch it from the counter, a set of manicured hands grabbed it. His stomach clenched when he spotted who those hands were attached to.

Erin.

"What are you doing here?" He kept his voice flat. She should be in California by now. She'd packed her shit up. Ready to move on with her life and leave everyone in her wake. Just like Reece had promised.

"What did you wish for?" Her eyes were wide, a little crazy around the edges. Erin had a carefree attitude about her most days, but he knew that she was in full control, a planner. Never one to seem frazzled like this.

He didn't know what the hell she was talking about. All he knew was that he wanted to get his damn bagel and leave.

Even though he should have walked away, for his own personal sanity, he indulged. "What wish?"

"The one you made on this." Jake did a double take as she held up the coin covered in Sharpie.

"How did you get that?" Seeing that reminder in *her* hands was an unexpected kick to the gut. She should keep it. They both represented the same things to him. Leaving.

She ignored his question. "When we were down by the riverfront. What did you wish for in the fountain?"

"Why does it matter?" *I wished for you.* A fool's wish, he realized. He'd never had her, never would. Anything with Erin was like a race dog chasing the rabbit. He'd gotten close enough, could even taste what it'd be like, but it just wasn't in the cards.

She mashed her lips together. Why was she here? He'd like his damn bagel back and to get the hell home.

"It matters to me," she said.

He blew out a breath. Honestly, he didn't want to see Erin right now. Looking so goddamn gorgeous in jeans and a tank top. Her blonde hair was pulled back into a loose ponytail, and a few waves framed her face. She was so beautiful it hurt. "I wished for you, Erin."

"I don't believe in wishes." Her thumb smoothed over the top of the coin. "I've never believed in them. But today, when I had to turn onto the interstate to go back, I just couldn't. I can't leave."

"Why not?" This made no sense. She'd wanted to leave from day one. It was Jake who had been an idiot for thinking she wanted to stay. Only fools hoped.

She threw her hands up in the air. "Because all this means nothing if I have no one to share it with."

"I get where you're coming from. I do, but I think it's better this way. I can't subject Bailey to any more pain."

Her gaze raked over him. "Bailey or you?"

"Both," he admitted.

"I am going to apologize to Bailey and make it up to her. But I'm begging you to please give me another chance. I know I screwed up. I seem to be doing that a lot lately. But I am here to stay. Because when I came back to Portland, I didn't just fall back in love with this town. I fell in love." She mashed her lips together. "I know we've only been seeing each other for a little over a month, but I'd like to keep doing that. The seeing-you part. And I'd also like to get to know Bailey better. I decided to take the interview with the school here."

"I'm happy for you. Sounds like you have a good plan going on." This was a lot to take in. He trusted Erin. She'd always been up front. But he didn't know if he trusted himself.

"Listen, I'm sorry. I screwed up. This sounded a lot better in my head when I was on my way over here."

"How did you know where to find me?"

She gave a wry smile. "It's the end of your shift. You're predictable."

"Boring, you mean." Maybe that was why Erin had decided to leave in the first place. She liked spontaneity. His life revolved around structure. A matchmaker's nightmare.

"Never. You're the best man I know. You know what's sexier than the bad boy you used to be?"

"What?"

"The good man you became. You have your shit together. I've never felt this way about anyone before, and it scares me."

"It scares me, too." So damn much.

"But you didn't run. You see danger, and you go toward it. I've never been that way."

"You stole from a public fountain. I'd say you have a bit of danger in you." He realized that the coin he'd been carrying around for years didn't hold the same weight as he thought it would when he saw it again. It was just a coin. There was no such thing as placing hopes on inanimate objects. But there was the woman in front of him whom he'd fallen for.

"I'm serious." She playfully smacked him on the chest. "I may not believe in wishes, but I do believe in you. I want to make this work. If you're willing to forgive me, please give me a second chance. I know you have Bailey to think about, and I understand if you want to protect her, but I am here for good. I'm not going back to California. I'll take a job here."

His brows shifted together. The wall he had built was back in place. He could feel it as if it were actual bricks. "Why?"

She shook her head. "What?"

"What changed your mind?"

"I realized I made a mistake and hurt the person I love."

He lifted a brow. Was she really admitting what he thought she was admitting? It'd been only a month, but what he felt for her went deeper.

"I think there's a whole line of people that fit that category. Can you be more specific?"

"You, you dummy." She pushed at his chest. "I love you."

A few gasps erupted around them, and a quick glance confirmed several of the coffee-shop patrons were watching them with rapt fascination.

Jake's pulse ticked in his temples. This woman. This firecracker who sparked something inside him. Made him believe in love again. Damn it, he couldn't pass this up a second time. "What about all your stuff in California?"

She looked up at him with hopeful eyes, ones that melted his resolve. "I'll need to have that shipped home."

"Home." He smiled. "I like the sound of that. Erin?"

"Yeah?"

"I love you, too." He tugged her to him, sweeping her into a kiss. Her lips were so damn soft, and Jake could spend forever exploring them.

She pulled away, those perfect pink lips pulling into a smile. "Thank God, or else this conversation would have gotten really awkward. Does this mean you'll give me another chance?"

He tucked a strand of hair behind her ears and cupped her cheek. They'd make this work. They had to because Erin was quickly becoming his everything. "You're holding my wish in your hands. You tell me the answer."

Her arms wrapped around his neck, and her lips met his again.

"Yes."

ACKNOWLEDGMENTS

First, I want to thank my wonderful editor, Maria Gomez, for taking a chance on my book. Writing this book made me fall in love with writing again, and I so appreciate you giving me the freedom to run with Erin and Jake's story. I'd also like to thank Andrea Hurst, who made this book infinitely better with all her suggestions and feedback. Thank you to the rest of the Montlake team for your kindness and enthusiasm.

As always, thank you to my agent, Courtney Miller-Callihan, for always being in my corner and saying, "Hell yes!" when I said I wanted to write about firefighters.

A special thank-you to firefighters/paramedics Brian Mintie, Garrin Duffield, and the rest of the crew at TVFR, who let me ride along and ask awkward questions and gave me great insight into the daily routine of firefighters.

Thank you to firefighter Andrew Burg for letting me pick his mind about all the technical terms. Any mistakes regarding firefighting portrayed in this book are solely my own.

Amy, Lia, and Chanel—my writing besties. Thank you for always being there. Also thank you to Danielle Gorman, who is both my trusted confidante and friend.

And saving the best for last, thank you to my family for always being so supportive. J and L, you are my everything.

ABOUT THE AUTHOR

Photo © 2012 Leahana Byrd

Jennifer Blackwood is the *USA Today* bestselling author of the Rule Breakers, Drexler University, and Snowpocalypse series. Aside from writing contemporary romance, Blackwood teaches English in Oregon, where she lives with her husband, son, and unruly black Lab puppy. When she isn't writing or teaching, you can find her binge-watching some of her favorite TV shows, such as *Supernatural* and *Gilmore Girls*. Visit her author website at www.jenniferblackwood.com, and follow her on Facebook at www.facebook.com/AuthorJenniferBlackwood and on Twitter at http://twitter.com/jen_blackwood.